VALE]

GU00838733

Cristina Hodgson

"One of those rare books that will make you both laugh and cry...often at the same time. Valentina is a story of love, loss, learning and yearning, with two stories about two courageous women cleverly crafted into one hugely entertaining tale."

Heidi Catherine,
***Award winning and Bestselling author of
"The Soulweaver"***

TO FRAN

For giving me the key to life more
precious than mine.

ACKNOWLEDGMENTS

There are many special people I would like to thank. A writer's life is a solitary one; you spend hours inside your own imaginary world. It's a lonely process, and it's important to have people who understand and support your need to express what's burning inside. I'm lucky to have the backing of many people. And for that I would firstly like to thank every single person who has gone out of their way to support me on my writing journey. For all of you who have bought my books, you are the reason I continue writing. For those who have left reviews and contacted me to tell me how much you've enjoyed reading my work, it is for you that I continue to story-tell. A special thank-you to each and every one of you. Impossible to name you all here, but you know who you are, especially: Ann-Marie L, Anna H, Andrés C, Alison F, The Barrs, Beverley Ann H, Cathy P, Cathy D, Claire H, Claire S, Danie T, Elisa L, Juliana C, Karen B, Katy J, Leisa S, Rachael B, Rosie C, Samantha C, Sarah J, Sarah V, Shamsiha, Sophie P, Suzanne H, Tessa R and Vici.

A huge thanks also to all those wonderful book bloggers who have taken the time to spread the word about my work and to all those supportive writer's groups that I'm honoured to form part of. Especially to 20booksto50k.

A huge shout-out to the following wonderful people who I'm blessed to call my friends: Alice, Dush, Aimee, Steph M, Steph R, Sara, Suzanne, Inma, Marina, Heidi Catherine, MG, Tita Anna and

Tito Paco. I thank you from the bottom of my heart to the tips of my writer's fingers.   ; -)

To my brilliant editor Sue Barnard. Writing is the painting of the voice; thank you for blotting out all those unnecessary paint drips.

Finally, to my mum, dad and brother... for giving me the greatest gift anyone could give another person, for believing in me, and for teaching me to do the same.

ABOUT THE AUTHOR

Cristina Hodgson, mother of two, born in Wimbledon, London, currently lives in southern Spain. Cristina had a long career in sport, reaching national and international level and still actively participates in Triathlon races and enjoys outdoor activities. In her spare time she also enjoys reading and writing. She won a sports scholarship to Boston College. After a period in Boston, she returned to the UK and graduated from Loughborough University with a degree in Sports Science.

A Little of Chantelle Rose was her debut novel. Amazingly, it has nothing to do with running!

Valentina is book II in the Chantelle Rose series.

You can find out more about Cristina Hodgson at www.cristinahodgson.com

FREE EXCLUSIVE CONTENT

Sign up for the author's New Releases mailing list and get a free copy of her short story *Three Against One* a true story about love, hope and survival.

Click here to get started:
Cristina's Newsletter
www.cristinahodgson.com

VALENTINA

Book II of the **_Chantelle Rose Series_**

PROLOGUE

The sun was setting leaving a golden hue all around, like fairy dust colouring a magical twilight. It would be autumn soon, and the leaves would fall russet and gold onto the ground below. Crisp autumn leaves that would twirl in the wind as they gently fall, to lie motionless on the floor until the wind blew and took them again. Mother Nature would whisper and do with them as she pleased.

He stood there, looking for one last time at the swirling water in front of him, then closed his eyes and sighed deeply. He could hear the water softly splashing as it followed its own path, the wind rustling the leaves and the evening song of a wood-lark nearby. Everything has a calling, everything has a moment, but he was lost. Lost to the enchantment, to the magic of nightfall, lost to her.

He turned to go, and with a heavy heart made his way back home. He walked this time, blind to the setting sun and the cool breeze that now caressed his whole being, gently blowing back his hair, like a lover tenderly caressing his handsome face as he moved along.

It was over. Downhearted he continued his way home.

Home? Could he call it a home when there was nothing to keep him there? Could there be a home without a heart?

He stepped through the front door. His mother was waiting for him, and stood quickly on seeing him enter. She wrung her hands together nervously then wiped them down the front of her dress in a habitual gesture of anxiety, stalling for time as she looked at him. He knew he had changed these last few months; the alteration wasn't physical, it wasn't even clearly emotional, it went deeper than that. Without a word his mother disappeared into the kitchen and returned with a dust-covered box, a little larger than a shoebox, and handed it over.

There was no need for words; he guessed what was inside. He nodded and tried to smile. It was time, he realised. Time to find his way, his identity.

First thing the following morning, before anyone stirred, he departed...

CHAPTER ONE

CHANTELLE

Pregnant!

I couldn't believe it. I tried not to panic. I sat there on the golden dune and looked at the twilight stars that had begun to shine. The sand beneath me was turning cool as the evening rays slowly disappeared. Sand that trickled through my toes as I pushed my legs forward and I lay back to look at the clear sky above. I briefly closed my eyes; the seagulls had gone quiet and all I could hear was little more than the calming lap of the ocean surf as it broke on the beach front.

Twenty-four years old and pregnant. But that wasn't the worst bit; after all, I wasn't that young! The shocking factor, stupefying if you like, was that I had no idea who the father could be.

I didn't know whether to laugh or cry. Both appealed. Thankfully, this stretch of beach was deserted, so if I were to cackle aloud and follow on with heartfelt sobs, no one would see me and worry about my mental state. I sat up again and felt a little dizzy. Well there was no point in totally freaking out just yet. Perhaps the queasiness I'd been feeling over the last few days was nerves due to my current emotional state. The bedlam of the last few months would have been enough to lead anyone to have some sort of possible nervous breakdown, so perhaps this was just a simple case of anxiety. Not that suffering from anxiety could ever be simple, of course.

I tried to calm myself. Perhaps I was overreacting a little, and there was no need to panic, at least not just yet. I stood giddily and had to momentarily close my eyes to steady myself. Composure returned and I made my way back to Lionel's bungalow. Well, at least he was going to be away for the next few weeks on his latest million-dollar film. For once I was relieved he was a Hollywood star and would be kept away from me on his blockbuster shoot. I needed time to figure this out. The first step, of course, was to take a pregnancy test.

I went to find Gabby. The least she could do after her psychotic scheming was lend me her car. But I had no real desire to see her again; as far as I was concerned, after what she'd done she should be behind bars. I walked up the path that led from the secluded beach to Lionel's secret bungalow (secret at least from the paparazzi, and secret to me until a few weeks ago). I'd always believed that this fabulous bungalow had belonged to Freddie G, Lionel's agent. But then, there was so much I had learnt and so much had happened these last few months that it was hard to keep track, even for little old me. In fact, especially for me, considering my current situation.

Lily-of-the-Nile, with its arching tropical leaves, ran around the perimeter of the bungalow. I followed it until I came to the partially-hidden gate that led to the main house. Lionel's family house.

Family! *Shit!* I hadn't really thought about it before, this is where his mum and dad lived too. I hoped to God that his parents (his adoptive parents, that is) hadn't come back yet from their annual rendezvous on their privately-owned Transatlantic yacht. Facing Gabby was going to be challenge enough; I had no desire to add to my obstacles a friendly chit-chat with my future in-laws. Who, come to think of it, I'd never actually met. In my giddy state. I wasn't sure I'd knock'em dead, British accent or not.

I peered through the gate and was relieved to see Gabby's 4x4 jeep parked in its habitual slot. I shot across the perfectly groomed lawn, rich in exotic flowers (Pink star tulip and Crinum lily to name but two), and thankful that despite everything I was still nimble. I was hoping that Gabby had left the keys in the ignition as she often did. I was about to open the door, praying that if it was locked I wouldn't set off the car alarm, when I heard a rich female voice coming from the veranda.

"Gabriella, honey, I'll be back later. Anything you need?"

I turned towards the voice, magnetised, despite my urge to shoot out of sight behind the nearest tree. The voice belonged to an elegantly-dressed, well-coiffed, middle-aged lady, who glided down the steps of the veranda and tuned to move in my direction. Without thinking twice, I opened the car door, dived into the back seat, and lay down, hidden out of sight. My heart hammered away as I heard footsteps approach. I held my breath in anticipation as they abruptly stopped, and it dawned on me that I'd just been terribly foolish to choose the back seat of the car as my hiding place. Just as I was mentally kicking myself for my stupidity, the door to the driver's seat creaked open. Rich perfume filtered through the vehicle, which rocked slightly as the woman sat down in the driver's seat and turned the key in the ignition.

I thought it best to make my appearance known before she hit the main state road; otherwise, I risked her swerving off the highway and down the cliff to the Ocean. We were about halfway down the private track that led away from the main house (well, mansion to be precise) when I popped my head up behind her and said rather innocently, "Hello!"

The shrill shriek and 360° spin was more petrifying than any funfair ride I had ever been on. Thankfully, the car engine stalled and the car shuddered to a stop before we crashed into the perfectly-pruned, animal-sheared boxwood hedge. I'd managed to smack my forehead on the driver's headrest and I was sure I would suffer from whiplash for a few days. The car mechanisms didn't seem too alarmed, though, as none of the airbags had opened.

I stumbled out of the back passenger seat, opened the driver's door, and helped the lady to her shaking feet. She slumped down again to sit inside the car, with her hand resting on her no doubt thundering heart. She'd gone as white as a sheet, and her hair… well, let's just say it wasn't quite so coiffed any more.

I peeked at her and gave her a shy smile.

"Sorry about that, Ms King, I didn't mean to give you a scare." A slight understatement I know; she'd probably grow a new streak of white hair from the sudden shock of me popping up like that. I didn't think I'd knock 'em dead, but for once, I'd actually underestimated myself.

She just stared at me with wide, chocolate-brown eyes, and then something in her look altered, as if she'd recognised me, or realized that I was indeed harmless. At least, as harmless as I could be considering this first encounter.

"Chantelle?" she asked in a trembling voice.

"Yes Ma'am," I replied, trying to sound as polite and imperturbable as possible.

"I'm Claire, John's wife, not Mrs King."

I stared at her. John, the chauffeur? The very same man who had locked me in the barn a few weeks ago, back in Kent? The man who had scared my best friend Tammy so much that she spent several days in a coma from the fright he'd given her? She had fainted and he'd left her on the cold frosty ground, and by the time I found her she was deathly cold. I shuddered at the very memory. John, Gabby's co-plotter? Participant in her psychotic scheming? I couldn't believe it. I actually felt like driving the car off the cliff and into the Pacific Ocean myself!

Now it was my turn to sink to the ground and sit in a stupor.

Gabby was Lionel's adoptive sister. Years earlier, when she was a young and easily-influenced girl (I say girl, but in fact she would have been in her early twenties at the time, so should have had more sense), she'd had her fortune told. Some hippy nutter had told her that she would only find happiness once her brother had met and settled down with the girl of his dreams, a so-called "Chantelle Rose." And for all these years, Gabby had believed it.

Lionel King, a Hollywood superstar, saw me, by chance, as an "extra" in a ghastly Brit gangster movie and sent his agent Freddy G to razzmatazz me up and offer me a million dollars to be an extra in one of his films. Well, not so much an extra as a body double for the nude scenes. Information I wasn't given on signing the contract, otherwise I would have shoved the contract up Freddy G's arse (and Lionel King's, for that matter). And that's putting it politely!

Gabby, to make sure that I didn't remain in the UK, sent John (the King family's chauffeur) to the UK after me and had him do all in his power to scare me into returning to the States. Over the last few months I'd received menacing letters aimed at driving me away from my beloved rural Kent and into the arms of my now fiancé Lionel.

What Gabby didn't understand or appreciate was that I had fallen in love with Lionel from the start. There had been no need for such dramatic methods. And the worst thing was, apart from seeing Tammy so affected by the whole scare, I had blamed Lionel! I thought that he had been behind the threats. Lionel, who had done nothing except shower me with love and affection from the very start. But I'd convinced myself that it had been him – and I messed things up quite dramatically. So much so that I now found myself in this very tricky and delicate situation.

I desperately needed to get a pregnancy test done to see if I was indeed preggers, and if that fear was confirmed I needed to find out who the hell the father was. Because there was a chance that it wasn't Lionel.

***

After the whirl on the private path, both Claire and I thought it best not to venture any further down the road. In our trembling state, it wasn't worth the risk. I wanted a pregnancy test, not a survival test. So I escorted Claire back to the main house and left the jeep in its parking space before disappearing back to the bungalow. Dusk was long gone by that time, the clear sky was filled with stars, and most stores would have been closed anyway, so I decided to leave pregnancy testing for the following morning.

Which is how, quite early the very next day, I found myself wandering around a drugstore at the nearest mall searching in vain for pregnancy tests. I was still quite distracted from the events of the previous evening, and my neck felt as sore as hell. As a result, my eyes kept zoning in on the painkillers, but I didn't want to take anything strong, just in case. If there was a little embryo growing, I wanted to keep it safe. But if I discovered that there was no baby, I'd skip the painkillers and head straight for the nearest bar and order a gin and tonic.

I finally found the mother and baby section. *Eeekk!* I didn't think I was ready to face so much pink and blue all at once. But by the time I'd gone down the aisle, it was as if all these lovely, cute baby things had hypnotized me into a pleasurable hormonal trance. And I was quite looking forward to the possible prospect of motherhood.

I came across Clearblue Ovulation Kits (*Don't miss your two best days to conceive*). Ironic, really, that you have about two days in a whole month when you're likely to conceive, and most couples take months or years to get it right. Except me, who seems to have got it right straightaway and almost without any practice. Put that way, I sounded quite exceptionally gifted. Shame it wasn't in an intellectual or athletic way.

I finally found what I was looking for: Clearblue Pregnancy Test (*Delivers over 99% accuracy from the day of your expected perio*d). Good enough for me, I thought, as I popped it into my shopping basket. I didn't think I'd ever got a 99% correct result in any tests in my life, so this was going to be a first. And with that I headed for the till.

I decided not to venture with the self-checkouts. I was always disastrous at trying to figure which way round I had to hold the bloody item up and beep it across the barcode scanner properly. I almost always ended up running the shopping bill to double the actual amount, so I always avoided them whenever possible.

I was just about to place the pregnancy test on the counter at the human-operated cash register, when the cashier turned to me and let out a little squeal:

"Ms Chantelle Rose! Oh my God! I can't believe it! Lionel King's fiancée? *The* Lionel King? Mr-Hollywood-Heart-Throb-Who-Is-Such-A-*Dream'*s fiancée?"

"I know, I find the idea rather a shock myself," I replied, and I did too. But I wasn't quite sure if she was shocked to see me in person and realised that there was nothing exceptional about me at all (except, as only I knew, my possible fertility predisposition), or she was shocked that given my new status I was actually doing my daily errands myself and hadn't sent some hired help to do them for me. But whichever it was, I was glad that she hadn't made my presence known by announcing it over the tannoy.

"Can I have your autograph?" she asked as she fumbled for a pen and piece of paper. I, at the same time, instinctively dropped the pregnancy test on the floor and booted it across the polished aisle, and watched despondently as the box skidded away. I couldn't risk flashing a pregnancy test in front of one of Lionel's aficionados; it would be sure to get to the press, and they would have a field day. I scribbled my name across a torn piece of receipt whilst, without looking, grabbed the first item I could find and placed it by the till.

The cashier picked the item up and her eyes widened in incredulity. She fumbled as she passed it over the barcode scanner and handed it back to me with the habitual "Have a nice day now," but with an added conspiratorial wink.

As I left the store I glanced down to view my new purchase – and was horrified to see a pack of XXXL glow-in-the-dark condoms, with a promotional sex toy strapped to the packaging.

Well, I thought, at least that will mislead the paparazzi if this bountiful purchase story, in more ways than one, is sold to the press.

CHAPTER TWO

Hired help, I thought, on seeing Sav, the Mexican maid who worked for the Kings samba across the bungalow porch as I arrived back at the unit. Why hadn't I thought of that before?

"Sav! Sav!" I called out, but she obviously couldn't hear me. As I got closer I realised that she was plugged into her Smart Phone, which was acting as DJ, and Marc Antony was being blared out and into her ears. I could quite distinctly hear the music from over a metre away, so her eardrums must have been taking quite a hammering. I reached out to tap her shoulder, but it was a bit tricky; she stepped forward, then backwards, sunk down and then leaped up again before whizzing around.

"Señorita!" she exclaimed, as I almost poked my finger in her eye. I had been aiming for her shoulder, but with this rumba lark, my coordination (unlike Marc Antony's singing) was way off key.

"Sav," I said, "can I ask you a favour?"

"Perdone?" She removed the plugs and turned the music off.

"A favour, *un favor*, for me please?"

She looked a bit blank, and I wondered if this was actually a good idea. With her woeful English, and my almost total non-existent Spanish, I had a good chance that she would come back with anything but a pregnancy kit!

"Could you go and buy me a pregnancy test?"

"Señorita!" she exclaimed once again, and I wasn't too sure if we were starting the conversation from scratch again.

"Pregnancy test... but shush... secret... *secreto! Mucho! Mucho! Embarazada."*

I wasn't too sure if I'd got that right. It sounded more to me that I'd just said I was very very pregnant, rather than it was a top secret. But Sav seemed to understand, as she gave me a quick squeeze and giggled as she patted my belly.

"Si, secreto!" And with a wink she was gone.

"Buy two," I said to her departing back. *"Dos, por favour."*

She turned and waved putting her thumps up in comprehension. I thought two tests was a good idea; with my luck I had a good chance that the 99% accuracy would have to be double-checked.

***

Sav turned up about an hour later, carrying a huge bag. Christ, I thought, on seeing the colossal carrier. She obviously had mistaken my instructions. I wondered what on earth she had bought; I just hoped it wasn't any more sex toys! After all, my love life needed much more than some kinky bits and bobs to sort itself out.

With a puff, she handed over the bag. She looked quite exhausted.

"Gracias!" I thanked her and stood awkwardly for a moment as Sav made no move to leave. She just stood looking at me, then at the bag, then back again.

"Ayuda?"

21

Help me? Err, no, I thought, I think I can pee by myself thanks! I handed over some money to cover the purchase (not that I really knew what I was paying for, though it certainly wasn't *two* pregnancy tests), but it seemed to be sufficient as Sav took the money and smiled.

"*Mi abuela es bruja,*" she said. "*Mi* Nana *es* witch."

Now it was my turn to stare at her. I wasn't too sure what she expected me to do with this information, or what reaction was appropriate. I couldn't quite figure out what I needed a sorceress for. I'd already had quite enough of sorceresses interfering in my life, directly or indirectly. One had been sufficient, and I hadn't even met her!

We stood for a while in silence until I gasped out loud. She probably thought I wanted an abortion or something, and would probably offer me some lethal cocktail. A Bloody Mary was quite lethal enough for me on a normal day; mind you, I felt I could do with one right now.

"*Noooo!*" I blurted out. "Abortion NO!" I added quite firmly.

"*Señorita!*" she exclaimed for the third time this morning, looking aghast that I could even think such evil thoughts. She was Mexican, after all. Birth was sacred for them, and I'd probably quite offended her.

"*Niño o Niña!*"

Ahhhh! I understood. Her gran could predict if it was going to be a boy or a girl. I wondered if she could also predict who the father was. Now that *would* be money well spent.

"*OK, gracias. No importa.*" It was fine, the sex of the possible child wasn't an issue for me at the moment. There was something far more important than that. But I was grateful for her concern and interest.

"Change mind, call Sav." She grinned at me and patted my belly again. "*Abuela* help. If sick, *Abuela* make you feel better." She skipped back down the garden path.

"Thank you Sav, remember big *secreto* OK!" I called out after her. I couldn't stress it enough. If this was to leak before I told Lionel in person, I'd be in big trouble. Possibly in more ways than one.

***

Finally alone, I stepped back into the bungalow and closed the door. I placed the bag, which was actually quite heavy, on the low oak coffee table and opened it. To my surprise, it was filled to the brim with Clearblue Pregnancy Tests. Well, at least Sav got the actual product right. But why so many? It looked as if I was about to venture out and try and flog these on the black market.

I counted them out. Twelve in total. I was going to need to pee like an elephant if was to have any hope of testing out all these! Then it clicked, and I actually chortled out loud. Twelve. In Spanish, *doce*. I'd said *dos* (two) and Sav had obviously thought she'd heard an extra "e" at the end making it sound like the higher number. Well at least she hadn't understood *doscientos*, two hundred. Otherwise, I'd be unloading a whole truckload of goods.

Well, this is it! My heart started pounding as I unwrapped one of the tests and skimmed over the instructions. Simple enough. Well, coordinating the

23

wee onto the slight marker was probably going to be a bit tricky, but then I decided that after dealing with the filming of nude scenes and then suffering the consequences of having stolen images of me naked plastered all over the world, wee coordination was going to be a cinch.

It was too! I managed to spread my urine over four of the tests, which, as I calculated, should be more than enough, giving me a 3.96 out of 4 chance of success. Or rather, of confirming accurately my current parental state of affairs. The three-minute wait for the digital word to appear that reads *Pregnant* or *Not Pregnant* were an eternity. They say, rather psychologists say, "time can stand still" or was that Taylor Swift? Anyway, that's pretty much how I felt: floating boundlessly. Mind you, saying that, my heart was about to hammer out of my chest, quite the opposite to floating really.

I glanced down at my watch: two and a half minutes. It felt as though an hour had passed. I unsuccessfully tried to suppress the urge to look over to the pregnancy tests, which I'd placed on the low table. But from where I was sitting the little screens remained blank anyway. Boy! When the manufacturers say at least three minutes, they really know their stuff!

I glanced down to look at my watch once again. Finally three minutes! Simultaneously out of the corner of my eye, I could see little print letters appearing on the screens. Except one that seemed to remained blank. I leaned over to read the words. I held my breath. It wasn't that I didn't want the child if I was pregnant. But as there seemed to be no guarantee of who the father could be, and no way of figuring it out, it was such bad timing. If I was to fall pregnant in a month's time, and I'd managed to sleep with just one person (I mean, how hard could that be?), I'd be ecstatic.

I cringed. This was so unfair; this whole incident made me sound like a right hustler. But I've never slept around. OK, I've had my share of boyfriends, but *never* to this level of doubt about my sleeping partners.

I braced myself against the low wooden oak table and looked at the test results:

PREGNANT 1-2 / PREGNANT 1-2 / PREGNANT 1-2 …

Christ! This was worse than I expected! What the hell did *Pregnant 1-2* mean? That there was one or two, or one out of two fathers?? Or that I had one child on the way or twins?? My legs gave way beneath me and I slid to the floor.

***

I recovered some minutes later and read the results again. I tried to assimilate that this was real, that this was happening, because I'd have preferred it to be a dream – (well, a nightmare, to be precise). I really didn't know what to do, whom to call, whom to confide in.

I went over the instructions once more, especially as the last test now read PREGNANT 2-3. Was I was having triplets?

As I skimmed over the instructions again I realised that the numbers signified the possible weeks I was pregnant. It seemed the deed was done around one to two weeks ago, or possibly two to three weeks ago. So really no help there, though I was relieved to learn that at least I wasn't going to push out a whole brood of little ones all at one go.

At any other point in time I would have phoned Tammy, my best friend from nursery days. But she was still recovering from the scare we'd all received just a few weeks ago (not even weeks, more like days, though it felt like a lifetime ago). And my parents, God bless them, were no longer with me either. My mother, sweet and gentle to the end, had suffered from that monster called cancer and had passed away when I was a little girl, and my father had followed some years later from a broken heart.

Mind you, I don't know how I would have explained to them that their precious little girl had lost track of her nocturnal partners and had got herself into a real mess. The shock of it would have been enough to rocket them up to high heaven, so perhaps it was just as well they were already there.

I had flown out to LA just two days before, to tell Lionel how sorry I was that I hadn't believed him. I had blindly assumed that Lionel had been behind the string of threatening letters I'd received, when in fact it had been Gabby all along. I wasn't sure if he'd forgive me for not trusting him, and for thinking he was capable to going to such extremes to keep me at his side. He seemed to forgive me, when I saw him just before he flew off on his private helicopter to start the filming of his new multi-million-dollar movie. He said he'd be away for three weeks, and that we could talk about it all when he got back.

I closed my eyes, and the image of him looking desolate (as I'd yelled the accusations at him back at the country cottage that I'd just purchased in Kent) came flooding to my mind. I'd really hurt him with my cruel words. I couldn't – and didn't even want to – imagine what his reaction would be if I told him I was pregnant and there was a chance he wasn't the father. The whole notion made me shiver.

For a moment, I considered the option of not telling him the truth, and making out he was the father whatever happens. He would never know. No one would ever know.

Except, of course, Robbie.

CHAPTER THREE

"Robbie."

I actually said his name out loud. I'd tried to push him from my thoughts, his rugged good looks from my mind. His beautiful sad smile as we'd said goodbye and his words: "If you're not happy, come back." But it was impossible. I've said it before and I'll say it again, if anyone was to whisper in my ear that they were caught between the love of two wonderful men, I'd say a little prayer for them, because it was a bloody nightmare.

I'd been blessed with three weeks all to myself: three weeks to think things through. To try and decide what I really wanted. More importantly, who I really wanted to be. I'd been lucky, more than lucky. I'd been given the love of two incredible men, and both had selflessly offered me a future. Which path I chose would be light years apart from whichever one I left behind. I also realised that once I'd reached a decision, there would be no turning back. Whatever I decided would be forever, with all the consequences. But I'd never counted on this added dilemma of not knowing who was the father of the child I was carrying. Perhaps I wasn't that lucky after all.

I wondered what Robbie's reaction would be. The shocking thing is, believe it or not, I have no recollection of the night we spent together. It had been after spending the whole day with Tammy at the hospital and I was feeling exhausted. The doctors had warned me that I needed to go home and rest.

Robbie, of course, had jumped at the chance to take me home and look after me. And he did just that! So much so that the following morning I'd found myself totally starkers in my bed, with his angelic face just inches from mine. The shock had been immense, and that's putting it mildly.

At the time, I'd just found out that John, the King family's chauffeur, had been the one leaving the menacing letters around for me to find, and I had assumed that Lionel, (my then fiancé; well then and still now) had been behind them, to keep me at his side. This would fulfil what he'd been told by some crazy soothsayer: that he would only be happy with a dark-haired, almond-eyed lady named Chantelle Rose. To be fair, that did sound a hell of a lot like me. The name, at least, was spot on!

It had made sense at the time, though it broke my heart to believe it. I'd turned to Robbie for strength; I'd been weak and he was there. He'd always been there and though it seemed like the perfect excuse, it wasn't an excuse. I'd have turned to Robbie regardless. Except, perhaps, with some sort of self-control – and then this mess I now found myself in wouldn't have happened.

It's not that I can't remember what happened because I was sloshed or anything. In reality it was much more serious than that – and it had happened to me before. Not the actual sleeping with someone and not remembering anything (once was definitely enough for that), but rather the memory loss. My mother passed away when I was a little girl, and I actually blocked out the whole incident for months. Gradually, over time, fragmented pictures started falling into place, and there came a moment, with the immense help of my father and professional child psychologists, that I could remember it all.

My mother had been my absolute hero. I had, of course, loved my father dearly, but the relationship with my mother had been unique. It was as if she knew that there would come a time when she would no longer be with me. Every instant at her side was incomparable and special. She would stay with me until I slept, softy stroking my hair, and be the first to smile at me on waking. There were times, however, when I would catch her looking distracted and upset. A tear would find its way down her cheek, and not even I could make her smile. She was my mother, my best friend, my everything. And one day she simply wasn't there anymore, and I never got to say goodbye. I was too young to understand, and far too young to lose her.

That period of my life just seemed to disappear; it went the very day my mother left us. Only much later was I able to remember my father telling me, with tear-filled eyes and a broken voice reflecting his own broken heart, that my mother had gone and that I would never see her again.

"She's gone to be with the angels," he'd tried to explain.

I'd hit him and told him I didn't believe him, and had run from the house and onto the main road. Cars had screeched to a stop, horns honked, but I'd kept running, blindly, tears obscuring my vision, stumbling as I ran, until my father caught up with me, picked me up and held me tight. I'd slumped in his arms and fainted.

The next clear moment I had was some six months later, when my father came home with a golden Labrador puppy. It was a female pup who came bounding into the sitting room and almost knocked me over in her excitement and licked my face in delight. It was the first time I laughed again. From then on, the pain started to ease and the memories gradually returned.

There are still moments, under extreme stress or anxiety, when I feel the threat of fainting. The nerves, tension or excitement get too much for me, and my body reacts in a way that I haven't yet learnt to fully control.

I have improved over the years, but the risk of fainting or temporary amnesia is still there. These memories losses have, however, always occurred when I've been under severe pressure or distress, and nothing like how I was on losing my mother. I had no idea why I couldn't remember the night with Robbie. I had been under a lot of pressure, what with the whole American adventure ending in disaster and deception, together with the extreme concern I'd felt over Tammy's health. I just couldn't comprehend how I could block it out when I'm sure it would have been magic.

I guessed it was just too soon after Lionel. I was still officially his fiancée, after all, and deep down I felt terribly sad. From the outside it probably looked as if I was using Robbie. But I would never do that. It had all just been too confusing, too much to take on in such a short space of time. It was the only explanation I could think of. It was either that, or in fact Robbie and I had actually managed to have terrible sex, and it had been enough to conk me out!

Robbie had never told me what had happened either. He'd simply said he'd wait for me to remember.

But it wasn't as simple as that. As much as I tried to remember, the whole night remained a blank in my mind. I'd given up on trying to recall the events and relied on the knowledge that at some point, when I least expected it, I'd remember.

I had this overwhelming urge to call Robbie, to hear his comforting voice over the miles. To feed off his strength, his vigour. Without giving it a second thought I retrieved my mobile from the bedroom and dialled his number. It was going to cost me a bomb and I hadn't checked the time zone, but I really didn't care.

The line buzzed in that funny way when calling abroad, and my heart started pounding. The ringing went on and on. He didn't pick up, and my heart sank. Just as I was about to hang up, the line clicked, and his masculine, firm, strong voice, answered.

"Hello?"

"Robbie!" I cried out shakily. "Oh Robbie! I just don't know what to do. I'm pregnant and I'm not sure who the father is. I know that we never cleared up what happened between us, but I need to know now. You have to tell me the truth. I'm desperate Robbie, desperate!"

It wasn't quite the opening lines you would expect in a normal conversation. I'd probably just given him the shock of his life and I'd totally skipped the polite *Hi! How are you, I hope I didn't wake you up. Weather good?* entrée, but there was no time for any pleasantries.

"Hello?" I heard called out once again.

Shit! Had he not heard me?

"Robbie?" I called down the line again anxiously; I didn't think I'd have the nerve to repeat the conversation all over again.

"Robbieeeee? Can you hear me?"

"Hellooo?" Silence, then "Bloody wanker." At least that's what I thought I heard before the line went dead.

I gasped and dialled again, but this time there was no tone. The line seemed to have been disconnected and now there was no way I could reach him and I had no idea if he'd heard anything I'd just said. Probably not. I mean you don't just say "Bloody wanker" to the supposed love of your life, do you? Or do you? Okay, I'd left him to return to Lionel, but I don't think I deserved that level of name-calling. "Hi gorgeous," would have been much more appropriate and appreciated, especially in my delicate state of nerves.

I needed some sort of positive feedback, other than, of course, the four positive pregnancy tests. I mean, it just wasn't quite the same.

CHAPTER FOUR

The following day, having waited for a couple of hours on standby, I found myself on a Virgin Atlantic flight back home to London. *If the mountain will not come to Mohammed, Mohammed must go to the mountain.* Or was it the other way around? Never mind. I wasn't going to worry myself over religious proverbs right now. What counted was that I was going to try to find out who was the father of this baby I was carrying, preferably before three weeks were up. Before I had to face Lionel and explain it all to him.

I was a little concerned that I'd had no contact whatsoever from my supposed fiancé in these last few days. He'd gone very quiet, not a call or a text had come through. I understood that being in the middle of an important shoot, his sleeping and waking clock depended on the scenes being filmed. I certainly wasn't going to call him because I didn't want to risk waking him or calling him off set, so I'd gone quiet too. This was actually to my favour. I needed time to play with as I figured this all out.

This was my first flight as a newbie mother-to-be, and it was terrifying. The instinctive need to protect offspring had been triggered to red alert. It was the first time ever that I paid full attention to the cabin crew's safety instructions. I actually put my hand up a couple of times to clarify some of the safety guidelines, ignoring the flabbergasted looks of my fellow passengers who actually started to hiss at me.

At take-off, I hastily fished out the safety pamphlet that was tucked into the chair in front of me and studied it as if cramming for my school A-Levels again. As soon as the safety belt sign had been turned off, I stood and paced the emergency exit route three times, memorising the steps so that on the last go I was able to shuffle from my seat to the emergency exit and back again with my eyes closed before plopping myself down onto my seat again. I turned beaming with triumph towards the guy sitting next to me who was gawking at me, but he didn't return the smile. In fact, he then rather rudely ignored me, looking aghast as he rapidly fished out his Kindle and immersed himself in whatever he was reading. When, in fact, he should have thanked me, because if there really was an emergency "Mayday, Mayday" I'd be the one to follow.

I was, however, rather glad that my frizzy hair was on the comeback, it had been professionally straightened for the weeks I'd been a body double, but now that look was wearing off. This natural mop of mine bore no resemblance to the exquisite image the press portrayed of me, thus keeping safe Lionel's reputation. Nobody (except the cashier girl at the drugstore, so top marks for her) associated him with this "Ms Chantelle – Control Freak – Rose". And for that, I was grateful.

***

The first thing I arranged on arriving back to London was a check-up with my GP. I was expecting the nurse to inform me that there was a two week waiting list, but miraculously there'd been a slot available for the very next day. I wondered whether my sudden stardom had something to do with it, because as soon as I'd said my name over the phone, there was a slight intake of breath and I was quickly informed that I could be seen the following morning. My old family doctor had retired a few months ago, and this was going to be my first appointment with my newly assigned general practitioner.

I'd spent the night in my bedsit off Streatham High Road. Despite my newly-purchased country cottage in Kent (thanks to the million dollars I'd earned for flashing my backside as a body double), I still fortunately had my London abode. This meant I was just a train stop away from the practitioner and my whole medical history.

I stepped through the door to my doctor's consulting room and sat down in the chair opposite her, with a large oak desk between us. Somehow, the solid table seemed to calm me. I was in need of being close to something strong and reliable, and as I seemed to be lacking in human strength or companionship at the moment, and I'd never been a high maintenance girl, so a wee bit of wood was good enough for me.

"Ms Rose," my GP began, "pleased to meet you, how may I help you?"

"I think I'm pregnant."

"Think?" she enquired, in a soft calming but clear voice. "You have doubts?" (More than you could possibly imagine, I thought, although not about the actual pregnancy.) "Have you taken a pregnancy test?"

36

"Yes, four."

"FOUR!" She repeated, surprised. "Is that because the first readings were unclear? Sometimes if you test very early on, the pregnancy hormones aren't detectable in the urine sample. Is this what happened?"

"No, all four tests read pregnant, but as they are only supposedly ninety-nine percent accurate, I thought that perhaps there was a zero point one percent chance, multiplied by four of course, which actually gives a zero point four percent chance, the readings could be incorrect."

The doctor looked at me blankly before giving me a warm smile. "No, if the tests read positive, you're pregnant. Only if they read negative is there a one percent chance of inaccuracy, due to the lack of detectable hormones in the body system at that early stage. So congratulations!"

She fiddled with her computer screen and started typing away as she continued:

"I'll arrange a follow- up appointment with a midwife. That will be in about three weeks. You'll have your first scan and you'll be asked a few simple questions with regard to health matters and hereditary illnesses. You'll need to think about any questions you'd like to ask then, which your midwife will be able to answer for you." (Or not,, I thought.) "I'll just take note of a few details now to start the process. Date of last menstruation?"

I took a while to answer.

"I'm not sure; the 20th of last month I think."

"Age of first menstruation?"

Don't pressure my brain cells too much, I reflected. In my hormonal, jet-lagged state I could come up with any foolish answer.

"Fourteen."

"Age of first sexual intercourse?"

Seriously! Were these questions necessary?

"Pass," I said, not sure if I could get away it. She didn't bat an eyelid, but her fingers paused over the keyboard waiting…

"Twenty-one," I said. Her fingers remained motionless. I felt like I was being tested by a lie detector.

"Seventeen… almost," I muttered.

"Name of the father?"

I gasped, I certainly wasn't expecting that question.

"Lionel King," was my quick reply; it came out without me really thinking about it. She turned and looked at me again and smiled at me heartily.

"Lionel King? Like, *THE* Lionel King, the actor?" she asked. She was obviously a fan because her eyes lit up.

"No, not LIKE the Lionel King. THE actual Lionel King," I said firmly. She looked at me in astonishment.

"Right," she noted, nodding as she typed away, obviously not believing me. She was evidently one of the few people in the world not to have watched the Oscar night, where Lionel had pretty much proposed to me in front of the millions. His exact words had been "If I could spend the rest of my life with a certain Rose at my side, I'd be the happiest man alive. Chantelle Rose, this is for you." Then he'd turned to offer the Oscar statuette to me. My frizzy hair may have been on the comeback, but I doubted that there were that many Chantelle Roses in the world who could boast to be on the receiving end of that dedication. And anyhow how could she not know!! The nurse who took my appointment call yesterday seemed to have known who I was with just a smattering of information.

"Okay," I interrupted her typing. "Don't put Lionel King down, put Robbie." Now *this* is where my answering started getting really daft.

She paused. "Ahh…Robbie…" she murmured, as if that explained everything.

"Surname?"

I hesitated and stuttered.

"Robbie… err… ummm…" *Bloody good question!* "I'm not sure, to be honest," I meekly replied. I could feel my skin crawl with shame, and I most certainly didn't improve matters by blurting out rather ineptly, "He's the town's handy man!"

"AHH!!…" Even louder now, followed by a slight "Tut tut… I bet he is! Handy, that is!"

There was a quick flash to my ring finger. No, I wasn't married, but in this day and age that shouldn't have been a cause for alarm. I was rather disappointed now that I'd taken off the huge "bling" Lionel had given me as an engagement ring. Its titanic size would have at least proved that there was an acknowledged partner somewhere. But I'd hidden it. It was so expensive that I'd have needed a bodyguard or two to escort me around South London if I was to have kept it safely on my finger. And I just didn't think that was practical. I was still trying to follow my mother's good teachings: *No need for fancy bits Chantelle, it will only lead you to trouble.*

39

And she was right about that.

***

Midwife appointment card in hand, I rather shamefully exited the GP surgery. Well, that didn't go quite as I expected. She probably thought I was nuts! At least I wouldn't have to face her again for a few weeks, and by that time I hoped to have the father's name somewhat clearer.

I was just making my way to Tammy's house (well, actually her parents' house in South Kensington, where she was currently resting up) when a woman who was skittering backwards down the busy street bumped right into me.

"Sorry," I apologised, when in fact I was the one who had been whammed into. The lady swung around, flowery bag following dangerously and I had to dodge it to avoid another knock.

"Excuse me, baby on board!" I added, though she didn't seem to hear me. Pamphlets had gone flying out of her bag and she was busy picking them up. Finally, she stood and looked at me. She gasped and peered at me closely as she mumbled, "Is it you?"

Oh Jesus! I thought, now I've gone and attracted some crazy woman who wouldn't let me pass.

She tried to cup my face in her hands, but I quickly sidestepped to avoid her touch. Physical contact from a complete stranger was not something I was partial to.

"I can't believe it! It must be you!" she continued, oblivious to the frown on my face and my not-too-happy stance. "But more beautiful, if that's possible, than I remember. You've flowered into a most exquisite and beautiful young lady, Chantelle!"

I paused in my attempt to elude her and it was my turn to stare at her. This stranger knew my name. She was middle-aged, somewhere perhaps in her mid- fifties, greying hair tied back in a low bun. Two bright blue eyes peered back at me from a creased but homely face, and there was something about her that did seem familiar.

"Chantelle Rose, the loveliest little girl I'd ever laid my eyes on, is now this striking young lady before me. Can't you remember me?"

"E- E- Err… no!" I stuttered. "Should I?"

"Oh Chantelle!" she exclaimed, "I wish you did remember me, you must! We used to play together all the time when you were a little girl, when your parents lived in Wimbledon Village. I used to take you to the Common and we'd fly kites and dip our feet in the pond." She paused here as if to give me time to recollect. "Do you remember now?"

I closed my eyes for an instant and it was as if I'd whisked back in time. I could feel the summer sun warm on my face, and hear the distant hum of busy bees gathering pollen together with the faint sweet chime of an ice-cream van parked across the green. I could hear children's laughter mixed with dogs excitedly barking nearby. I was stripped down to my shorts and vest, dipping my feet into the cool pond water, gurgling with delight as I paddled in. The barking became louder and louder as a huge English sheepdog barged past me and I was suddenly knocked off my feet and spun around to land right on my behind in the middle of the pond, up to my chin in muck. I had turned to look for help, bravely trying to keep my tears at bay. I was only about six at the time, and though I find it quite funny now, the little girl in me then had been frightened. I hadn't expect to fall in the water. My clothes had got soaking wet and the blow had disorientated me. Vainly I'd searched for a familiar face amongst the bustle of people lounging around and started to panic.

"Mummy, Mummy!" I'd cried out in alarm, and was quickly scooped up by some tender, loving arms, which had held me tight.

"There, there Chantelle. It's all right. I've got you now." I was wrapped in a warm shawl, which smelt of lavender, and taken home in those comforting arms, dripping ice cream I'd been bought on the way and dropped off to sleep under the hush sweet lull of a lullaby.

I opened my eyes.

"Sally? Is it you?" I whispered, as the memories flooded back. And I, quite ashamedly, started crying. I'm not talking a couple of tears that trickled down my face. I'm talking sluice-opening tears that just came out in floods, with no self-control whatsoever. I couldn't stop. I fumbled unsuccessfully around my handbag for some tissues. Sally, thankfully, was better prepared than me and handed me a whole new packet of Kleenex. She just looked at me with a sorrowful smile, but seemed to understand my need to just let everything go. I was aware of a few odd looks coming my way, but thankfully, my vision was too blurred by the tears to properly focus on any of the bystanders. It was as if I'd kept locked up inside me, over all these years, the pain and loss I'd felt for the death of my mother. Seeing Sally, who'd been like a second mother to me, had triggered off all this pent-up emotion for my beautiful, loving, caring mother who'd been taken so young. Too young. I missed her so much, I couldn't bear it!

"Pregnant, are you?" Sally queried softly, which brought me round to some sort of self-control almost instantly.

"Why do you say that?" I snivelled. I mean, after all I was only just a few weeks pregnant. Maybe I'd put on a pound or so, but surely it wasn't that obvious.

"Hormones, dear. You can only cry like that, for no apparent reason, when you're pregnant. One moment you're as happy as a buzzing bee, the next you're sobbing your heart out. But it's a wonderful feeling isn't it, pet?"

If you say so, I thought. Personally, if you ask me, it's dead embarrassing.

"Let's go and have a coffee, love, and you tell me all about it." Sally gently linked her arm through mine and led me to a nearby coffee shop off Old Brompton Road. I could do with a drink too, even if it was just non-alcoholic. I'd started to feel a bit shaky and my hands trembled slightly. Surely so much emotion wasn't good for the developing embryo. Pregnancy hormones should be limited to provoking solely laughter, joy and happiness. What was the point of bellowing like I'd just sat through a heart-rending session of *Bambi, Dumbo* and *Annie* all rolled into one?

We sat down at one of the coffee tables near the entrance. I ordered a decaf, as there was little point in getting my nerves any more taut than they already wcre, and a huge Pumpkin Scone, finished with sweet vanilla icing, cinnamon and pumpkin drizzle. After all, as they say, "there's a bun in the oven," so I may as well have a real one.

"I still feel sorry about your mum." Sally spoke quietly, and placed one of her warm hands over mine and gave me a quick squeeze. "I used to babysit you when she went for her medical check-ups," she continued as she slowly stirred her iced green tea. "She seemed to be getting better, and then suddenly one day she said to me, ´Sally I'm just not strong enough, I love them both so much it hurts, but I can't fight this anymore… Please tell them I'm sorry. Sorry that I'm not strong enough, sorry that I won't be able to see her flower into the beautiful woman that I know she will become and whisper every day into her sweet-smelling hair how much I love her. I will always love her, even though I'll no longer be here to see her grow, to pick her up when she falls. Tell her to be strong and tell her to love, to love with all her heart no matter what happens, because that's the secret lesson we all have to learn to find true happiness...` And that was it, the very next day she passed away. You know, she was the most beautiful, loving and caring woman I'd ever met. Isabella Gravachi, as exotic as her name. It's no wonder that your handsome dad was smitten with her. She spoke the Queen's English better than me, but fooled your dad with her soft Italian lisp."

By this point, tears were once again streaming down my face. I'd long since run out of tissues, and the sugar sachet wasn't doing a very good job of blotting my now runny nose.

"Anyway," Sally continued. "Let's not run away with ourselves, this should be a happy reunion. How's your dad?"

"P-P-Passed aw-w-way, almost t-two years ago n-n-now," I managed to stutter. The tears kept flooding out and I was just about to start using the tablecloth as a huge handkerchief when the couple at the table next to me handed over, in unison, a packet of tissues each. I nodded my gratitude and smiled feebly.

"Pregnant," I explained, and their faces lit up in awe, as if I'd just performed, in front of their very eyes, the most magical trick in the book. But, thinking about it, "conception" *is* the most magical trick in the book, so I guess I had. And if you then take into consideration my unique technique (a mystery even for me, because quite apart from my mental blank with Robbie, I'm now not too sure what the hell happened to the condoms I used with Lionel), I think I just about outshone David Copperfield!

Sally, after offering me condolences for my dad, in an effort to cheer me up reached out across the table to hold both my hands in hers.

"Let's have some fun," she said and turned my hands palms upwards. "Let's see what I can read here."

Oh God, help me! I thought. Fortune-telling at the local café! This is all I need. With my hormones running wild, I'll probably end up believing every single word she makes up.

She glanced down at both my hands, her hands underneath tenderly supporting mine. She turned both hands around and then palm upwards again. I

45

started to fidget. At least this sudden uneasiness I was starting to feel had managed to halt my tears. I was tempted to remove my hands. I really had no need to hear that my love-line was a shambles, that my lifeline was much the same and that my marriage-line was non-existent, because I already knew all of that. I didn't need a fortune-teller to point out the obvious. But I sat there mesmerised, and held my breath in anticipation. Or perhaps, better said, in apprehension.

"You have a strong life-line, Chantelle, full of vigour and energy. You are suited to outdoor life. Find your mantra in the big outdoors; this will maximise your natural vitality and guide you to personal fulfilment."

By the big outdoors, did she mean *al fresco,* like camping? Or the world, like travelling, because I didn't think it was physically possible to jet about any more than I already did. I'd started to pop across the big pond now on an almost daily basis, and it certainly wasn't improving my natural vigour. Quite the opposite, in fact.

"Your head-line is long, Chantelle." She traced her finger from my palm edge between my thumb and forefinger across the centre of my palm and slightly downwards toward the end. "This line reveals your wisdom, thinking and creative ability, strain capacity, self-control and more." She paused for a moment to smile at me, whilst I thought, well that's good isn't it? If it's longer, it must mean I'm wiser with better self-control… or perhaps not?

"Your line shows you have a clear mind, you are responsive, good at thinking and more considerate than others." (That didn't sound quite like me right at this moment. My mind certainly wasn't clear, and I doubted Robbie thought I was very considerate, leaving him the way I had. Saying that, I had tried to call him again that very morning, but his line was still dead.) "The line steeps downwards a little." Sally continued tracing it once more with her fingertip. "You are fertile of imagination," (Quite right! But it's not the only place I'm productive) "and you have a high creation ability and artistic flare. Do you like painting?"

"Not really."

"You are also easily influenced by emotion." (Well, that was obvious; I'd just spent the greater part of the last hour crying my eyes out.) "You perhaps spend a lot of money when in a bad mood." (Not quite I thought, unless or course, you count buying a huge country cottage in Kent on a total whim, though I wasn't in a bad mood when I purchased it, quite the contrary. Perhaps, going on the scale of things, bad mood purchasing would have counted if I'd landed myself with a castle.)

"And now your love-line, Chantelle." Sally paused once more to look at me. Her honest blue eyes held mine for an instant before she returned to gaze at my hands.

"The third major line in the palm." She traced the line, just above the head-line, starting from the edge of my palm under the little finger, across the palm, ending between the middle and forefinger.

"The heart-line is your love-line; your line is deep, clear, curved and unbroken, with a fork at the end." (I started to panic. What did the fork mean?) "You will love deeply and will always be clear about your feelings. You are a born romantic and can

47

speak your feelings openly. The fork at the end means that you are popular, loved by many." (Two was, by far, more than enough, thanks!) "Your line ends where the Mount of Jupiter joins the Mount of Saturn," (she'd lost me there) "and it indicates that you will have one true pure love."

I sighed with relief. Now I just have to figure out who it is. Or was.

Sally looked up at me again. "I see confusion, though, and this is not from your palms; there is an aura of tension and turmoil about you which is blinding your inner light. You have to let your inner self guide you. If you block yourself from your instinct, you may choose incorrectly and you will be lost forever. Let your instinct guide you, trust yourself, who you are and what you want to be. Don't be influenced by others, Chantelle. You are strong, always have been, but you have doubts now about something and you are lost. Let your inner mantra guide you. Let it choose for you, that way you will never be wrong. Listen to your heart, Chantelle, and you won't be let down."

We fell silent. Wow! I needed more than just a decaf to assimilate all this information.

"I can read Tarot cards as well," Sally continued. "Fancy a go?"

"NO!" I exclaimed. That was quite enough for one day. "I'm meeting with a childhood friend," I hastily added. I didn't want her to think I was being rude.

"Quite alright, pet." She nodded. "But before you go, let me tell you a secret." she whispered. "I've never told this to anyone as I would lose my fortune-telling reputation, but I may as well tell you.

I've travelled the world, and every time I've come across any handsome young man who's asked to have his fortune told, I'd tell him that he will meet this beautiful, exotic lady, with luscious dark hair, soft olive skin and with huge, honey-coloured eyes." She paused for dramatic effect. "And that only with this lady would he find true love." She started to cackle out loud, as I stared at her in disbelief and started to feel a bit nauseous. "And I would tell him, she'll be called…."

"Chantelle Rose," we said in unison.

CHAPTER FIVE

I was about a five-minute walk from Tammy's house, but it was going to take me a good half hour to get there. After my encounter with Sally, I found myself sitting on a park bench trying to gather my wits.

I couldn't believe it! My beloved "second" mother, Sally, was the hippy nutter who had convinced Lionel that he would only be happy-ever-after on meeting *ME!* If there was any truth in her fortune-telling words, the last bit about me was totally fallacious. She'd even admitted as much. She'd said the same words to hundreds of young, easily influenced men, and I doubted very much that they were all unhappy and still searching for a so-called "Chantelle Rose." At least, I hoped they weren't, otherwise I was at risk of having prospective husbands popping up at every global corner!

As I sat there in shock, it was a while before I realized my mobile had started vibrating and quickly fumbled for it before the ring tone started. I still hadn't changed the tone, and what had previously been my tactic to identify my ring tone in an instant amongst many on public transport was starting to make me uncomfortable. It attracted too many odd looks when what I yearned for right now was discretion. So as I unsuccessfully fumbled around my handbag to reach for the vibrating device, the now unwisely selected donkey *Hee-Haw* bray started screeching out in true *Old MacDonald* style. Some nearby dogs started barking frantically and running around in circles looking rather confused.

I quickly answered without checking the caller ID, certain that it was going to be Robbie.

"Hello!" I answered breathlessly.

"Hi, Doll!" I knew in an instant it wasn't Robbie. He would never call me "Doll," especially, at least, not after "wanker". And anyway, the American twang was unmistakable.

"Hi Lionel," I replied. I knew my voice was a bit flat, but I really needed to talk with Robbie to get him to tell me exactly what happened the night we spent together before I broke the good (or bad) news to Lionel.

"You don't sound very happy to hear me." His sorrowful voice came down the line and I could feel tears welling up inside me again.

"No, no! Of course I'm happy," I replied, but my voice was emotional and tight.

Silence… I sniffed as I waited for Lionel to answer.

"Are you crying?" He sounded concerned.

"No, no," I replied quickly, clearing my voice and trying to make myself sound cheerful. "I just seem to have come down with a bit of a cold or something."

"Where are you?" he asked. "You sound really distant, and I can hear scads of dogs barking as if you're at some pedigree championship or something?"

"London."

Silence again. I wasn't sure if he was trying to figure out what the hell I was doing in London, when only three days before I'd been in his arms and in LA, or why there were so many barking dogs in the UK's capital city.

"Ohh!" he murmured after a while. "What'ya you lost in London?"

Nothing! I wanted to say, though I wasn't too sure if that was true. London was where I'd been born and brought up, cosmopolitan and unique, rich in heritage and cultural diversity (well, at least for the moment, until Brexit really kicks in and leaves us with only insularity and minimum culture). I loved it, as I did the whole of the UK, despite the dismal weather. But, I hesitated in my thoughts, I may lose you, Lionel, if I don't sort out the mess I'm in quickly.

"I'm on my way to see Tammy. She was still so weak when I flew over to apologise to you, that I felt uneasy about how she was getting along and wanted to come back and see her." That, at least, was true. "And as you said you'd be away for three weeks, I decided I could make the most of it and be here with her."

"Wow! She's one lucky girl to have you care about her so much. Let me know if she needs any medical care paid for. I feel bad about what's happened to her too. Gabby really took things too far."

"Thanks, Lionel, that's very generous of you. I'll tell her, she'll really appreciate it, but I think it's all under control." Our NHS was teetering with all the financial cutbacks, but the staff had all been amazing and Tammy had actually recovered quickly. "I'm just getting to her house now. Can I call you later?"

I was desperate to end the conversation as quickly as possible before it got any more intimate. I was lying – terribly – and Lionel didn't deserve this from me. Or from anyone, for that matter.

"No worries," came his (still gloomy) voice, so out of character from his habitual cheery tone. "I'll call you." And with that the line went dead, and I was left staring at my mobile phone and feeling utterly wretched.

***

"I'm so confused!" I cried out to Tammy, who was, thankfully, looking sprightly, well and fully recovered. To prove it, she called out, quite candidly, in her characteristic, honest way, as soon as she saw me walk through the door.

"Bloody hell, Chantelle! You look shocking. What the hell's happened? Your eyes are all puffy and red and your face is all blotchy! Have you broken up with Lionel or something? I always thought it was a bad idea. Hollywood heart-throbs aren't for us normal girls. I said so much to Ray just the other day. I said: 'He'll only break her heart. She's much better off with Robbie!'"

I sunk down to sit on top of her beanbag, which cushioned up around me, partially swallowing me, and rested my head back for a minute. We were in Tammy's bedroom (which was actually bigger than my flat off Streatham High Road), and the pale peach décor was pleasantly calming.

I sighed deeply. Where to begin? On the night we realised that the one leaving all the threatening letters was John (the Kings' chauffeur), he had seriously scared her; she had fainted and knocked her head giving her concussion. From the shock of it, coupled with a night spent on the freezing ground, she'd fallen into a semi-coma which had lasted several days. Though now fully recovered, she was, as far as I was concerned, unaware of the complete mess I'd managed to get myself into.

Tammy's boyfriend Ray was Robbie's best friend. We had met them (or rather been rescued by them) about six months ago during a weekend getaway to the country, when Tammy had managed to get her expensive Jag (a 21st birthday present from "Daddy") stuck in the mud. I'd been swept off my feet by Robbie's amazing looks (I know that sounds superficial and rather childish, and as my mum would have pointed out: *It's what's on the inside that counts, my love...* Exactly, Mum!), and things hadn't been the same since.

The day after being rescued by our rural knights on a tractor, I'd received a phone call from Freddy G – one of the world's leading and most sought-after movie agents. He'd been asked by Lionel King, his top star and the biggest name in Hollywood to date, to watch *The Business* (a tatty British crime film) and observe the girl in the red catsuit – and offer her a role in his next big production: an action-packed, multi-million-dollar-budget film.

And, of course, I was "the girl in the red catsuit." The rest is history...

"I'm pregnant." I said the words out loud, no more than a whisper.

There was a moment of utter stillness, as if everything was trapped in time, before I heard a huge intake of breath from my friend, who was, I believe, for the first time ever, stunned to silence. I turned to look at her. She'd gone quite pink and her mouth opened and closed several times, but nothing came out. Which was a first, because Tammy on a good day could get more words out of her mouth per minute than even the most expert football or racing commentator.

I was the one to break the silence, by adding, "And I don't even know who the father is." Not that this additional information was going to help Tammy recover from her sudden muteness. But she did flush an even deeper pink, and it was a while before she exclaimed in delayed shock:

"Shit, Chantelle! How many guys have you slept with?"

"I don't know!" I blurted out, feeling wretched.

"Bloody hell! This is worse than I expected!"

"I know," I replied. I closed my eyes and leaned back into the huge beanbag again, wishing it really could swallow me up. I felt numb, and it all seemed a bit surreal.

"So, I know that Hollywood is famed for drugs, sex and rock and roll, but seriously, Chantelle, I didn't realise you would fall for it." By this time she had plopped herself down next to me. "So tell me, was it just one big orgy?"

I forced my eyes open again to look at her. She was staring at me; her eyes looked as if they were going to pop out of her head in expectation. I actually laughed aloud; well, it was more like a throaty chortle. My voicebox couldn't cope with much more than a hoarse sound after today's crying binge.

"Sorry to disappoint, Tammy. I only gave my body and soul to Lionel whilst over in Tinseltown. That's not the problem. The problem is, I just can't remember if I slept with Robbie or not."

Tammy's eyes, which were already bulging, looked at me unblinking, urging me to go on.

"I had one of my memory lapses the night we spent together, and as much as I try to remember, I just can't. Now I'm pregnant and I have no idea who the father could be. There's a chance it may be Robbie and I need to find out before I tell Lionel I'm pregnant."

"You haven't had a severe memory lapse in years, Chantelle. Why do you think you can't remember your night with Robbie? It couldn't have been that bad could it?"

"The memory lapse, or Robbie?" I wryly asked back. "I'm sure that if Robbie and I had slept together it would have been amazing, but for some reason the whole night remains a huge blank – and when I asked Robbie about it, he just told me that he preferred to wait for me to remember. His exact words were: *Would you remember if it was the most magical night of your life?* Because if it was, he would wait."

Tammy's big blue eyes now glistened; tears were on the verge of spilling out of them.

"That's so beautiful," she whispered. "I hope you do remember soon then, before it's too late."

"What do you mean by that?" I asked, feeling a slight uneasiness building up in the pit of my stomach.

"He's leaving the country. Didn't you know?"

CHAPTER SIX

Leaving the country? Shit, that was quick! I'd only just left the country myself. And he'd said he would wait! Christ, talk about running away at the first sign of trouble. And that's without even knowing the possible dilemma he's in.

My mind was in a whirl, which is how I found myself the very next morning driving down to Kent as fast as I could (which, considering that my new parental state had triggered road safety to red alert, was actually the slowest I'd ever managed to do). I'd checked the rear and side mirrors so many times on the journey down that my neck felt really stiff as I pulled up outside Robbie's family home. I hadn't even bothered to stop at my cottage first. There was no time to lose, and Robbie's phone was still on the blink. Even Ray, who had tried calling Robbie for me, hadn't had any luck. What the hell is the point of having an iPhone, which is actually more sophisticated than the computer programme used on the Apollo 11 mission which landed two men on the moon, if you're not going to use it! Because, quite frankly, "Houston, we have a problem."

I knocked on the front door. Silence. I knocked again, my heart thumping steadily and quickening with each passing moment. I strained my ears to see if I could pick up any noise from inside the house, desperately needing to hear a masculine voice that would confirm that I hadn't arrived too late. Finally, after what seemed like an eternity, I heard steps approaching and a female voice hushing a dog that had started barking. The door crept open and I found myself looking into the kindly brown eyes of Robbie's mother. It was a while before she seemed to register who I was. But then she let out a loud gasp.

"Chantelle! Come in! What are you doing here? Robbie told me you'd gone back to the States. Come in, come in." She opened the door and motioned me to enter.

I hesitated.

"Hello, I just really need to speak with Robbie. His phone doesn't seem to be working. Is he here?"

"No, love, you've just missed him."

"So he'll be back soon then?" I sighed with relief. If I'd just missed him, I was sure that meant he would be back soon. I bloody hoped so. I stepped into the house and fondly patted the Collie dog's head as I moved through to the kitchen, with Robbie's mum leading the way.

"Tea?" she called over her shoulder to me, as I frantically tried to remember her name. I'm terrible at remembering names. In this case I couldn't believe I was struggling to remember hers, because I'd actually signed the preliminary contract of the purchase of my country cottage with her. She was the owner of the town's estate agency which she ran from this family home. So it was shocking that I was struggling to remember her first name, and forget about remembering her surname. I'd already nicknamed her son Robbie as the "town's handy man" to my GP just yesterday morning. Molly? Polly? It was something like that, I was sure.

"Yes please, Holly." To which the Collie dog started barking excitedly, running around in circles.

I'd obviously got someone's name right, but I wasn't sure if it was quite the right "person."

Robbie's mum turned to me and smiled. "Dolly." She said.

"Yes, right! Of course, sorry Dolly." I sheepishly apologised as I bent down to fondle the Collie's head and hide my crimson face from Robbie's mum's gaze. As she pottered about putting the kettle on, I patted the dog's head once more and was mortified to read the name *Dolly* written on the dog's tag. What the hell!

It was a relief when Robbie's mum placed some mugs down on the table and I could quite clearly read *Robbie* on one and another name on the other mug, which I reached for quickly to get a better look. *Fanny*. But thankfully it triggered my brain cells.

"Thanks Myfanwy." I sipped the warm, milky tea.

"So, have you returned for good then?" Myfanwy asked politely, but her keen eyes, which seemed to scan me for information gave her away. Innocent though the question seemed, I had a feeling that there was a lot lying on my reply. She would be looking out for Robbie's interests, and I couldn't blame her. And I was sure that if she thought I was just playing around with his feelings, she would be quite frank and tell me to stay clear.

"Err, not sure really." Which was as true a reply as I could give. I honestly hadn't really thought what I expected – or hoped – Robbie would to say to me. In many ways it would be a relief if he just said that we hadn't actually done anything, that it had been nothing more than just an innocent kiss. Not, of course, that an innocent kiss translated to spending the night naked together of course, which is how I'd found myself on waking that morning. But it would save a huge headache. I could feel one coming on now.

But somehow I had to tell Robbie. For some reason I just knew he would say it was going to be OK. That we would figure it out. That I had nothing to worry about. That Lionel would understand! There, you see, I was feeling better already. A drop of tea really could work wonders.

I fidgeted in the chair trying to think of something to say that wasn't on the lines of *You might be a granny soon*. I risked being sprayed by tea as I was sure she'd splutter from the shock.

"Nice weather for this time of year isn't it?" It was the safest topic to broach, and if you like your facts and figures it was actually the most normal thing to say. After all, we Brits are renowned for talking about the weather. And, of course, our ability to queue.

"Yes, nice," Myfanwy replied. "Good weather for flying."

I nodded my head in agreement. Not that I was sure what she meant. Was she insinuating that I should get on the next flight back to LA? Or was flying a little pastime of hers and her light aircraft was just parked in the back garden waiting for take-off? I hoped she wouldn't ask me to co-pilot. Driving out of London had been challenging enough.

"So, do you think Robbie will be back soon?" I tried to keep my voice level; I really needed to keep calm. But I was desperate to see him again.

So the last thing I was expecting to hear was, "Oh no love. Not for weeks, I should imagine. Or perhaps ever. He's gone to Argentina."

***

Argen-fucking-tina?

Just around the corner, then. Christ! What was more amazing was that I didn't actually faint from the shock. Though I must have turned an ashy pale, as Myfanwy looked at me, concern etched on her face. She moved around the kitchen table to stand next to me, as if to steady me if needed. I felt shaken to say the least. Well, that certainly explained why Robbie's phone seemed to be dead; it was obviously in flight mode. And there was no other way to contact him. He was one of the few left who refused to have Facebook, Twitter or Instagram, and although he had email he never bothered to check it. So how on earth am I going to reach him now?

I must have said the last bit out loud, as Myfanwy placed her hand softly on my arm and gave it a gentle squeeze.

"If you love him, go after him," she said quietly.

I must have looked at her as if she'd lost her mind. She was expecting me just to rock up to a nation with a massive landmass, the eighth largest in the world to be precise, and find one person out of about forty-four million? I had a better chance at winning the Euromillions jackpot six times over! I shook my head as I felt tears welling up in my eyes.

"Because you do love him, don't you?" I could hear Myfanwy softly ask, but I continued to shake my head trying to clear my dazed mind. "Is that a no?" she continued, seemingly puzzled. "Young love is funny, lass, but you don't fly halfway around the world just to say hello. You don't drive all the way down to Kent just for a cup of tea. You don't look like you've just had your heart wrenched out of your body when you realise that you've arrived one day late, unless you love him, of course?"

"But you don't take off without saying goodbye either though, do you?" I whispered back.

Besides, there was more at stake than just my heart. But I couldn't possibly tell her that.

***

We remained silent for a while. Even Dolly the Collie dog had gone quiet. Myfanwy moved back to the other side of the kitchen table, picked up her now empty mug and took it to the sink.

"Stay here for a moment, will you, Chantelle?"

"Yes, of course." But I was miles away. What to do now? Return to Lionel and be honest with him, tell him what had happened, that I'd spent the night in another man's arms? I inwardly cringed, but it was probably the best thing to do, even if it meant an end to everything.

I closed my eyes and sat in silence for a while. I was startled when I suddenly heard Myfanwy return and noisily place something in front of me. I opened my eyes and looked down. Before me was an old-looking shoebox filled with letters and what looked like a leather diary. *What the hell was this?* I looked at her in puzzlement.

"Take it," she said as she pushed the box towards me.

"What is it?" It looked as if it held personal information, and I really didn't need anything complicating things more than they already were.

"It's from his mother."

"Whose mother?" I naïvely asked back, though my heart thumped at the realisation of what I had in front of me.

"Robbie's biological mother. Take it, and find out the truth for yourself. And please, if you can, bring him back."

CHAPTER SEVEN

I made it back to my cottage in a trance, the shoebox tucked safely next to me. Myfanwy had also given me a sack of provisions. "Just to get you through the next couple of days, lass," had been her words as she'd handed over a loaf of bread, some homemade cheese, eggs, milk, freshly-squeezed orange juice and various other comestibles. I was a girl with a mission, and couldn't waste time popping to the local store to stock up. There was no time to lose. At least that was the impression I'd got from Myfanwy's urgent look as she'd waved me off.

Little did she know that she was betting on the wrong horse. There was no way on earth I was flying to Argentina to get her son back. The very idea was crazy – and that, coming from me (who's capable of signing contracts to show off my nude butt without checking first), just showed how messed-up the very notion really was. It looked as if my coming motherhood was finally knocking some sense into me. And about time, too; after all, what would be the good of jumping on the next flight to Buenos Aires? Besides, with my Spanish (or rather lack of it), I was bound to end up in trouble.

Finally inside the cottage, I opened the curtains and let the sun's rays dance across the sitting-room floor, bring out the coppice gleam of the wooden floorboards, reminding me of the last time I'd sat here, with Robbie just inches from me. His tender look had penetrated my heart as I'd told him about my childhood loss, when my mother had passed away and triggered these temporary memory losses. But he'd understood. He'd held me tight in his powerful arms, and whispered to me that he would wait.

But he hadn't waited. He'd gone before I'd had a chance to remember what had actually happened the night we spent together. Before I could figure out in my heart what I wanted. And now I'd lost him.

I left Myfanwy's provisions in the kitchen and moved back to the sitting room. It was early afternoon, and the room was warmed by sun's rays filtering through the windows. I placed the box on the coffee table and opened it. There was several letters and what I'd originally seen, a leather diary. Out of the diary fell another letter which I opened with trembling hands; the paper was scented and looked relatively new. The writing was a beautiful slanted calligraphy. I closed my eyes for a moment. I knew I was about to embark on a journey that would take me to some unknown place where a lifetime of secrets would to be revealed, and I wasn't sure if I wanted to know what all these letters and diary contained. I had a feeling that I was going to get myself involved in something that, perhaps, was better left for someone else to discover. Who was I to read such personal information?

But, for some reason, Myfanwy believed in me. More than I did myself perhaps. She was relying on me to somehow bring her son back. I didn't think that was possible. But there was only one way to find out. I opened my eyes and started to read.

***

Dear Mr Garcia,

Further to our telephone call this morning, I have enclosed the diary and several letters that need to be urgently translated into English. As I've already said, the translation is imperative and I insist on the utmost discretion of the information revealed within. As discussed, I will transfer the money today and look forward to receiving the translated text by the end of next week.

If you have any queries, please don't hesitate to contact me.

Yours sincerely,

Valentina Mendoza.

PS: For the sake of comprehension, I recommend the reading and translation of the diary first and then the letters. Please translate this letter also.

I read the letter again, and realised my hands were actually shaking. I was going to need more than a drop of chamomile tea to get me through this box of secrets, but it was the strongest I felt I could have in my current pregnant state. Valentina, was that her name? Robbie's biological mother? Could this be a Pandora's Box? Would there be hope at the end? More importantly, would it confirm that there is also another son? I glanced back down at the letter before folding it away and my eye caught the date. My pulse quickened suddenly.

The letter was dated the very day I'd sat on a rickety old stool, nearly two years ago now, when I'd been an extra in that ghastly gangster film. The very day that was to change my life. It was the film that Lionel spotted me in. The very film that made him send his agent after me, to razzmatazz me up into agreeing to participate in Lionel's upcoming multi-million movie. That very day changed everything. And from the looks of things, not just for me.

I took a deep breath and picked up the leather-bound diary. "Let's find out what happened to your granny then, shall we?" I said out loud as I placed a hand tenderly on my belly. With the other hand I opened the diary, and once again began to read.

CHAPTER EIGHT

VALENTINA

San Rafael. Friday 7ᵗʰ September 1984.

I've just had the most amazing birthday. Fifteen today! Papa took me over the family vineyards at first light, as of custom on every birthday since I can remember. (I've never been to school on my birthday, and that alone always makes it a special day). I love riding with him over the plains. We left at dawn. It's Spring now and we were enveloped in a warm blanket of early morning mist as we started off at an easy trot. I was riding Lady. I was a bit concerned as she's almost twenty-five years old now. She used to be Mama's horse, but Mama doesn't ride any more. Mama doesn't do anything any more. She just sits on the porch, looking over the Valley, a sad figure, shrouded in black as if in mourning, like when Abuela died.

"What's wrong, Mama?" I've asked a thousand times. But she just looks at me as if I'm not really there, and tells me that I'll understand when I'm older. But I am older now, surely. I'm fifteen years old now! But I wasn't going to worry about her today. I was with Papa, it was our special day and as we broke into a gallop and my hair fell loose and cascaded down my back, I felt free. Papa glanced over at me, a carefree smile on his lips, mirroring my own sense of liberation. The fresh morning air was caressing our faces, bringing a rosy shine to our cheeks. I felt like when I was a little girl and I would ride behind him, holding him tight, urging him to go faster.

We rode south of the city along the Diamante River, immersed in a landscape of mountains, valleys, sun and water. The horses knew the route without us having to guide them. Papa rode his beautiful black Criollo stallion, named "Beauty" after Black Beauty. I was on Lady. I had outgrown my schooling pony years ago. But Papa had refused to get me my own horse. He had told me time and time again that Lady was a safe horse: noble, docile and steadfast. Even under a summer storm she would remain calm. But I was desperate for my own horse. A yearling that could gallop as fast as the wind and take me higher up on the rocky terrain where all you could see was the snowy peaks of the Andes mountain range and the Diamante river, born from the glaciers on the Maipo, stretching from east to west and all that could be heard was the whistle of the wind and the harsh caw of the Crowned Eagle overhead.

Our family land encompasses thousands of hectares of production land, at five hundred metres above sea level, and the Continental, almost desert climate, gave us our famous white Chardonnay and Sauvignon and red Merlot, Syrah and Malbec wines. I knew that the limestone sandy soil was imperative for the wine production, but I didn't really pay attention to much more. I was going to be an actress. As soon as I turned sixteen I was leaving to go to drama school. Not that my parents were aware of this yet. But it was my dream and I just knew Papa would support me. I always got my way in the end.

Which is why when we reached the Fernandez horse ranch, just below the Andes range, north of our hacienda home and Papa told me to slow down. I grew excited with the knowledge that, finally, I would get my horse. I'd always wanted an Appaloosa, white with black marks. An American Indian horse, to match my wild heart. And there she stood, impatiently tossing her head and pawing the soft ground below. I slipped off Lady and handed Papa her reins as I ran towards the young mare. She was beautiful. Her long thick mane was patched black and white like the rest of her. She looked at me through intelligent dark eyes and sniffed my hand which I held out for her to inspect before I patted her on her neck. She stilled her anxious pawing and let me caress her behind her ears. She was perfect.

"Can I ride her now, Papa?" I'd called out over my shoulder. But it was another voice that answered me.

"Not yet, little girl." I hadn't taken in the person holding the horse's halter and turned now. Angered by being called "little girl," I could feel my face flush with indignation.

"Excuse me." I'd hotly replied back.

And out of the shadows, stepping around the horse, came a man. My eyes locked with his. For a moment, we just looked at each other. I believe that something happened in that split second. At least for me. My heart raced and I was at a loss to continue any rebuke. He had the most unusual eyes. One was a brilliant green and the other a sapphire blue. He held my look, daring me to question his comment, challenging me with his eyes to deny that I was indeed no more than just a little girl. I was neither a girl nor a woman just yet, but the way he regarded me stirred something in me and I fell silent and was the first to break eye contact.

I turned to look back at the beautiful Appaloosa, though all I could see in my mind's eye was his face. His unique eyes, his strong jaw, his well-structured facial features. His dark hair which he kept back in a short ponytail enhancing all the more his broad forehead and olive-brown skin. I had seen him before, but never so close up, and had never realised how handsome he was: his tall wiry frame, powerful from physical labour and horse riding. They called him the horse whisperer, and he was renowned in the area for his gift with horses. He could tame the wildest mount. His real name is Rafael, he is the Fernandez son. His father had owned the horse ranch, but had been killed in a plane accident about two years ago, and now the ranch was run by his widow Carmen and his son Rafael: this young man before me. Even though he had called me a little girl, he was actually not much older than me, only some three of four years. Enough to have reached manhood, and forget what it is like to be in that awkward stage of adolescence.

There was a moment of silence before Papa reached us.

"Thank you, Rafael. When will she be ready?" Papa asked.

"She has a strong will and will be hard to tame, but I know how to earn her trust, she will follow me and allow me to ride her soon. You will be able to take her in the next month or so." This had been Rafael's reply, but all the while he'd looked at me as if he was talking about me instead. I'd felt myself blush and was relieved when Papa continued:

"Perfect. You will come to the party tomorrow night. No?" Papa was referring to my birthday party, which we held at the main family home every year. It was a huge social event, all the rich families of San Rafael came, even some from Mendoza travelled in. The capital city of our province held great importance for our family, we bore the very name on our family crest. We were Mendoza.

Rafael hesitated for an instant before answering; "Only if Valentina wishes me to come."

It wasn't a question, rather a statement, and caught me off guard. He knew my name. Of course everyone knew my name. But for some reason I was surprised to hear him say it. His intense gaze was on me once again.

"Of course," I answered. I was trying to sound as if I really didn't care whether he came or not. But I was breathless to hear his reply.

"In that case, I'll be there," he'd said as we'd turned to leave.

"Great," Papa had responded, giving Rafael a friendly slap on his back as we moved to continue with our ride.

"Tell your Mother to come too," Papa had insisted, as we mounted our rides and moved off at a steady trot, but my heart was beating wildly. As wild as the Appaloosa we'd left behind.

***

San Rafael, Sunday 9th September 1984.

It's 4 am and I can't sleep. I've just come in from the birthday celebrations and I'm far too excited to go to bed. The house seems quiet now. I can hear a faint murmur as the last of the party guests, who are still milling around outside, collect their belongings and say a final farewell to Papa who has waited to see them off. Mama had retired to her room hours earlier. Indeed it was the first time I stayed up after her on my birthday. It had been a great social gathering this evening. I was finally fifteen; this season an official debutante in the Mendoza society.

I had dressed in a flowery blue dress that hugged my body. For once I'd been able to choose my outfit and had opted not to wear the typical two-piece embellished outfit that the ladies usually wore with a very full skirt, designed for comfort and practicality while dancing. But the dress I'd chosen, despite its tight fit, was actually like a second skin and made dancing just as easy. I had walked into the garden area, my arm linked through my father's and together we'd greeted the guests. My heart was beating rapidly throughout, in anticipation of meeting Rafael once again, but he was nowhere to be seen. The guests had gathered and I had smiled at all of them as they complimented me on how grown-up I looked. A real beauty, they all commented to Papa, who beamed in pride.

My father looked extremely handsome too. Dressed in typical *gaucho* clothes, his brightly-coloured *faja* worn around his waist over his shirt, enhancing his still trim frame. There was no doubt that we were father and daughter. I'd always been told that I looked just like him. We both have dark blonde hair and smokey grey eyes, but despite the somewhat northern European look, we also had the dark Latino skin. The contrast was quite striking, or so everyone says.

The dinner buffet had been laid out to one side of the main house. The front porch embraced the tables and chairs which had been decorated with dark maroon ornamental coverings to match the floral garden that was alight with fairy lights and decorative candle torches which had been dug into the rich soil beneath and held up by large spokes. The buffet was accompanied by trays and trays of barbecued *asado*. There could not be an Argentinian feast without an *asado*, grilled meat on an open fire. Just as there could not be a *fiesta* without tango. I did the opening dance, in open embrace, with Papa. I'd had dance lessons since I was a little girl, but tango was in our blood as much as we are Mendozas. My feet were light on the dance floor as my father glided me around to the beat of the music. The tango had originated in the 1880s, in the lower-class districts of Buenos Aires and Montevideo, along the River Plate, the natural border between Argentina and Uruguay. It is part of our heritage and we are proud of it. As the music slowed and the guests clapped, I was caught unawares by a voice behind me, speaking to my father.

"May I have the honour of dancing with your daughter, Sir?"

My heart started beating rapidly – and it had nothing to do with the dance that I'd just performed.

"But of course, Rafael," my father had responded as I'd turned to face the horse whisperer. As our eyes locked I tried to maintain a cool composure and somehow indicate to him with my dark stare that I was still offended that he'd called me "little girl" the previous day. It was too little success as he took no heed of my cool look or curt smile, and without waiting for me to acknowledge any willingness to dance with him, he took firm hold of me in his warm, work-hardened hands. He pulled me close in a tight embrace as the music started again, his left hand holding my right hand firmly in his as he placed his right hand in the middle of my bare back just below my shoulder blades. I tried not to quiver under his touch as in turn I placed my free hand at the centre of his back.

I closed my eyes for a moment and breathed in his fresh cologne, spearmint mixed with sandalwood and sweet musk. He smelled of the wilderness, open air and freedom, and as I opened my eyes and tilted my head up towards him I was startled to find his lips just inches from mine. I pushed back with a jolt. We were in the middle of the dance floor, the centre of attention, and I could feel my face blush in modesty. The music picked up, and thankfully I was able to follow the rhythm despite my shaking legs. I let the music flow through me, and as we circled around in a tight embrace *slow, slow, quick, quick, slow*, I mirrored his moves. Not once did he take his eyes off me and I was aware that his hand had moved and was positioned low down on the small of my back. We danced the next three dances together and not once did he let go of me. Then my cousin Nacho interrupted us to dance with me, and the magic was broken. Out of the corner of my eye as I twirled around I could see Rafael dance with some of the other young ladies, but his gaze searched me out time and time again.

Finally I was able to free myself of Nacho, but by then my mother was waiting for me, shrouded in black as always, her face sunken and pale. She looked older, and there was a streak of white hair in her head of dark locks that I hadn't noticed before.

Beside her was Santiago, the son of our family's solicitor. I'd met him before; he was in his early twenties if I remembered correctly, but still had pimples all over his face and a puppy-fat roundness that he hadn't shed with the years. My mother beckoned me to her, and as I approached, she drew me close and whispered in my ear as she led me toward the young future lawyer.

"Santiago is a better suitor than that horse trainer. Listen to me, Valentina: for your own sake, stay away from Rafael. He'll lead you to trouble." And with that she disappeared and left me in awkward silence with Santiago. Eventually Santiago started a one-sided conversation and told me all about his University studies at the school of Law in Mendoza, and how the university is the oldest and biggest private non-profit institution in the region of Cuyo. But I wasn't listening; I was looking out for Rafael who seemed to have disappeared. What would my mother know about the feelings that had been provoked by Rafael's touch? I was fifteen now, a young woman, old enough to make my own decisions. Old enough to excuse myself from my mother's ideal suitor and seek out the man I wanted to spend time with.

I hesitated near the dance floor searching for Rafael. I had been offended by his comment the day before, and had wanted to make it clear that I had not been impressed, but now I was just more concerned in seeing him again before the night was up. It was late now, and some of the party guests had already left. Papa was dancing in the candlelight. I wasn't surprised to see that it wasn't with Mama, as she refused to participate in anything merry any more, and I smiled at him as I moved on. It was when I rounded the garden hedges that I heard a soft "coo" calling from further down the garden path.

Curious, I moved down the darkened trail. I knew it wasn't a bird making that soft sound at this time of the night, and my heart quickened with each pace. As soon as I got level with the far side of the garden, past our fruit orchard, I felt someone reach out from the bushes, and a hand went over my mouth to stifle my startled cry. Before I knew it, I was held tight in Rafael's arms. My breathing became shallow, and I could feel his own quick, warm breath on my cheek. I looked up into his eyes, one the colour of deep forest pools, the other of glacier meltwater. He moved his head down towards me and with rising anticipation I closed my eyes as his lips found my own and for what seemed like an eternity we were locked in an electrifying embrace.

I had never been kissed before, at least not like this. His tongue had hungrily urged my mouth open and as it searched out mine and they touched, it was as if an electrical current charged down me, to the very tips of my toes. I never realised that one simple kiss could contain so much passion. But it wasn't a simple kiss, it was more than that. I don't know who broke away first, we seemed to move as one. But when we did finally relax our hold of each other it was with sudden urgency as there were voices approaching in our direction. A soft female laugh floated over the spring night towards us. I tried to break free and run back to the main house, but Rafael held me back for a moment.

"Valentina," he whispered, "come to the ranch tomorrow. Tell your father that I need you to help me tame your mare. Promise me you'll come tomorrow." There was an urgency in his voice that betrayed his unwavering gaze.

"I'll be there," I excitedly whispered back, and with that ran all the way back to the house and to the safety of my bedroom where I sit writing this. My hands still shake with excitement and it's hard to keep the pen steady. I will try to sleep now, but I doubt sleep will come.

***

San Rafael. Sunday 9th September 1984.

It's still Sunday, but late in the evening. I hardly slept last night. Despite going to bed so late, it must have been well past 5 am when I finally dozed off. I was awake before 9 am and had quickly dressed in my riding habit, excited about going to the Fernandez Ranch. Part of me actually felt I must have dreamt up the magical night. I couldn't quite believe that I had been in Rafael's arms just hours before, and that he'd kissed me with such passion. I laughed out loud and blushed at the same time as I recalled his warm embrace. He obviously didn't think I was such a little girl after all.

I skipped down to our dining area. I had no appetite to eat anything at all, but I didn't want my parents to suspect something was amiss and ate my breakfast as best I could before I informed Papa that I was going to help Rafael with my new mount. Papa didn't look the slightest bit surprised, but it was a long ride to do on my own and he said he would accompany me. This wasn't exactly my plan, but, realistically, I didn't think I would have been allowed to do the whole ride alone, so going with my father was a far better option than not going at all.

As we approached the ranch, the day had broken into a beautiful spring morning and I was feeling quite warm as we trotted through the main gate. I could feel my cheeks flush and was glad that it could be blamed on the warm weather and fast ride out, rather than my expectation of seeing Rafael again. And there he was waiting for us. He nodded at my father first, who had dismounted quickly, then turned to me and smiled. A brilliant happy smile which made my heart leap. But he courteously kept his distance in the presence of my father as we made our way to the paddock.

"What will you name her?" he asked me as we walked along. I hesitated for a moment before answering. I was so distracted at being in his company again that it took me a few seconds to realise he was taking about my mare.

"Dancer," I answered. It seemed fitting, too, considering that I will always, at least I hope I'll always, remember dancing with Rafael. I wanted a name that would somehow entwine Rafael and me together in memory of our first dance.

He nodded in response and discreetly winked at me as a modest smile played on his lips. We continued in silence until we arrived at the large circular corral where Dancer was frolicking around, kicking up dust as she reared up and then bucked back. She really did look quite wild but stunningly beautiful. On seeing us arrive she neighed and broke into a wild gallop right up to the far fence which I thought for a moment she would try and jump. Thankfully she just skidded to a halt and trotted back to the centre again in high graceful dancing steps, an apt reflection of her name. I positioned myself on the highest rung of the wooden fence, Papa beside me, and watched in expectation as Rafael jumped into the circular corral and made his way towards Dancer.

He let out a soft low whistle as he approached the mare. Her ears twitched and she let out a soft neigh in reply and sniffed the air and stepped a pace towards him. He whistled again, this time softer, then approached her slowly, holding out his hand for her to sniff. She moved towards him until her nose twitched near his head. In one sudden wild movement she reared up, and my heart leaped in my chest as I thought she would come crashing down on him. Rafael remained still as Dancer landed her hooves just inches from him and once again she was off in a wild gallop around the corral.

Rafael at this point settled himself in the centre of the corral and sat on the ground. Finally Dancer stilled and raised her head to look in Rafael's direction. His dark head gleamed in the late morning's rays. He was looking at the ground directly in front of him and though I couldn't hear what he was saying, his lips moved as if chanting to himself, or rather to Dancer who now shook her head, shaking out her generous mane. She snorted as she nervously pawed the earth and lowered her neck towards the ground and sniffed, then she reared up and bucked and stampeded to the far fence.

Rafael remained still, softly chanting magical words that only Dancer seemed to hear. Slowly she moved towards the centre of the corral, snorting as if trying to identify any possible danger. But Rafael was far from a danger to her. His soft chanting floating over to me in a hushed whisper. I couldn't make out what he was saying, it sounded like the old Quechuan indigenous tongue, but I'm not familiar with the language so I couldn't be sure.

Dancer approached cautiously until she was just a metre or so away from the horse whisperer. My pulse quickened. She leaned towards him until her nose touched Rafael's dark hair. His chanting seemed to hush for a moment, then it began again – but this time in an eerie sing-song tone. I was reminded of the Inca Empire that used to inhabit the Andes mountain range around us.

Slowly Rafael shifted to kneeling and held his hand out once again for her to sniff. As she inquisitively continued her examination he casually rose to standing. She remained still as he now caressed her neck, from her ears slowly down to her withers, then back up to her cheek and jaw and then rested his palm on her muzzle. He then leaned close to her neck and rested his head on her as he continued to caress her.

The first simple and natural bonding had taken place in such a way that it seemed as he had done nothing, but as Rafael now started to walk way, Dancer kept at his side. If he paused, she paused beside him. If he walked on, she kept pace. Now and again he would stop and caress her face and neck again and whisper in her ear before moving on.

The whole performance had probably taken no more than an hour, but Dancer had calmed. As they slowly circled around the corral together, the mare seemed more like a puppy than the fiery mount that had been waiting when we first arrived.

Rafael paused near me and beckoned to me. Slowly I climbed down on the inner side of the fence and walked towards them both. My eyes stayed fixed on Rafael who smiled at me encouragingly. Instinctively I held my hand out for Dancer to sniff, and caressed her slowly as I had seen Rafael do.

"Speak to her," he whispered.

I felt a bit foolish, but leaned in close to her and told her how beautiful she was, that I'd named her Dancer and hoped she liked the name. I promised to look after her and that we would be friends. I turned to Rafael to see what other advice he would offer me, but he was no longer there. I'd been left on my own with Dancer, and as I stroked her neck one last time before I moved back towards where Rafael was standing watching with my father, Dancer followed me.

***

San Rafael, Friday 14th September 1984.

Finally it's Friday, and I'm back from high school and writing my diary again. This whole week has really dragged. I could hardly concentrate on my classes, my thoughts constantly going back to Rafael and to Dancer. I was anxious for the weekend to arrive and have an excuse to go and see them both. After all, Rafael needs my help. Doesn't he?

Every time I think back on how we'd said goodbye last Sunday I find myself smiling. We had stayed for a quick refreshing *yerba mate* (tea that originates from the Guarani indigenous culture). The tea leaf is quite strong, and considering how little I'd slept the night before, it was a relief to have some strong natural caffeine as we still had quite a long ride back home. As Rafael had offered me the tea in a calabash gourd with the silver *bombilla* straw to drink from, his fingers had lingered on mine as I took hold of the mug to drink from. Our eyes had locked for a moment, and it seemed, at least to me, as though the world had stopped for a split second before it started spinning again at an electrifying pace, matching the fast beat of my heart.

As we returned to our mounts Rafael walked close to me. His hand "innocently" brushed mine a couple of times on the way, and I felt ridiculous happy. If my father noticed, he remained silent. He wasn't like Mama. There was a mutual respect between the two men, they were both *gaucho* cowboys. The wilderness was part of their persona. Both were as sturdy and strong as the rocky mountains around us. As beautiful as the clear blue sky above us. Men of my heart.

As soon as I'd walked in from high school my father had informed me that Rafael was on the phone and wished to speak with me. It was just as well that Mama hadn't answered, I wasn't sure if she would have passed on the message.

My voice shook, much to my embarrassment, as I answered the phone and heard Rafael's strong robust tone down the line.

"Valentina, Dancer has really progressed this week, but I'd like to do a new exercise with her. I plan to lead her out to Lake Los Reyunos in the company of my horse who will teach her calmness. Will you come too? It will be a whole day out, we need to bring food and drinks."

"Of course," I'd excitedly answered. He'd kept on talking, but I was so exhilarated about spending the whole day with him that I could hardly concentrate on what he was saying. Thankfully I did catch his last few words, informing me that he would call for me at eight o'clock the following morning. I wasn't too sure how I was going to get away with spending the whole day with him without Mama trying to stop me, but thankfully Papa told me he would take care of it.

But now I can hear them arguing. It's been a long time since I've heard them speak in raised voices. Mama's shrill voice can be heard loudly down the corridor: "The Fernandez family are trouble, always have been. Hasn't she done enough!? And now him. I won't allow it!" I can hear father hush her as she now breaks down and sobs, an eerie sound in the quiet of the night, and I inwardly shiver.

***

San Rafael, Saturday 15th September 1984.

Something's not right.

I've come home to an empty house. I've searched all over the place, but Papa and Mama are nowhere to be seen and I can't find any note from them anywhere telling me where they've gone. I'd quietly entered their bedroom in case I'd been mistaken and Mama was actually sleeping. But nothing. The bed had been carefully made, her clothes had been neatly pressed and put away. The room smells of lavender. As long as I can remember, this has been its characteristic aroma. It helps Mama sleep, or so she always tells me. It's a spacious room, the base tone used in its decoration is a soft light green, mirroring the green vineyards that surround the house. Then there is the en suite bathroom to one side and the writing desk right by the window. Mama often likes to sit there, though she doesn't write much, rather just gazes out of the window and into the open fields below.

As I neared the window I noticed an open letter on the desk, and moved over to read it. It was addressed to my mother, Maria Pérez de Mendoza. I scanned the letter quickly, worried that at any moment my parents would return and find me snooping in their bedroom, for I doubt the letter was intended for my eyes. It was only a few sentences and I was able to memorise it:

85

Dear Maria Pérez de Mendoza,

I hope this finds you well, however I imagine you know full well what I need to discuss with you, and pleasantries are unnecessary. In fact whether you are well or not is of no concern to me.

Meet me, without fail next Monday, in the Plaza San Martín at 12 o'clock noon. Come alone. If you don't come, I'll take matters into my own hands.

Carmen Gonzalez de Fernandez

Rafael's mother! What did she have to discuss with my mother? I panicked that perhaps she too was against me spending time with her son. But then I noticed the date: over two years ago. And if I carefully recalled, it was the same time Mama stopped laughing, the same time my mother changed from her beautiful smiling carefree self to an old lady shrouded in black.

And now I can hear someone pounding on the front door in the dead of the night and I don't know what to do...

CHAPTER NINE

CHANTELLE

Bloody hell!

I'm not sure I can read much more of this. I had a good chance of getting the jitters, in my own home and in broad daylight. I'd best kept my thoughts off the fact that my current home was nestled in the depths of rural England, surrounded by dense forest, with the closest neighbour well over a couple of miles away and mobile telephone reception, if I needed to make a hasty call for help, as unreliable as the weather. Getting neurotic over this diary wasn't going to help me much.

But I did double-check that the front door was locked and the chain was on, and for added security I placed a kitchen chair under the door handle. Not that a bargain buy IKEA chair was going to do much if someone decided to break in through the front door. I doubted there was even enough proper wood in the structure to cause a splinter, let alone prevent someone determined to get in. Still, it obviously helped psychologically, because seeing the chair in position I suddenly felt soothed and much more secure.

My thoughts went back to Valentina. I hoped to God she wasn't going to go into explicit detail of when she pops her cherry. I'm not sure I could handle reading the details. She is supposedly my child's granny, after all, and there are some things I'd rather not think about.

I skipped to the last page of the diary, thinking that perhaps that way I would be saved from having to read all the sinister details, as obviously something goes terribly wrong. But it really didn't help much as I read the final sentences:

I'll never forgive any of them. My life has ended before it's even begun....

I sat still for a moment on reading these sad and quite obviously bitter words. What had happened? How was it that someone who'd had their whole life before them could end up in such distress? Valentina had come across as quite a strong-willed young girl, someone used to getting her own way. How could she lose everything? Surely her parents would have protected her. At least her father (who obviously doted on her and let her get away with her every whim) would have helped her. Unless, of course, something had happened to him? I shuddered.

There was only one way to find out. I picked up the contents of the box again. I still had a fair bit of the diary to get through and then all these letters. Jesus, it was going to be like cramming for my A-Levels again. It was still mid-afternoon. I figured that if I could pull off an all-nighter, I should have everything read by morning.

I headed to the kitchen to make myself some coffee. I doubted that a decaf would see me through till morning, but it was going to have to do. I switched on my sophisticated Nespresso coffee maker. The machine had been an expensive gift from Tammy's parents as a thank-you for the way I'd looked after Tammy while she'd been in the hospital. Together with its sleek metallic design, pre-programmed settings and backlit controls, I wouldn't have been the slightest bit surprised if it took off and circled the room, before pouring its contents into the coffee mug I had waiting. If I hadn't known better I could have mistaken it for one of those new-fangled drones. Personally, I wouldn't go near one. I'd a good chance of blinding myself if handed the controls for one of those machines. I'd only just figured out how to use the coffee maker without trapping my finger in the capsule compartment every time I used it.

I gazed out of the window and my thoughts turned to Robbie and Lionel. Valentina may have found herself in trouble, but I wasn't far off her in despair. I was, however, determined that although I'd managed to get myself into a mess, I would take control of the situation and follow my heart. I did have strong, loving feelings for Lionel, but I was also well aware that I'd been overwhelmed and very much influenced by the Hollywood magic. Were my feelings really genuine? I'd been totally swept off my feet, but who wouldn't have been? I mean, honestly, who could come away from being wined-and-dined by one of the most attractive and wealthy men in the world and not fall for him like I had? I was no Mother Teresa, who would have most probably taken the million dollars for the needy and walked away with only a slight flutter of the heart. She would not have been swayed from her mission as I had been. But then again, she had been canonised – whereas I, well, I'd been knocked up. There was a huge difference.

Returning my thoughts to the diary again, the more I read about Rafael, the more I realised that there was no doubt Robbie was his son. I didn't blame Valentina for falling for him so quickly. Didn't the same happen to me with Robbie? I wished I could remember our night together. For some reason I felt it would help me figure out which way to turn. Not that that sounded very intelligent – basing my future life, more importantly, my child's, on the memories of a one night stand. God! That seemed so frivolous.

I stood for a moment longer gazing out of the window. The branches of the trees swayed in the autumn breeze, leaves swirled to the ground, covering it in a rich blanket of reds and yellows as they settled. There was something about this place, this cottage, that generated peace. Lionel may have joked about the fact that I would be bored out of my wits if I lived here by myself. But I wasn't so sure. I had London just over an hour away if I craved a bit of excitement; I could enjoy a night out at the theatre followed by a candle-lit dinner, and be back at my haven in little over seventy minutes. It was perfect. I sighed deeply, peacefully. Despite my initial feelings for Lionel, I wasn't too sure I could be a Hollywood wife.

As if on cue, my phone bleeped with an incoming text. And I was sure it had to be him.

I reached for my phone. The sender ID was an unknown number, but only Lionel would text: *Hi there! I miss you.* Without thinking, I punched back my quick reply: *Miss you too!* And I did. I rushed back to the sofa and settled down, a goofy grin on my face, waiting to read his reply.

-Really?
-Of course!
-Wow! I feel so much better! Can I call you?

-Yes, please!!!! ;-) xx

As soon as I'd pressed the *Send* button for my last text I felt a bit anxious. I'd have to tell Lionel at some point about being pregnant, and I wasn't too sure if it would be wise to tell him about my current reading material either. Err, shit! Perhaps I shouldn't have sounded so eager to speak to him. And now the phone was ringing and I didn't know whether to answer it or not.

Gathering my wits about me, I pressed the button to answer the call. I'll just play this by ear, I thought, as I tried to make my voice sound chirpy.

"Hi Hun, how are you?"

There was a slight pause before I heard: "Really good thanks!"

"Vivien!!" I shot back down the line. *What the hell?* For fuck's sake; I'd just started flirting with Lionel's ex! This was all I needed. And now I actually had to pretend that I was over the moon to hear her screechy squawk down the telephone line.

Vivien, who had been dating Lionel until he saw me in that ghastly gangster film and ditched her for me, on a fantasy that he had built up over the years from his meeting with Sally, my second-mother-turned-fortune-teller. Vivien, who loved Lionel so much that she had tried to kill herself when she realised that he no longer wanted her, but wanted me: a run-of-the-mill London lass who had just rocked up to Hollywood a few weeks before, and in an instant had crushed her lifelong dream of being Lionel's wife. She had hated me from the start and had made it clear, but when she'd tried to drown herself one stormy morning in the Californian surf, I, of all people, had saved her – and she had turned into my number one fan.

As I heard Vivien ramble on about the progress she was making at getting over Lionel, I was more than a bit unsettled by the fact that whilst I was unable to get through to Robbie and that Lionel hadn't bothered to phone me back or text me since our last call (which had ended rather abruptly), Vivien had searched me out with far more enthusiasm and ease than either of my "lovers." I did worry about that, and it wasn't the first time she'd showed more interest in finding me than the men in my life had done. I sighed. I really didn't have time to psychoanalyse all this all just yet. I was desperate to end the conversation and get back to the pressing urgency of finding out what happened to Valentina. So I was stunned to hear Vivien meekly ask, "Can I come and stay?"

Christ, no! I was lucky I hadn't said it out loud! "Err, I'm a bit busy right now Vivien."

I could hear her voice tremble down the line. "I still love him you know."

"Yes, I know." And I did. I was also aware she wasn't saying it to spite me or to make me feel bad. She was just been downright honest and open. Admirable traits really, and much more than I could say for myself.

"Hang in there, Vivien. I'll call you tomorrow if you like, and we can chat again, how about that?" I was concerned that she might try something silly, and I was hoping that I could somehow keep her occupied.

"That would be great Chantelle. Don't worry. I've learnt my lesson. I owe my life to you and I won't mess up again, but I'd love to chat again when you get a chance."

I sighed with relief.

"Great, it's a phone date tomorrow then!" I put my phone down and smiled. The closest I was getting to sexing was with Vivien. Just bloody brilliant!

***

My coffee had gone cold, so I had to heat it up again. I also grabbed one of the bed duvets to keep me warm as the autumn afternoon started to cool, and made myself a cheese and pickle sandwich to see me through the next few reading hours.

I skimmed over the letters before picking up the diary again. One letter caught my eye as it was addressed from Valentina to Roberto. Who the hell was Roberto?? Then it suddenly clicked: Robbie. Oh my, this was her first attempted contact with her son? It was dated just over eighteen months ago.

Dear Roberto,

I'm not sure if you'll ever read this, if this letter will reach your hands at all. But after searching for you all your life, I can only try. I'm not sure what information you have been given about your birth. I hope that you have been loved and well taken care of. That alone would ease my pain. Just knowing that you had been treated well, I could one day begin to forgive those who separated us.

It's important to try to forgive. Just as I hope one day you'll also forgive me for not doing more in my power to keep you. To find you quicker once I'd

93

lost you. Thirty-one long years have passed and I'm now no longer the young girl who was able to hold you tight for one brief moment before you were taken away. If I close my eyes I can still see your tiny dark head as it rested on my breast and smell your warm powdery vanilla scent. Your tiny hands that circled my fingers and squeezed tight in a reflex to never let go. But I let you go. Even if I could forgive those who took you away, I'm not sure I'll ever forgive myself for not preventing it. But I was only sixteen. I was so young. Too young to know that on letting you go, my life would end.

Six months ago my mother passed away, and her thirty-year-old secret was finally revealed. I won't go into details here. I have left you my diary that has been translated into English and all the letters about what happened, in the hope that you will read them and at least understand that I would never have let you go if I'd been told the truth.

I live in the hope that though you now have your own life, you will one day come and see me. I will never attempt to take the place of your adoptive mother, who will suffer with this also, but at least if I could see you just once again in this lifetime I will die in peace when the time comes.

Roberto, did you know you had a beloved brother? But he died when he was just two months old. I've never been able to find out what happened to my other dear son. Only you.

I love you, always have and always will.
Valentina Mendoza.

I broke from reading the letter, my heart pounding. Holy shit!! She doesn't know? Of course

94

there was a brother, but he didn't die, he's very much alive...

CHAPTER TEN

VALENTINA

San Rafael, Sunday 16th September 1984

I've hardly slept. Mama and Papa still haven't come home. On hearing the banging on the front door I'd crept back to my parents' bedroom and peeked through the curtains to look below and see if I could spy who was outside in the dark. I'd been careful not to turn any lights on and there was a great uneasiness in the pit of my belly as I peered below. I could see a couple of men standing around, but it was so dark I couldn't tell if I knew them or not. Their voices were muffled by the closed windows, which I didn't dare open, not wanting to alert anyone that I was actually inside.

Suddenly I head the front door lock turn and squeak open. I didn't know what to do. I ran into my parents' bathroom and locked the door. The tiny window in this bathroom opens on to the dining room terrace, and I calculated that if I eased myself through the window and was able to land safely onto the terrace floor, I had a chance of escaping. As I quietly made my way, in the dark, across the bathroom floor towards the window, my feet crushed broken glass. Something had fallen and had broken on the floor, which also felt slippery and wet underfoot. But I didn't think about it much. I was desperate to reach the window and escape.

"Valentina, Valentina!" I heard called out. I was so scared. Who had come to get me? Where were my parents? My heart pounded and I couldn't think straight. I stumbled on the wet glass and slipped to the floor. By this time the voices were nearer.

"Valentina, are you here? It's me, Teresa!"

I held my breath. Teresa? I waited in silence, my heart thumping, for the woman to call out again. I had to be sure that the voice was indeed that of Teresa, the family housekeeper who had been part of the household for as long as I could remember.

"I'm here," I called out in a shaky voice as I turned the bathroom light on. I let out a shrill cry of alarm as I saw blood all over the floor and a scattering of pills and broken jars. I stumbled to the door, opened it and fell into Teresa's arms.

Teresa embraced me firmly and rocked me, hushing me as if I was a small child.

"Your mother has fallen ill," she told me, in a voice tight with emotion. "She'll be away for a few days."

"Ill?" I'd seen the pills on the floor, the blood. I didn't need her to confirm that by "ill" she meant that my mother had tried to take her own life. But why? What had happened?

And now I sit waiting nervously for Papa to come home and explain it all to me. For a brief moment, I'd considered phoning Rafael. I was desperate to confide in someone. But something held me back. I had a feeling that somehow his mother was involved, so I thought it best to wait and see what Papa said.

I'd had such an amazing day with Rafael yesterday. How could such a magical day end in such tragedy? Rafael had picked me up, as arranged, early in the morning. I'd woken early and dressed with care, picking out my newest riding jodhpurs, cream tone, with a black strip down either leg which matched the black knee-high leather riding boots. Rafael had seen me in riding clothes before, but these jodhpurs seemed to hug legs like second skin and highlighted my slim figure. It was still early spring and the cool air made me shiver as I'd waited on Lady by the main gate to the estate. I was wrapped in a warm olive green poncho, but I realised that the early morning breeze wasn't the only reason I was shivering.

I was so nervous about seeing Rafael again. We were going to spend the whole day together, alone, and I couldn't contain my excitement. I'd packed a picnic basket and even sneaked into the wine cellar and poured half a bottle of Pinot Noir into a small flask I had found. I never drank (to be honest, I didn't really like it), but I was sure that sharing a glass with Rafael would be special. As I shivered once again I could hear the clatter of hooves in the distance before Rafael actually came into view. His shoulder-length hair was loose and danced with the breeze which pushed it back from his proud, chiselled face. His sparkling white shirt, partly unbuttoned, flapped in the wind as he galloped closer, astride his huge white stallion and leading Dancer behind. He slowed to a canter as he approached. His solemn, tanned face broke into a brilliant smile on seeing me, and for a moment I was left breathless. He had to be the most beautiful man I'd ever seen, and I couldn't believe that he wanted to spend time with me, that he's kissed me with such passion the week before. I could feel myself blush at the memory and offered a shy smile.

We rode away from San Rafael towards the Lake Los Reyunos, some thirty-five kilometres away. I haven't been there often, it isn't really a lake, rather a man-made dam that had been inaugurated just over a year ago. As we kept off the main road, and wound through the tracks towards the lake, Rafael told me all about how, towards the end of summer, he had been commissioned to cross from San Rafael to Santa Isabel in the Pampas region on horseback, leading a herd of cattle that was coming in from Santiago. It was a journey of about two hundred and forty-six kilometres. He told me that while cattle could be driven as far as forty kilometres in a single day, they would lose so much weight that they would be hard to sell when they reached the end of the trail. Usually they were taken shorter distances each day, and allowed periods to rest and graze both at midday and at night. Rafael calculated that if he moved the herd about twenty-four kilometres a day, they would maintain a healthy weight. Such a pace meant that it would take about ten days to ride out with the herd and another four days or so to return.

And he's asked me to go with him!

I'm in such a state of nerves. I'm filled with anguish over what's going on with Mama. But I can hardly contain my excitement at the thought of going with Rafael. My parents will never allow it. Especially now. But it's decided. I'll just escape when the time comes.

***

San Rafael, Monday 17ᵗʰ September 1984.

Papa finally came home late last night. He looked drained, his face creased with concern. He's refused to give me details about what's happened to Mama. Why does everyone treat me as if I'm still a child? It's so frustrating. I didn't want to cause Papa more pain, but I need to know if she'd tried to kill herself. But all he told me was that Mama has been unwell for some time now. "Mentally unwell" were his exact words. She needs special care and attention and would be away for some weeks. And no, I couldn't go and see her, he'd added, before I even had the chance to ask.

I feel sad. I have never been really close to my mother. She has never been able to show me affection. It's as if there's an invisible wall between us. It has been there for as long as I can remember, and in recent years it has got worse. I've always had a nanny to look after me and play with me. Papa has always been my hero, but if Mama isn't well, I do want to go and visit her. Perhaps if we were able to get closer I could help her somehow. But right now Papa isn't willing to listen to me or even suggest a visit.

To keep my mind off Mama (and, I imagine, any idea about going to visit her), he had asked me about my day with Rafael. I told him how Rafael had waded into the River Diamanté with Dancer, who followed him trustingly. There, though the current wasn't strong, the water which swayed around Dancer's legs prevented her from bucking and Rafael was able to lean over her withers and back. At first Dancer's tail had swished nervously, damp and heavy from the water, and her ears kept swivelling rapidly as if trying to pick up anything that would tell her that she was safe. Her nostrils flared, but Rafael continued to caress her and murmur to her softly, and she'd slowly seemed to relax. Rafael continued whispering as he stroked her mane and patted her firmly on the neck. When Rafael finally turned towards me and made his way back towards the river bank, Dancer followed.

We allowed the horses to graze nearby as we laid out our picnic lunch in the shade of a large Luma Apiculata, whose golden orange bark seemed to sparkle and glow as the sun's rays filtered through the evergreen leaves. It felt quite magical.

I certainly didn't tell Papa, of course, how Rafael and I had lain together on the soft moss-covered ground and how we'd kissed passionately. Rafael had unbuttoned my blouse and I'd felt a surge of dizziness as his fingers had explored my body. He whispered to me as he had to Dancer, except it wasn't in an eerie native tongue but clear sweet words that I will remember forever. How my grey eyes were like shimmering pools, two moons that reflected off the dark lake water on a brilliant summer night. Like smouldering smoke that made him catch his breath every time he looked into them. I could feel myself blush as he'd whispered to me, teasing me with butterfly kisses on my neck and down to the curve of my breasts.

He'd made me feel older than my fifteen years. His words were not like those of the boys in my class at high school, who were clownish and would fool around, immature and silly. His had been those of an experienced and worldly man, older and wiser than his nineteen years. I'd felt like a grown woman under his touch. I was used to being in control, flirting with the boys in my class and making them feel unsettled if I got too close to them. I'd found it amusing how they would back off and turn red if I gazed at them a little longer than necessary. But with Rafael, there'd been no backing off. He had taken me to a completely different level.

I didn't tell Papa either about our plans to go down to the Southern planes together. I can't actually believe Rafael has asked me to go with him. We've known each other all our lives, our families being two of the most well-known families in the area. But we don't really *know* each other. I've seen Rafael often enough from afar, but never really paid him attention. I've always been more interested in the horses around him. But being with him has changed me, and now my whole world has spun into a different sphere. The idea of crossing the plains with Rafael and Dancer is more that I could possibly have dreamed of. We are to work over the next few months to tame Dancer so that I can ride her. We will leave in the first week of December, and I'm to tell no one because it's clear if my parents find out, they'll probably lock me away. Not even Papa will consent, I'm certain of it.

Rafael has assured me that we would face the music when we arrived back. I know we're both being very simplistic. I'm sure that when I disappear Papa will have the whole countryside turned out with *gauchos*, police and the military until I'm found. But Rafael had said it in such a reassuring way I believed him. A half smile played on his lips as he'd caressed my face with his strong hands and brushed a strand of hair away from my face and tucked it behind my ear. I had actually thought for a moment that he was going to tell me he loved me, but then he'd turned to gaze into the distance. A peaceful silence had fallen between us, with just the soft breeze which whistled through the tree tops and the soft neighing of the nearby horses.

It got late and it was time to return. What I hadn't expected was to return to an empty house. Now there are new feelings stirring within me, bringing out the woman in me and closing a childhood door forever. But another door has also opened – a tragic one at that. I've got mixed feeling, growing excitement at my upcoming adventure and concern over Mama. When will she be back? And not just from hospital, but from the dark world she has fallen into...

***

San Rafael, Friday 21st September 1984.

Again the week has dragged really slowly. There has been no sign of Mama. The only information I've managed to extricate from Papa is that she needs time to recover, but is in good hands and progressing well. I'd turned to Teresa our housekeeper for information, but this was futile. She keeps her distance and looks at me with pity, as do the other house staff who all hush when I approached. School is just the same, the other kids all seem to be murmuring behind my back and fall silent when I pass. I haven't done anything wrong, but for some reason I seem to be treated as if I have some invisible but deadly contagious disease, at least that's how everyone was making me feel. Only Flavia, my best friend, has been the one to tell me that I shouldn't worry. She'd hugged me tight but hadn't asked any awkward questions. I'd been tempted to tell her about Rafael and the plans of our escapade, but, of course, I couldn't, at least not yet.

Rafael phoned me on Tuesday night. He'd just learnt the news about Mama from his mother and told me how sorry he was. I didn't ask how she'd heard, and there was a long pause and the line crackled, filling up the awkward silence before we'd continued our conversation. I wasn't sure if he knew that for some reason his mother may have played a crucial part in the current situation my own Mama was in. Carmen Gonzalez de Fernandez had a role to play in this I was sure. But what she had done in the past was surely in the past now. Why had my mother turned to such drastic measures now? And why doesn't anyone want to tell me anything?

My only comfort is that tomorrow I will join Rafael and Dancer again. We have exactly ten weeks to go before our adventure together is due to start.

***

San Rafael, Tuesday 9th October 1984.

It's been just over three weeks now since Mama's suicide attempt. I can say it now, though I'm still filled with anguish and despair when I say the word out loud. She came home last night. If I thought she'd aged in the last couple of years, these last few weeks have taken a dramatic toll on her, both mentally and physically. The deterioration has been quite dramatic. She had long ago lost the beauty she'd been famed for, but now she didn't even look human. It was a frail skeleton form that shuffled through the door as I'd run down the stairs to greet her. I halted on the last step and my eyes filled with tears on seeing her look so fragile. What on earth had happened?

My father sent me a reassuring smile and Teresa had quickly gone at my mother's side to help her and lead her to the master bedroom. My mother didn't even look at me as she shuffled past. I was lost. I didn't know what to do, what to say. I wanted to run to her and hold her tight and tell her that all would be well, but I'd been frozen to the ground and couldn't even find my voice to say hello.

Mama has remained in her room ever since. I knocked on her bedroom door when I got home from school today. Nobody answered, so I slowly turned the handle and opened the door and stepped through. The curtains were drawn, and Mama was sitting by her writing desk. She had pen and paper at hand, but the page was blank. I gave her a soft kiss on her forehead as she turned to look at me. For a moment her look was as blank as the paper on her desk: empty of feelings, recognition or acknowledgement.

She turned to look back out through the window and motioned me to sit. I took my place at the windowsill and waited for her to speak.

"Valentina," she said. Her voice was barely audible, no more than a whisper, and I moved closer to hear her properly. I knelt down next to her and took her cold hands in mine, although it was my heart that turned to ice as she continued. "You must never see Rafael again. You won't understand now, but believe me, you mustn't go near him. He'll only fool you into believing he loves you, but he doesn't. He can't. I only want what's best for you, Valentina, and Rafael will be your destruction if you continue to see him and spend time with him. Please promise me you'll never see him again."

"But Mama!" I exclaimed in shock and anguish at hearing her words. "How can Rafael be of danger to me? Anyway, I have to see him; he's taming Dancer for me. He's only a few years older than me, Mama, how can he possibly harm me?"

"You'll understand when you're older," was her simple reply, and then she threatened me with something that I couldn't possibly allow to happen. "See him again and I'll sell Dancer."

CHAPTER ELEVEN

CHANTELLE

What a bloody cow!! Jesus, the poor kid! I'm not sure if Valentina's mum has a reason for her threats or not, but what a way to really make someone feel terrible. I'm finding it really hard to have any good feelings towards Maria, Valentina's mum. I do feel sorry for her, because she obviously had a terrible time if she to tried to take her own life. But Jesus, just let your daughter go and enjoy life! The memories of my mum are so incredible and positive I couldn't imagine that there could be mothers out there who would make their own daughters' lives a misery.

I didn't know how this story was going to end, but I really needed to speak to Robbie. I fished my phone out again. I hadn't put it on silent mode, so I was surprised (especially considering the donkey bray it has as a ringtone) to see that I had a missed called from Tammy that I hadn't heard, and a text from Myfanwy, which I certainly didn't fancy reading at all. I felt I was under too much pressure. Robbie's biological mum and grandmother were giving me a headache as it was. I really didn't need more stress from his adoptive mum. I suddenly twigged that I'd get two mothers-in-law with Robbie, which considering that a lot of mothers-in-law are renowned for interfering, a double dose may not be so advantageous.

I quickly texted Tammy telling her that I'd arrived safely. I had promised to text her on arrival and completely forgot, so she was probably worried sick. As for Myfanwy, well, I wasn't going to worry too much about responding to her yet. I'd still got half a shoebox of letters to get through, and I desperately needed to talk to Robbie first.

It was mid-afternoon. I had no idea what the time could be in Argentina, but I really didn't care. I dialled Robbie's number and my heart thumped on hearing the tone. The previous times I'd rung him, there had been no sound at all, but this time there was a distant tone. *Please, please, please answer*. I felt all shaky and a bit sick to be honest, my whole future could depend on this call and I actually didn't have a clue how I was going to phrase things. I should have done a minimal rehearsal of what I was going to say before I'd dialled, but it was too late now as the line clicked, silence...

"Robbie?"

"Chantelle?"

"Robbie?"

"Chantelle?"

Oh for fuck's sake, I thought, we could go on like this forever! But I couldn't get any other words out.

"H-h-how are you?" I finally managed to stammer out, thinking *Get ready, because when you ask me, you're going to get the shock of your life.*

"Err... fine" came his seemingly not too thrilled voice on hearing me. I really didn't know what I was expecting him to say, but he didn't sound over the moon to hear me, and I certainly wasn't expecting that. Especially not after his parting words the last time we were together: *"If you're not happy, come back. I'll be waiting for you…"*

"I'm in Argentina," he went on, which took the meaning of "waiting" to a whole new level. I guess he thought I was the one who was going to be shocked by his revelation. Little did he know what I had in store for him – and his location, although it didn't help, was the least of my worries.

"I know," I replied.

"You know? How do you know?!" he sounded startled.

Now I'd got his attention, and we were just warming up.

"I'm at the cottage, and your mum Myfanwy…" (as there were now two mothers, I thought it was a good idea to name the mother in question to avoid confusion, not that *I* could personally get any more confused than I already was) "…has given me the diary and letters to read."

There was a sharp intake of breath.

"Why has she done that? Those are private letters, Chantelle. Don't tell Lionel about them until I sort this all out."

"Well, Robbie, he has a right to know too. He's just as much a part of this as you are."

"Fine, do whatever you want then."

Silence.

This conversation wasn't going how I expected, and I still hadn't even told him the main reason for phoning. For some reason Robbie sounded distant, almost like a stranger. Which, if I was honest with myself, he was really. What did I really know about Robbie? Or Lionel for that matter? Robbie has always seemed the more serious of the two, but reassuringly strong, sensible and reliable, like an old oak tree, unwavering under a gusty storm. I guess it wasn't really surprising that he had taken off so soon after reading the letters and diary. He would have thought it was his responsibility to find out the truth and to fulfil his biological mother's wish to see him, even if it was just once more, in her lifetime. Robbie was caring and unselfish and totally down-to-earth, which is what drew me to him, as well as his rugged good looks. He was kind and considerate. At least that was my perception of him, which is why I wanted to tell him first about being pregnant, not just because he held the key, but because he would advise me selflessly. He would give me his honest opinion, and I, on the contrary, was selfishly relying on him to guide me on the right road.

"Robbie, I know that you're far away and that you've got important issues to sort out right now, but there is also something very important that I need to tell you." I paused before I went on to make sure that Robbie was listening, that the line hadn't gone dead like last time, that this time he could hear me properly.

"Go on Chantelle, what's wrong?" Could I perceive a slight note of concern in his voice?

"I'm pregnant, Robbie." I actually choked on the words and I could feel tears welling up and my throat burning with tension.

Silence.

"Robbie?" I gasped out, panicking now that his reaction wouldn't be as positive as I'd thought. I'd been naïvely thinking he would drop everything to be with me and tell me that we'd be fine. There was always a "we" in my mind when I thought of Robbie, but now I suddenly felt very much alone.

"Congratulations," came his stilted reply.

"What do you mean, congratulations?" I certainly didn't feel like celebrating.

"I'm happy for you," he went on as I remained silent, trying to understand this sudden change of attitude. Robbie sounded distant. There was no tenderness in his voice. No emotion. It was as if I'd just told him that I'd had a wisdom tooth out, or that I'd adopted a puppy. I started to panic.

"I'm happy for you and Lionel," he added, as I slumped down on the sofa in silent bewilderment.

"But... but..." I managed to get out after a moment of awkward muteness. "Didn't we... err..." (how best to phrase this!?) "... have sex too?" I cringed as the words came out. How totally humiliating is this? I put my hand to my head and closed my eyes as I felt my cheeks burn in shame and my heart thumped waiting for his reply.

Silence once again. This was like torture. I would have much preferred the wisdom tooth option, have them all out at one go, rather than face this awkwardness. And if it was a temporary awkwardness I could deal with it. But *pregnant,* and all that that word encompassed, didn't feel very temporary to me.

I could hear Robbie clearing his voice before he continued.

"No, Chantelle, we didn't have sex. We spent the night together, but it wasn't sex." He paused here as the thumping of my heart was now joined by blood that pulsed in my head. "Sorry if I made you believe anything else."

111

"Right," I said, sounding all prim and proper despite the feeling that I was falling to pieces, that my world had been shattered. It was now that I realised that though it was actually easier to have just one "father" in this sorry affair (not that I was sure "affair" was the right word here) it was Robbie that I wanted, Robbie that I needed, and Robbie whom I loved.

You might be thinking: How could she possibly be in love, it's lust surely, she's just met the guy! Call it whatever you want, but I'd never felt this way before. Discovering this on the phone with Robbie, who had gone as cold as ice on me, certainly didn't help. Of course Lionel was any girl's dream. He was the Hollywood star with the charisma, looks, personality and wealth to go with it. But our whole relationship had been based on misconceptions. He had be blinded by what Sally, the so-called fortune-teller, had told him at an early, vulnerable age, about meeting a dark-haired, almond-eyed lady by the name of Chantelle Rose. Fair enough, that was me. But it was just a little trick that Sally had used. It wasn't *really* me. Then, by chance Lionel saw me in that fuck-awful gangster film and for him, it had been a game. To woo me, to captivate me, to win me over. And now this little game had tied us for life.

Why the connection with both men, and why I seemed to somehow be the missing key, was something I was yet to discover. Things always happen for a reason, or so they say. But I couldn't see any logic in being pregnant by the wrong guy. It certainly wasn't my smartest move. *Chantelle, my dear what have you done?* my mother would have asked sweetly. As for my dad, well, he'd have put me through the wringer!

"Right," I said again, clearing my throat which was tight with emotion. I could feel hot tears building up, threatening to spill out. "Umm... OK, thanks Robbie. Err..."

For crying out loud, what the hell was I meant to say now? I didn't want to end the conversation, but there was little more to be said after his statement that nothing had happened between us. I couldn't possible tell him how I felt, when the father was another man? When Argentina, far away as it was, felt actually close in comparison to Robbie's emotional distance?

"Chantelle?"

"Yes," I squeezed out, willing my voice not to tremble and give me away.

"I've got to go, but really I'm happy for you, for both of you. I hope you'll be happy too."

"OK" I whispered back in a broken voice.

With that, the line went dead. Tears gave way as I buried my head into the arm of the soft sofa, wishing for the first time ever to be with Mum and Dad.

***

A wave of dizziness overcame him. A shard of ice thrust deep into his heart, chilling him and draining him from the life that beat within. He had lost her, to a future that lay far from his arms. He could no longer compete for her love now. It would be best to let her go. She would be better off without him. What else could he do?

113

***

I must have fallen asleep as I woke with a start. My head thumped away and my eyes felt puffy and swollen from crying. I snivelled and searched for a tissue.

"Come on, Chantelle," I mumbled, trying to pull myself together. What was it I had said to myself not so long ago? That I could do this. With or without Robbie. With or without Lionel. I had a life to live, and inside me a new, precious, little life was also growing. I was glad that the baby was totally unaware of the complete mess I was in. "Sorry littl'un," I sighed out loud, thinking I wasn't exactly the best role model.

But I knew I was strong enough to do this by myself if necessary. With one thing and another, losing my dear mother at such a young age had marked me and made me a loner. *An independent young lady* is how I like to phrase it. I could and would sort this out. (I was also as stubborn as a donkey, which I proved to myself on an almost daily basis!)

I still had to figure out what the hell I was going to say to Lionel. I realised now that I couldn't possibly marry him. Despite having his child growing inside me, my feelings for him weren't so clear. I thought I'd loved him, and in a way I did – but if I was honest, what I loved was the part of him that was like Robbie. The part that was considerate and kind. He had a freaking awesome body too, juvenile as it was to admit it.

Bloody hell, what a mess I was in. Could things possibly get worse?

It was the Hollywood side of Lionel, that made him who he is, that I couldn't handle. The superstar. The fame. The show, the razzle and dazzle. It wasn't for me. I'd rather be blinded by a summer storm than the flashing camera lights. It was a totally different world where I would never fit in. Where I could never be happy. I sighed. There wasn't much else for it but to finish reading the diary, find out the truth, and then tell Lionel everything. If I could at least help him with his past, there might be hope for my future.

I settled back on the sofa again, wrapped the duvet around me, rubbed my eyes and picked up the diary, ready to continue where I'd left off. But before me, the pages blurred and all I could see was Robbie's face. My heart thumped and I closed my eyes briefly, I didn't want the image to go away. He was talking to me, and I tried to slow my shallow breathing. It was all coming back to me and this was not the time to faint with the stress of it all. This was my chance to figure out what really happened that night.

I got another flash. We'd just arrived back at the cottage. He'd driven the van for me as I was feeling light-headed after spending the whole day at the hospital at Tammy's side worried sick. It had not been the homecoming I'd expected. Nothing had been what I'd expected. I'd have been less shocked and much more at ease if I'd just spend the last twenty-four hours trying to climb Mount Everest in flip-flops. The jet-lag was setting in too. Robbie parked the van outside the cottage gate and turned the engine off. We'd driven in soothing silence and now he turned to me. I could see the flashback of events now, as if played in slow motion. He held my eyes in an unwavering gaze and tenderly reached over and brushed my cheek with his warm hand, cupping my face for a second.

"How are you feeling?" he'd asked.

"Pretty crap," I'd answered sorrowfully. "I can't believe it. I can't believe Lionel could do this; go to this extreme just to have me at his side. It's been a pretty shitty day to be honest." I broke eye contact and sullenly stared before me into the surrounding countryside.

"Stay here." And with that he got out of the van, opened the gate to the cottage and the front door before returning. He moved with such a confident stride. His tall, strong frame seemed to push back invisible cobwebs, cobwebs that had been clouding my judgement, and everything around me. But as he approached, my bleary mind seemed to clear as the sky does when clouds move off, leaving a brilliant blue – as blue as Robbie's eyes as he looked at me again. He was just inches from me and my heart gave a little leap. Surely such good looks so close up couldn't be good for my health. I was in danger of cardiac arrest as it was with the latest upheavals in my life; there was no need to add his devastating good looks to all of this.

"It's been an ugly day," I sighed "Tell me something beautiful?" The words slipped out, I was trying to bring some light conversation back into this dark day. Anything to keep my mind off Tammy's delicate state and Lionel's betrayal.

He leaned forward and with one swift motion had me in his arms. My heart didn't just leap now, it pounded away, and I wondered if it would pop right out and onto the floor. I hoped not, I didn't need things any more dramatic than they already were.

"Chantelle Rose," he'd said. This got me really befuddled. Was this a question? Was he checking that I knew my name? Because, though I was prone to memory lapses, I think it would take more than just a dizzy spell for me to forget my own name.

"Yes," I'd answered slowly, a silly giggle bubbling inside. It was either that or close my eyes and wait for his passionate kiss, because surely that's what would have happen in a soppy film. But this wasn't a film, it was real – and knowing my luck, he had no intention of kissing me at all, and the situation would then have left me feeling frightfully stupid, eyes closed in anticipation, putting him, in turn, in a terribly awkward position.

"You asked me to tell you something beautiful, so I've said your name."

"Ohh!" I stammered. I certainly wasn't expecting this degree of romance and hung on to his neck as he strode up into the house, kicked the door closed as we walked through and placed me softly on the sofa. Which, giving credit, was quite an achievement; slim though I am, I'm a five-feet-niner. Tammy at five-feet-three, is what I would call petite, whereas me, well, I'm bloody massive. So to have carried me up the garden path and over the threshold and not trip up on the way or start puffing from the exertions was quite remarkable. In fact, quite in line with what would have happened in a soppy romance. Perhaps happy endings did exist in real life after all.

I started to shake. Nervous shivers. I couldn't get any words out, and had to fight the silly giggle that was threatening to erupt. I knew Robbie was aware that I was a bit odd. He'd seen me in action before. I'd jumped through a window pane in his presence and had rolled about in mud down by the river on the very first day I met him. So I didn't think nervous laughter would scare him off any more than my habitual behaviour, but I didn't want to risk it.

"Are you cold?" came his concerned voice. "Stay here." And with that he disappeared upstairs appearing back again, a moment later, armed with one of the duvets and a couple of pillows. He placed the cushions with delicacy underneath my head and wrapped the duvet around me. I was in fact feeling really hot, especially having him so close to me. The shivers had nothing to do with being cold, but I couldn't find the words to tell him that. I was wrapped up like a cocooned caterpillar, just my head poking out, sweltering, flushed and red-faced but, much to my mortification, I couldn't stop shivering, so poor Robbie ended up throwing another blanket on top of me, tucking in the edges for added warmth. In truth I was about to explode from fire burning within, and conscious if that happened I would leave Robbie feeling really startled.

Luckily I was left alone for a moment, not that you could really call it lucky, as Robbie had gone off to get some wood for the sitting room fire which he was going light, to warm me up properly! Little did he know that I was on the verge of stripping off to my underwear as it was I was so warmed-up. Or perhaps, come to think of it, this was his plan, and he was cleverer that I realised.

It wasn't long before Robbie had a roaring fire going, whilst I subtly untangled myself from the beddings.

"You look much better," he said as he turned to me, warmth in his eyes as he gave me a shy smile. Not that there was anything shy about Robbie really. He was in total control and moved with confidence as he set about the cottage, tidying up my out-of-place trainers and my jacket that had been strewn across one of the armchairs. Thankfully I was able to stop him just before he reached for my pongy socks. "You just sit still, put your feet up and I'll get dinner ready," he went on, as I just looked at him in silent bliss. If my mother, God bless her, had been alive, I'm sure she would have whispered into my ear: *For the love of God, Chantelle, hold on to this one!*

I must have dozed off, for on waking I found Robbie had laid the dining room table, with freshly-cut flowers in a vase in the centre. A tantalizing smell drifted in from the kitchen, there was soft slow music playing from my small portable music system, and I started to give credit to my mum's wise words: cuckoo though I may seem most days, I would be really crazy to let Robbie go.

Not that I was sure what Robbie would have to say about the matter. He seemed keen. At least he'd done a bloody good job in getting this smoochy setting ready. Lights turned low, the flames from the fire danced with the shadows, and Robbie, as I tried to suss this all out, standing before me, held his hands out to hold mine. He drew me to my feet and into his warm embrace as he whispered in my ear.

"Will you dance with me?"

I wrapped my arms around his neck in answer and rested my head on his powerful shoulder taking in his earthy, spicy scent, of oak moss and sandalwood, or Hugo Boss bottled, if you want to be spot-on. For a moment I was taken back to those school discos, where I was lucky to get a dance in without having my feet trampled on. I usually towered over my dance partners, too, their head snuggled into my armpit, which, frankly, took away any tinge of romanticism. But this was no school disco, and as the music slowed I stood mesmerised in his strong embrace. He bent his head to the base of my neck where his lips lingered and softly brushed my skin, and I felt an electrical current charge through my body. Slowly, with kisses that set my skin alight, he continued up my neck, up to my earlobe which he playfully nipped before caressing my face with his strong hands and tenderly turned my lips up towards his. I held my breath and closed my eyes. I couldn't quite believe I was here in his arms as he held me tight and as his soft lips brushed mine I knew this is what I'd wanted from the very start. From the very first day I'd met him. I wanted to feel his touch, his warmth, and as our lips parted and his tongue hungrily sought out mine there was nowhere else in the world that I wanted to be, except here and now.

This wasn't revenge because of what I saw as Lionel's betrayal. There were no feelings of guilt as my tongue explored his and my hands moved to unbutton his shirt. I should never have got myself involved with Lionel on more than a professional level, but I'd been swept away by the Hollywood magic, by his charismatic personality, and by the fact that he looked so much like Robbie who stood before me now. Robbie who I wrongly believed had been dating Tammy, and also who I wrongly believed had been the one sending me the menacing letters, before I suspected Lionel of the same thing, when all he'd been trying to do was show me who he was – incomparable and more than I could ever wish for. Robbie and I stood there as one, and as he slowly removed my clothes and laid me down on the soft rug, before the dancing flames of the fire, and we made slow and passionate love, I actually thanked Lionel – because I was now free to be with the man I'd wanted from the start.

***

I woke from my reverie with a start. Oh my God! We did make love! Holy crap, I thought as everything came flooding back, but not just in front of the fire place, but then again on the stairs, in the bath tub and once again (as far as I can remember that is) in the bed! For fuck's sake, no wonder Robbie had looked at me in total shock when I'd told him I couldn't remember. How could I not have remembered that most incredible night? And it wasn't just about making love, it was everything. The ease I felt being with him. The magical words he'd whispered to me throughout the evening, how my liquid, honey-coloured, almond-shaped eyes had captivated him from the start, how my full, generous lips had been tantalising him since that very first day we met, how he loved my outgoing, independent, reckless self, ready to take on the world (although the world I really wanted was a quite country life), how I wasn't afraid to speak my mind and fight for what I wanted. He'd added that I was a true friend and that despite my independent nature I had a heart as passionate and fiery as dawn on a new day.

I flushed on remembering everything. As well as being something of a poet, he was a also true gentleman: caring, selfless and kind. Bloody good-looking too. Quite right, Mum, I'd be bonkers to let Robbie go.

But he had gone – and the miles between us had nothing to do with the distance I'd perceived in his voice. I didn't understand the sudden change in his attitude towards me. I guess if he believed the child growing within me wasn't his, he would keep his distance. But he'd sounded cold and withdrawn even before I'd revealed that I was pregnant. So what had happened? I refused to believe that his loving words had all just been from the heat of the moment. He did love me, I was sure. But for some reason he wanted me to believe otherwise. Unless something had happened there in Argentina that changed everything.

But what could he possibly have found out about his past that would affect his feelings towards me?

I looked down at the diary. It was time to go back and continue reading where I'd left off. I had a feeling that, for whatever reason, my future also depended on Valentina's past. But before I opened the diary again I picked up my phone. I had two important texts to send.

The first was to Robbie:

"You once asked me if, with time, I would remember the most magical night of my life. The night we spent together, because if that was so, you would wait for me to remember. And I have remembered, but the word "magic" doesn't do it

justice. Words can't explain how you made me feel that night and how you make me feel now..."

My heart pounded as I pressed the *Send* button. I was quite chuffed with my verse too; it wasn't quite a Shakespearean sonnet, but good enough for me. In fact, I anticipated a call from Robbie straight away. But the phone remained silent.

My next text was to Lionel:

"Hi Lionel. I hope you're well and the shoot is going great. Phone me when you can, we need to speak."

My heart also lurched on sending this text. But I knew in my heart that I needed to tell him as soon as possible that, despite everything, even though there was a part of me that loved him, there was a greater part of me that loved someone else.

CHAPTER TWELVE

VALENTINA

San Rafael, Friday 12th October 1984.

I was in shock after hearing Mama's words about how I couldn't see Rafael again. I couldn't believe that she had threatened to sell Dancer if I disobeyed her.

What had I done? Why was she being so cruel to me? I couldn't contain my tears as I'd asked Papa about Mama's words, openly crying as I sought to know the truth. But all Papa had told me, as he held me tight and rocked me as if soothing a young child, was that I wasn't to pay any attention to Mama, she wasn't well. That, many years ago, the Fernandez family had let Mama down and the bitterness she had felt all these years was now surfacing again. But I wasn't to worry, Dancer would not be sold, but perhaps I should wait a bit before spending time with Dancer or Rafael again.

I was, however, able to sneak a phone call to Rafael yesterday evening. His voice vibrated concern as he spoke to me. We arranged to meet today (Friday), during my last class. It was PE, and if I could fake a bad stomach ache I knew I would be excused from the lesson. PE was one of my favourite classes, after Drama, and if I was to say I wasn't feeling well, I knew the teacher would let me sit the class out as I would never miss a class unless I was truly unwell. And by the time the PE class came around I was actually feeling quite queasy anyway. Would Rafael be waiting for me outside? Would someone see me leaving the grounds and raise the alarm? Would my parents be called?

However I did escape unseen and Rafael was waiting for me as arranged. I fell into his arms in relief.

"What had happened to our families to cause my mother this grief?" I'd asked him.

He shook his head. Apparently something had happened many years ago, but he said he knew nothing more. Our fathers had been great friends, but something had happened and the friendship had ended. Though my father had made attempts to get the families together again, the distance remained. Rafael had observed a closer relationship in the last two years between his mother and my father, but hadn't really given it any importance. My father often stopped by the ranch and drank tea with Rafael's mother, Carmen, but surely that could be just normal. If my father had once been great friends with Rafael's father, perhaps he felt that by spending time on the Fernandez ranch, he could somehow make up for the years of friendship that had been lost after the plane accident two years ago.

Rafael told me not to worry, that the past shouldn't affect our future, and that we would continue seeing each other secretly. We would still cross to the Southern plains, down to Santa Isabel, together. He gave me a quick passionate kiss and hug before I slunk back into the school grounds, pretending that I'd been there all the time, though I wasn't too sure if I could blame my flushed face rumpled clothes and ruffled hair on my supposedly upset stomach without causing suspicion.

As Rafael said he knew nothing, I still I couldn't understand why my mother was behaving as she was. Why was she so sad?

And a thought has suddenly come to me as I sit here writing this. I shudder to think, but could it be that my father is having an affair with Carmen Gonzalez de Fernandez?

***

San Rafael, Saturday 20th October 1984.

It's mid-October now, the days are getting longer and hotter as the summer draws closer. I've been observing Papa all week. Surely if he was having an affair I'd notice some signs of it. I remembered him dancing with someone at my birthday party. But in my search for Rafael that night, I hadn't noticed who my father held in his arms. It hadn't been Mama, of that I was certain. I realised that even if they were so unhappy together, they couldn't get divorced as this was not permitted by law in our country. I'd heard of several cases of people falling into a legal limbo, left perhaps abandoned by their spouses, but unable to legally be free. My country is heavily Roman Catholic, and the church, apart from the official law, would condemn divorce as immoral and a threat to the family.

But why should two people who are unhappy together, for whatever reason, be trapped in a loveless marriage? They had been happy once. I was sure. I remember them laughing together often, such a handsome couple too. My father, Gabriel, tall, elegant, an imposing presence. When he entered a room, everyone turned towards him, magnetised by his charisma. And my mother Maria, despite her now desolated figure, had been renowned for her beauty. She quite proudly boasted that she had indigenous Mapuche blood in her. Her raven-hued hair hung down her back shiny and straight, her macchiato skin soft and smooth, and her black eyes like two dark pools. I used to wish that I had looked more like her when I was younger. But I was just like Papa in both looks and personality. Now, over the years and with the growing distance I felt towards Mama, I was glad that I took after Papa and not her.

Papa would never let someone stop him from finding out the truth, and that's what I was going to do. My mother was going out later, to spend the weekend with her sister, my aunt Gloria. I used to love going to my aunt's house, because Nacho would be there, and I loved him as if he was my brother. He was the one who interrupted my dancing with Rafael at my birthday party. If it had been anyone else, I would have refused to change dancing partners, but Nacho was my cousin and best friend after Flavia. If my mother was going to spend a few days with her sister, perhaps Nacho might be able to find out something. I, in the meantime, will search my mother's writing desk as soon as she's gone. If I could find more letters, I might find out what happened to make Mama change so drastically.

***

San Rafael, Sunday 21th October 1984.

I've found three letters. One is the letter I came across from Rafael's mother Carmen Gonzalez de Fernandez to my mother Maria Perez de Mendoza, asking to meet her in the town square to discuss an urgent matter. Another is from our family solicitor, Sr S Castro, dated quite recently, informing my mother that her request had been discussed with great interest, and that as one of the oldest families in San Rafael alongside the Mendoza family, the future union of these two families would without a doubt be most advantageous to all concerned.

I have no idea what business project my mother was planning with the Castro family. It was bad enough her insisting that I spent time with Santiago, the son, as she had done at my birthday party. But as the family business isn't a priority to me right now, I'm more concerned at finding out the truth behind Mama's melancholy state, I didn't bother finishing that letter, as it went on to discuss legalities of the Mendoza estate and was of no interest to me.

But the third letter caught my attention straight away, as I could see that the original paper had been torn into pieces and then taped together again. There were pieces missing and it was quite hard to read. I didn't recognise the handwriting and there was no way to determine to whom it was addressed and who actually wrote it, as the opening and end pieces were missing. But my pulse quickened as I read it – twice so as to memorise it – and re-write it now:

It's been many years now, but as much as I try, I cannot forget how it used to be between us. I try not to think of that dreadful day which changed everything for ever. If only I could go back. If only we could go back to how it used to be. I will never forget what happened, but over the years I've learnt to forgive, and though our lives have followed different paths, I believe that somehow we could join them together again. We have lived our lives for too many years now in the pretence of something that doesn't exist. You cannot possibly love her as you did me. And I have never loved anyone as I did you. I used to believe that I would get over you, that my heart would find happiness, but then I hear of you, or someone says your name, and I know that I was only fooling myself. I could never be wholly happy without you at my side. I should feel bitterness by what you did, but we were young and innocent. It was a lifetime ago. I need to see you again; despite everything, we could somehow start again. Please agree to meet with me, we need to talk...

There are a lot of feelings in this letter. Could it be from Rafael's mother? I didn't recognise the handwriting to be my mother's, but it had been written by a female hand; the words *"You cannot possibly love her as you did me"* indicated as much. A beautiful but poignant love letter. But, of course, if it had been for Papa's eyes and my mother had found it, it's no wonder that she was so sad and desolate. No wonder she kept herself in mourning, her heart would have been broken on reading this.

It suddenly made sense. Didn't I hear Mama say the day before I went riding with Rafael "The Fernandez family are trouble, always have been. Hasn't she done enough?" It also explained why Mama didn't want me to spend time with Rafael, who would be a constant reminder of his mother and the pain she's inflicted on our family.

But I have to see Rafael. My feelings for him aren't going to change because of what I've found out. I have time to myself as Mama is at her sister's house. I also need to visit Dancer.

CHAPTER THIRTEEN

CHANTELLE

I'm so confused; this is like a never-ending mystery series. I only flew home to see Robbie to try and figure out my own future. It had initially seemed a pretty simple and straightforward idea. But now I'm sitting here trying to figure out what the hell happened to his biological mum, grandmother, grandfather and their seductive neighbour! And all I've actually figured out is that I love Robbie and he's buggered off to the other side of the world. I was totally disheartened to see that he hadn't even bothered to text back either.

I grabbed a notebook and jotted down all the pointers I could think of to try and clear up this mystery. I glanced once again at my mobile and realised I hadn't replied back to Myfanwy. I was quite amused to read her text.

Where are you up to?

It was like getting ready for the monthly book club meeting. I felt like texting back: *I'm really struggling to finish. Did you get past page 47? Does it get any better, or is the reader just left feeling more and more confused with each passing page?* Not that I was really struggling to finish to be honest. It made engaging reading, but I really had so much on my mind that I just found it quite hard to concentrate.

About half way, I texted back. Though I did feel like adding, *Could you just give me a summary of the events?* Actually that was quite a good idea. Like when I used to pop to my local library and select a synopsis of the English literature book we were reading at school to summarise the work without actually having to read it all.

I continued with my scribbles on the note pad. So we had:

- Valentina: Robbie's biological mum.
- Rafael: By the looks of things, unless there is a real, unexpected twist that I just haven't seen coming, Robbie's biological dad.
- Gabriel Mendoza: Valentina's handsome dad
- Maria Pérez de Mendoza: Valentina's heartbroken mum.
- Carmen Gonzalez de Fernandez: Rafael's mum (or seductive neighbour, depending how you looked at things)
- Teresa: The housekeeper
- Santiago and the Castro family. (Poor Valentina hasn't quite picked up on the clues I think, but by the sounds of it, her mum plans that she gets hitched to the pimpled-face, chubby son of the solicitor).
- Nacho: Valentina's cousin, almost like a brother to her.
- Flavia: Valentina's best friend.
- Rafael's father: Name? If it's been mentioned I can't remember it. Anyway, the father who'd lost his life in a plane accident two years earlier, which if I thought about it seemed to have triggered off the revelation of the secrets that had been kept hidden. At least one of the letters that had been found was dated in that period of time. Of course, Rafael's mum on finding herself a widow hadn't wasted time

trying to seduce her childhood sweetheart, and wasn't very subtle about it by the looks for things. Sending letters demanding to meet her rival in the town square sounded like a bad Western B movie!

Sitting here trying to piece the information together, I felt a bit like when I'd played *Cluedo* with Tammy when we were younger. Mr Mendez did it in the bedroom... but to whom and with what? Which actually made it sound a bit sleazy to be honest! Something didn't feel right, but I couldn't put my finger on it. Rafael had said that both fathers had been great friends, but something had happened.

My train of thought was interrupted as my phone bleeped with an incoming text. I glanced at the screen quickly praying that it would be Robbie. Surely after reading my soppy message he would text back with something? But the text was from Myfanwy:

Keep going. Read it carefully though, as there is a crucial piece that I just couldn't figure out and perhaps you will. (Myfanwy obviously holds me in great esteem and thinks I'm awfully clever, bless her. Unfortunately the only thing I'm exceptional at, which she is yet to discover, is getting myself into a mess.) *I know Valentina is Robbie's biological mum, but he's my son too and I really miss him.*

"So do I," I whispered back, but just sent her a Emoji winking face and a couple of thumbs-ups.

Then a thought came to me. Could it be? I went through the scatter of information in my mind again. The torn letter. The plane accident which triggered certain other events to take place. The young couple in love. Valentina's father trying to keep the peace. But the clue was in the letter that Carmen Perez de

Fernandez, Rafael's mother, had sent to Maria, Valentina's mum, just before the airborne tragedy. What were her words? Something on the lines of:

I hope this finds you well, however I imagine you know full well what I need to discuss with you, and pleasantries are unnecessary. In fact whether you are well or not is of no concern to me.

Meet me, without fail next Monday, in the Plaza San Martín. Come alone. If you don't come, I'll take matters into my own hands.

If I was having an affair, I certainly wouldn't want to make it public in the town square. But if I'd discovered something and had to confront someone about it, I probably would choose a public place, relying on the fact that the other person wouldn't want to cause a scandal and would keep quiet as I laid down the facts. The more I thought about it, I was sure that I was right, and as I picked up the diary once again, I cried out loud:

"Oh Valentina, you've got it all wrong. It's not your father who was having an affair – it's your mother!"

Chapter Fourteen

VALENTINA

San Rafael, Sunday 21ᵗʰ October 1984.

I've just come in from spending the afternoon with Rafael and Dancer, I've hidden in my room and closed the door with the lights turned low, my father has gone to collect my mother and they aren't back yet, but they will arrive any minute and I want them to think I'm sleeping. I don't think I could face either of them right now.

I told Rafael about my suspicions that his mother and my father were having an affair, but he quite adamantly refused to believe me. He'd actually looked at me in shock, a look which then turned to pity as I'd kept on insisting that someone was trying to break up my parents' marriage. At that, he'd held me tight and told me that his mother would never get involved with another man. She'd dearly loved his father and still did. Though she no longer dressed in black, her heart was still broken by her loss.

But that didn't explain the letters, the threats, the tension I perceived between the two women. I tried to forget about my worries and it wasn't long before I was immersed in the exhilaration of watching Rafael with Dancer. As soon as Rafael commenced his indigenous chant, it took just a moment for her to neigh softly in response whilst her muscles seemed to relax and she lowered her head,

135

her eyes partially closed. If Rafael told me he could hypnotize horses I would have believed him. And Dancer wasn't the only one caught under his spell.

They came close together, and Rafael caressed Dancer all along her neck, towards her withers, massaging her mane then returning towards her jaw and muzzle. She remained still, as if in a trance, as he patted her back and loin a couple of times before easing himself up on to her back and continuing to caress her neck and mane. If Dancer had felt the change in position, or some added weight on her back, she didn't show it. She stepped forward, hesitatingly at first, but with encouragement from Rafael, her steps became steady and sure. They circled the corral once before stopping in the centre. Rafael repeated the whole procedure several times, Then with a final pat on Dancer's neck, Rafael slid from her back and made his way over to where I sat, mesmerised by what I'd just witnessed. A wild horse had been transformed into a docile mount under his touch, spellbound by his magic. Just as I was.

"Next time you come I'll show you a trick," he said as he approached. (Another one, I thought, as if what I'd just seen hadn't been a trick? In which case, I wondered what amazing performance awaited me on my next visit.) A carefree smile on his lips set off his handsome features all the more. "And then it will be time for you to ride her, just in time for our adventure in December." His smile played havoc with my insides as I looked down into his clear eyes. He placed his hands on my waist and effortlessly lifted me down from the fence where I was sitting, and into his strong embrace. His lips lowered to brush mine before he whispered in my ear, "You will come with me, won't you?"

It would have been impossible for me to say no, even if I had wanted to.

"Of course," I answered, surprised that he would think otherwise. I would have followed him to the ends of the earth with my eyes closed.

***

San Rafael, Friday 26th October 1984.

I've just received some very disturbing news and I just don't know what to do. My cousin Nacho has been to visit. He looked distraught and I had thought that his mother had fallen ill or something. It has been an extremely tense week as it is, with Mama spending much of her time locked in her bedroom and Papa out most of the day. I was beginning to feel a bit uncomfortable around Papa, too. How could I tell him that I'd come across the letters from his lover? How could I look into his eyes and not read the deceit behind his concerned look? But what really frightened me is that Nacho has told me that he overheard our mothers talking last Sunday, and that my mother has decided that it's best for my future and for our family's future if I marry Santiago as soon as I turn eighteen.

I can't believe it. I'm shaking with rage with the thought of it. Who does she think she is deciding on my future like this? Surely Papa won't allow it. I won't allow it. It's my life and I certainly won't marry Santiago. I can't think of anything worse. I feel sick. I don't even feel like writing about it. It's a horrible idea.

I'm meeting Rafael in secret again tomorrow. I've told Mama and Papa that I'm going into town with Flavia to spend the day with her, not that there was much to do there, except wander the streets and sit in a café or two. But I doubted they would double-check with Flavia, and I desperately need to speak with Rafael. Surely he would help me with thinking up ways to stop this marriage going ahead.

***

San Rafael, Saturday 27th October 1984.

We have a plan. As soon as I told Rafael about my mother's idea to marry me off to Santiago, his faced turned to thunder. There was a look in his eyes that I'd never seen before. I actually shivered from the ferocity in his voice and his indignation that my mother could possible contemplate forcing me to marry a man who meant nothing to me. His voice softened (I imagine on seeing my alarmed look), and he told me that we would sort something out.

In the meantime, it was my time to ride Dancer. Rafael had driven over in an open-top jeep to pick me up and take me back to his family ranch. We had met just a couple kilometres from my main family house, at the far end of a trail that was partly hidden by the surrounding vegetation. It was a bumpy ride back to the ranch, as Rafael took a cross-country track across the land and off the main road to avoid being seen by any workers who used the road and would recognise me in his presence and take the information unintentionally, or not, to my parents.

On arrival at the ranch, I positioned myself once again on the upper rung of the wooden fence that circled the corral. Rafael entered with Dancer close behind. He winked at me as he positioned himself in the centre of the corral and turned to face Dancer. At the same time I felt someone behind me and was startled to find Carmen Gonzalez de Fernandez suddenly right beside me. She looked at me through huge friendly almond-shaped honey-coloured eyes. Her smile was like a sunbeam and for a moment I was left breathless. I hadn't expected to see her, and suddenly felt intimidated by her presence. But I have to admit she must be the most beautiful woman I've ever seen. Even more perhaps that my own mother before her decline. This was the first time I'd been so close to her in person. She's tall with long, wavy, chocolate-coloured hair that she'd tied back in a low plait. She looked young, though she was probably the same age as my own mother, somewhere in her late thirties perhaps. Her soft olive skin shone in the sunlight as she turned once again to me with a homely smile. She smelt of jasmine and exotic flowers.

I wanted to be rude to her. She was causing so much turmoil in my family, but I found myself smiling back at her and together we sat in comfortable silence to watch Rafael and Dancer.

Rafael had gone through his routine of patting Dancer along her neck, withers, back and loin, whispering to her to whole time. Slowly she got down on her knees and rolled until she was lying on the dusty ground. Rafael knelt down next to her and

139

placed his head down on her neck. I had heard of this technique Rafael used, though I had never witnessed it myself, and it was quite spectacular. The bond between man and beast was complete. Rafael had won Dancer's trust and loyalty, and I was impressed beyond words.

Eventually Rafael got up and moved towards me.

"It's your turn to ride her now," he announced.

I climbed down from where I was sitting, high up on the fence, and walked over to Dancer. I had ridden bare-back many times and swung over onto her back easily. Dancer patiently remained still until I gently pressed her sides and she moved forwards, slowly at first, as if floating over the ground as we circled the corral, but seemingly always understanding my instructions. She moved with such grace and calmness that it was hard to believe that she was still a young mare and had only been ridden a couple of times.

"Well done, Valentina," Carmen called out softly as I approached "You ride well." She stood up and turned to go, then said, with genuine concern in her voice, "I hope your mother is feeling better."

I would have liked to have replied, *She would be if it wasn't for you*, but something held me back. Carmen had sounded sincere; there didn't seem to be a hidden message in her good wishes, and I felt confused.

Rafael dropped me off, back near my family home, by the same hidden track where we had met earlier in the day. He walked around to my side of the jeep to lift me out. He held me in his strong arms in a passionate embrace and kissed me with such tenderness that I was left dizzy.

"I've been thinking all day," he said. "When we leave in December to cross down to Santa Isabel, we don't have to come back. We can start a life together. I will always have work with the horses, we won't struggle for money. I can teach you. I've seen how you are with the horses. I see how they respond in your presence. You have the gift also. We could do this together. What do you say?"

I didn't say anything at all. My throat was tight with emotion. I just nodded. There was nothing I wanted more in the whole world.

CHAPTER FIFTEEN

CHANTELLE

"I know how you feel, Valentina." I whispered aloud. I would have probably done the same too. Elope with the man of my dreams. Well, I would have likcd to, but right now the only thing I could elope with, or rather lope around slowly with, is with my soon-to-be-huge belly. And, quite honestly, it's just not the same.

I stood up and stretched. My phone remained blank. Nothing, no texts, no calls, not even a bloody call from the often annoying sales team of a telephone network asking if I'm interested in a contract phone. Another one? I mean really, what do they think I'm using to answer their call in the first place?

I peered out of the window. Dusk was falling. I moved back to the kitchen and opened the back door that led to the garden. I thought it would be a good idea to get outside for a moment and stretch my legs, hoping also that the brisk evening air would help clear my muddled mind. I breathed in deeply, taking in the tangy rich dampness of the soil. I did double-check that the kitchen door wouldn't close and lock me out. That would be all I needed, getting locked out of my house, again! I wouldn't even be able to get through the front door now either, having my bargain IKEA chair still in place.

I slipped out into the darkened garden and wandered down to the greenhouse that was towards the centre of the grounds. The air smelled of damp earth, Petrichor, if you want to be technical about it, an earthly smell which I loved. Next to the greenhouse grew a large oak tree. As I approached I spotted a carving on the bark facing the house, which I certainly hadn't noticed before. It was a rather large heart, with some initials engraved inside. My heart skipped a beat, it must have been Robbie, he was the only one who had access to the cottage and grounds.

I stepped closer in anticipation. Could he have carved our initials into the oak? I peered, surely it was a sign of his feelings for me, despite not wanting to admit them now. I ran my finger over the carving. I could faintly make out a C facing upwards and what I could only imagine was a half-finished R. What a sweetheart, he'd obviously carved out the first letters of our names in some sort of code. Perhaps it was in ancient Greek letters or something. And you know you're really smitten with someone when you do that, surely? I was about to lean forward and do something even more soppy and kiss the bark, right where the heart was, when I heard a sudden rustle from the undergrowth on the far side of the grounds.

I remained rooted to the spot as a dark figure appeared from the shadows, running towards me with blinding speed. I didn't know whether to scream or try to climb the tree, but the only sound that came out of my open mouth was a very subdued and rather squeaky "Help!" Just as I was about to try and sprint back to the kitchen door and lock myself safely inside, it dawned on me that the figure coming my way was a loping figure with a wagging tail and lolling tongue. Before my imagination could take wing any further, I was set upon by a hairy four-legged bundle of excitement.

"Dolly!" I cried out in shock. "You've just scared the hell out of me!" I was totally relieved on seeing what was behind this sudden ambush, but my legs felt really shaky and I felt the urge to sit – collapse, to be specific.

"What are you doing here?" I asked patting the dog's soft head, to which she responded with a string of excited barks. "Let's go back indoors shall we?" I added. Before I turned to go I took one last look at the carving in the bark and as I peered closer again the letters actually looked more like a V and a slightly wonky L. Why the hell had Robbie carved those initials in the bark? But I didn't give it much more thought, as, with bounding, yapping dog at my heels I made my way back to the brightly lit kitchen.

As I moved inside, Dolly obediently sat on the step on the outside of the kitchen and cocked her head to one side, ears pricked, looking at me through intelligent brown eyes. Her tail thumped the ground a couple of times before it continued with its frantic wagging.

"You can come in if you like Dolly." Dolly immediately bounded into the house, almost knocking me over in the process. "Let's tell Myfanwy you're here shall we? She'll probably be worried sick searching for you."

I fished out my phone and texted Myfanwy that Dolly was with me. That I'd almost wet myself from fright at seeing her dog appear out of the blue was information that I thought best to kept to myself. Myfanwy's reply came back quickly:

I know. I sent her.

That threw me a bit. I knew collie dogs were intelligent, but surely running through the open fields looking for a complete stranger isn't quite the same as rounding up sheep. Or is it?

Another text came through:

I thought you could do with some company. The cottage is a bit isolated, after all, and Dolly's a fully-trained sheep dog and guard dog. If in doubt just cry out ATTACK.

"Attack?" I said out loud – to which Dolly started growling, looking a bit mystified as to where the threat was coming from. She quickly moved to the front door and hunched down next to the IKEA chair, hackles up, tail raised and stiff, and a low throaty growl escaped from her as she sniffed around.

"It's OK Dolly, come here girl, false alarm!" I called out, though I observed it had served as a good practice drill. The word certainly worked, and Dolly obviously knew what she was doing.

I wish I could say the same for myself, and I have to admit it was reassuring having the dog with me to keep me company. I settled back on the sofa after placing a bowl of water on the kitchen floor for Dolly to drink from and gave her some slices of cured ham as a treat for doing her job spot on. She had found me in a flash.

"Clever girl," I said to her as I patted her head while she curled up on a rug next to the sofa and laid her head on her paws keeping her unblinking eyes on me. And it actually crossed my mind, was Dolly guarding me? Or supervising me? Making sure I was reading the diary entries and not messing around?

And I wondered what the command for that would be? *Find, confirm reading, snap at heels if deviation occurs*?

It was then I realised I had a text from Freddy G. It wasn't from Lionel, but considering he was Lionel's agent, it was good enough.

-There's been an accident. Don't panic. (A bit late for that!) *Lionel's OK, he's just taken a bit of a knock to his head and is under observation.*

-Are you sure he's OK? How did it happen? I quickly texted back, and sat in growing alarm, despite Freddy G's words not to. But how could I not panic? Whatever my current feelings for Lionel, I still cared for him. Whatever path my life took, I would always have fond memories of our time together. Lionel had made me laugh, many times when I was feeling lost and low. And now, he was injured and I wasn't at his side (as, perhaps, I should be), and it suddenly sunk in how unfortunate this accident really was. How was I going to be able to tell him our engagement, relationship, call it what you like, was over now? I mean, you can't break up with someone whilst they're lying on a hospital bed, or can you? I could hear the doctor's reassuring words now: *Your fiancée has returned your engagement ring, it was a sticky and unpleasant procedure, but we're pleased to announce that your head's now fully functional and intact!* Put that way it didn't sound so bad after all.

Perhaps I should take advantage of the situation. Just as I was mulling over this new possibility, another text from Freddy G came through.

-Lionel's perfectly fine, seriously don't worry. I'll keep you posted. It happened in one of the car

146

stunt scenes. The car flipped when it shouldn't have. We're looking into why, but the important thing is that he's fine and I'm sure will get discharged in the next couple of days.

-OK, thanks for letting me know Freddy. Just keep me updated please.

There was nothing much I could do, except get on the next plane back to the US and go and sit by Lionel until he recovers. I probably owed it to Lionel to do that. But I needed more time to sort myself out, and right now I didn't think playing Florence Nightingale was the best course of action. Surely it would confuse matters even more if I rushed to his side, only to rush away again almost immediately. Especially if he was suffering from concussion. I didn't want to cause any permanent damage by sitting with him and reassuring him that he was going to be alright, and then buggering off to be with Robbie. It didn't seem logical, even in my head.

I would wait until tomorrow and decide what was best. If I thought his injury was serious, I would go to be with him. In the meantime, I didn't have time to waste. I needed to finish the diary, and quickly!

CHAPTER SIXTEEN

VALENTINA

San Rafael, Sunday 4th November 1984.

This time next month I will be starting my new life. I'm not sure how I'm going to bear to say goodbye to Flavia and Nacho when the time comes, especially as I can't tell them about this decision I've made. I just hope that one day they will understand, and that, somehow, with time I will be able to restore some sort of contact with them. But only the future will tell. I don't even want to think about how heartbroken Papa will be. But he's responsible for most of this. If it wasn't for him, I'm sure such drastic measures would not be needed.

It hurts, deep down to the very pit of my stomach, when I think about it. I often find myself now waking in the middle of the night sweating, and I gasp with relief on realising that I'm still in my warm, soft bed and that I haven't left – at least not yet. But there doesn't seem to be another solution. Stay and I will have to marry Santiago. Leave and I go with nothing, but I save my heart. As exciting as the idea had sounded when Rafael first discussed it with me, it has turned from a fifteen-day adventure into a life-long journey, and, if I'm honest, there is a part of me that doesn't want to go. And the negative feelings that engulf me haven't anything to do with leaving everything I've ever known behind to start afresh. That doesn't scare me. It's something else, but I can't pinpoint what it is.

As the days pass and December looms closer, I can't help but feel something may go wrong. Terribly wrong. Rafael reassures me all the time that it's our only option. That it's our time to live our lives now. Our parents had their turn. The world was our oyster now, and that with him it would be a brilliant one. He would look into my eyes and cradle my face in his warm, strong hands, holding my gaze and, as with Dancer, my nerves would calm and I would give way to his loving touch.

**

San Rafael, Friday 30th November 1984.

We leave tomorrow, well in just a few hours to be exact. When the house is quiet and everyone is sleeping I will slip out into the middle of the dark night and not return. I can't believe how dramatic that sounds. I haven't written much in this diary lately as I've been so caught up with the preparation of this secret adventure that I've had little time for much more. I've been feeling more positive about this decision over the last few weeks too, especially since I overheard Papa agreeing with Mama, that perhaps it was best for me to consider a future with the Castro family. How could Papa agree to such an idea? How could he betray me this way?

It was with a sad heart that I said goodbye to Flavia yesterday. She has no idea about my plans, and it's better that way. She'll get questioned over my whereabouts for certain, and I don't want to get her into trouble. I gave her an extra strong hug as we left school yesterday and told her how much I loved her and always would. To which, of course, she looked at me a bit confused and surprised, but smiled back and told me she loved me too, that I was the best friend anyone could have. I will always remember her words. She is the best friend I could ever wish for and I will miss her terribly.

I have, however, told Nacho my plans. I couldn't resist. I needed to share it with someone, and I thought it was best that he knew where I was going. Someone from the family, but someone I could trust. Nacho is my soulmate; we've known each other so well since childhood. He has promised not to tell anyone, and I believe him. He understands why I'm going and has given me his blessing. I will miss him terribly too. He is like the brother that I always wanted and never had.

I will take this diary with me. I was thinking of leaving it behind. But I don't want anyone finding it, and I want to record the journey anyway, so that I will always remember with detail the first days of the rest of my life.

It's time to sleep now, though I doubt sleep will come. My bag is ready. I'm only taking a few light clothes with me. Rafael has been in charge of taking everything else: our food, water and sleeping mattresses.

Tomorrow night I will sleep under the stars and in his arms.

***

Salto de las Rosas. Saturday 1ˢᵗ December 1984.

We've made our way down to Salto de las Rosas in the Cañada Seca district, some twenty kilometres south of San Rafael, though the actual kilometres travelled today are a little more via the cross-country tracks we have taken. The cattle, a head of three hundred, had been resting up at the Fernandez ranch this last week, and now Rafael and I, together with two other *gauchos* and four dogs, have started our journey south.

The plan was to move south slowly along the Rio Atuel, which acts as a natural border with General Alvear. There are several good pastures which we would come across on the journey, ideal for the night stops and grazing on the way.

Despite my initial nerves, there was something about riding out at the break of dawn, as the early sun's rays kissed the tops of the mountains, covering the ground in a soft golden hue, the early morning silence broken by the lowing of the cows and clip-clop of the horses' hooves as they hit the dirt track. The dogs barked excitedly as they ran around keeping the younger calves together and inside the herd. I was comfortably settled astride Dancer who responded to my light touch as if the two of us were one being. Rafael sat proudly, not far from me, on his mount. He would turn to look at me and his smile would brush away any doubts that I could possibly have. This was to be my life now, I had done away with comforts for a freedom that couldn't be expressed in words. I felt like the rare Harpey Eagle, that can sometimes be seen soaring high over the

151

plains on this northern side of Argentina, wild and free.

How could I have possibly doubted that this decision would be the best for me? This is who I am and who I wanted to be. Not the wife of a snooty lawyer, going to ladies' day at the local club once a week and pretending I was interested in crochet and caviar as I sipped my tea like the sophisticated British ladies I'd so often heard about. I was Valentina, not even Mendoza anymore. But more importantly I was ME.

I can hear Rafael calling me now as I write this. I have come and sat on a rocky ledge as the last of the rays fall warm around me. Tonight I will lie in Rafael's arms. We have already prepared our bedding, away from the camp. The two other *gauchos* and the dogs will be in charge of the herd tonight. Rafael has already told me he has a surprise for me, and I'm excited to see what it is. I have a gift for him also, something I have never given to anyone else. My most intimate self.

***

Villa Atuel, Sunday 2th December 1984.

We have travelled a bit further today and have stopped near Villa Atuel. We left early and as the herd was moving well, Rafael opted to continue a few more kilometres than originally planned. He wanted to make as much distance as possible between ourselves and San Rafael. I had wanted to stay in his arms all day. I had felt like a grown woman before, but it's incredible how one magical night can transform a person. I felt as though I'd just emerged from a cocoon into a beautiful, magical world, where my wings had suddenly spread and discovered that they are the most vibrant colour blue. Like the Morpho butterfly, which looks like a normal brown insect, but as it takes off leaves you speechless at its beauty. This morning I woke to a beautiful new world, where nothing will ever be the same as it was before, where I have grown, both physically and emotionally. My new wings, which flash an electric blue, are untouchable.

Rafael called me as I was finishing my diary entry yesterday. He smiled at me indulgently as he would on finding a child playing with its favourite toy. He loves the idea that I write all my feelings.

"Have you finished?" he'd asked as he'd moved towards me and gently kissed my forehead as I closed the diary and put it away in my saddlebag. With that he gently took hold of my hand and led me to where our mattresses had been laid out. A blanket had been spread and arranged with our dinner: smoked ham, cured cheese, fruit, bread and water. He'd smiled at me apologetically. "Sorry I can't offer you anything more sophisticated, and I'm afraid that this is going to pretty much be our menu for the next ten days, but I do also have this for you."

By this time he had pulled me down so that I was sitting next to him on the blanket, then reached into his shirt pocket and pulled out a small package. With shaking hands I unwrapped the delicate paper and opened the small jewellery box, and there sitting on a velvety cushion was a beautiful, jewel-encrusted white gold ring. The tiny studded diamonds ran all around the perimeter of the ring and on the inside there was a very fine engraving which read: *My world begins and ends with you* and then two tiny initials *V & R*.

My eyes misted over and I was caught for words. Did this mean he wanted to marry me? I didn't know what to say. I know I had already left everything behind to be with him. But, nonetheless, I wasn't expecting this.

"I hope," he'd said, "that soon you'll be able to stop running away to avoid your marriage to someone else, because you'll be wedded to me."

A passionate kiss was my answer to his sweet words. He eased me down until we were lying, side by side. His hands brushed over my skin, sending electrical currents down, deep within me, leaving me tingling and eager for more. It was the first time his hands lingered lower, down below my waistline and I, without shame or self-doubt encouraged him as I untied his trousers and pulled them gently down. Rafael moved to lean over me. His lips left a trail of burning kisses all over my body and I gasped out loud as he lowered his lips to my breast and then below. I caressed him the whole while, willing him not to stop. I throbbed with the heat of the moment. I had never experienced anything like it before and when he paused for a moment and told me that he could wait, we didn't have to continue, that he wanted to make sure that I was ready. I moaned that it was something I wanted just as much as he did. I whispered to him that the moment couldn't be more perfect, and that I couldn't be more ready. And with that, he gently pressed himself on me and we made love in a way I will never forget.

It was perfect, his tenderness a total contrast to the wildness that surrounded us. But it was this wilderness that made us who we are. Rafael was a man of the great outdoors making love to me under the starlit summer sky, where the beauty of the open plains met the magic of the night. The glittering moonlight was our soft blanket, the twilight owls were our guardians. In peace I slept in the arms of the man who had made me a woman in every sense, and I couldn't have wanted it any other way.

We woke at first light and made love again. I still can't believe it's real, that I'm not dreaming this whole wonderful experience. I now wear the ring. It fits perfectly and sits snug on my ring finger. I wear it with pride and joy, though I have taken it off a couple of times, just to re-read the engraving. We rode close together today and the whole while Rafael would look at me, a soft smile on his lips, a contrast to the hungry look in his eyes. I've found myself smiling childishly all day, anticipating another night of passion in his arms.

Rafael has gone now with the other *gauchos* to round the herd in for another early start on the road tomorrow. I can hear the dogs barking, from where I sit. The barking seems a bit more excited than normal, and if I strain my hearing, it sounds as if there are horses approaching rapidly.

I've just stood up to see what I can observe from my resting place, half-hidden under the shade of a cluster of *Lophozonia Alpina* trees. I'm shaking now. I can't believe it. I can't see the riders well and I hope I'm mistaken, but I would recognise Nacho anywhere.

155

More to my concern is that Santiago is with him. There is fear rising inside me. I must stop writing now. I desperately need to hide.

***

Villa Atuel, Monday 3rd December 1984.

Today I must return with Santiago and Nacho. It's early morning and before the others stir and gather camp for another day I sit here looking out over the open plains. In the distance I see the mountain peaks to the West; the very same mountain range that had seemed to offer an open door to a new life, now appear to close in on me, suffocating and trapping me.

Rafael had held me tight during the night, but this time we didn't make love. My heart is heavy with sadness. Seeing that we'd been tracked by Nacho and Santiago, my first instinct had been to call Dancer and ride through the night, as far away from them as possible, but I heard Rafael frantically calling my name. There was concern etched on his handsome face as he'd found me. Was it Mama? What had happened now? Surely Nacho would never betray me, unless there was a life-threatening situation. But it was too late for me to aid Mama. I may have betrayed her as a daughter by leaving everything behind and disappearing, but she had betrayed me too: betrayed my childhood, my innocence and my trust. I was not returning for Mama.

What I hadn't expected was for Rafael to gather me in his warm embrace, hold my chin up so that my

156

eyes met his in an unwavering gaze as he told me that whatever happened he would come for me, but that I had to go back. My father had had a stroke, he was in a critical condition, and I had to return. Tears welled-up and blurred my vision just as the sun hazes the horizon under the harsh midday light of a scorching summer sun. But there was no oasis in this vision, only the cruel reality that Papa has fallen ill, and I shiver to think that it's all because of me. Whatever he had done, even if he had been unfaithful to my mother, I would never have wished him any harm. He was my rock, and he had fallen.

I didn't need Rafael or anyone to convince me that I needed to return. I would have left straight away, but it had been close to nightfall and it was too dangerous to ride so late. Besides which, the horses needed to rest. We were to leave at first light.

Now, as soon as I pack this diary away I will go and saddle Dancer. With Rafael's promise to come back for me in less than fifteen days, I will, with a leaden heart, go home.

***

San Rafael, Tuesday 4th December 1984.

I have been at the hospital all day and I am exhausted, though Papa is actually better than I feared. From what I had been able to gather from Nacho on the ride home, my parents had discovered my absence late on the Saturday evening. They had assumed I'd been with Flavia or out riding, but when dusk fell it became clear that something was wrong. They had called Flavia who obviously didn't know

157

of my whereabouts, and that is what triggered the alarm that something was amiss. Papa had quickly driven over to the Fernandez ranch but all that Carmen could tell him was that I had not been there and that Rafael had left that morning, commissioned to drive a head of cows down to Santa Isabel. It must have been then that Papa had realised what I had done. I'm sure it didn't take long from him to figure it out, knowing me as he does.

I've sat at Papa's side all day. He is a strong man and is recovering quickly, though I will never forgive myself for causing him this suffering. His eyes lit up on seeing me, and his smile, though slightly pulled at one side, warmed my heart. He tried to speak, but at first the words wouldn't come out. I hushed him and told him not to force himself, that I was here now and that I was terribly sorry, I never expected that my actions would inflict such pain. He shook his head hard on hearing my words and I was somewhat confused. Again he tried to speak, but I couldn't understand what he was trying to say. And it wasn't long after this first strain of seeing me and of trying to tell me something, that he feel asleep.

I'm sitting here trying to figure out what Papa was trying so hard to tell me. There had been an urgency about it; almost as if he was warning me. But the urgency had made talking all the more difficult for him, though I do believe, analysing things carefully now, that what he had tried to say, or at least what I have been able to put together from his hoarse slurred tone was something like: *This isn't because of you. Don't believe anything she says.*

Remember you are my daughter and I will always love you.

This, at least, is what I understood, but it seems strange – and something else seems strange which I have just remembered now. When we rode off yesterday morning, just as Nacho, Santiago and I were leaving the camp and Rafael was waving me goodbye, Santiago had quickly turned his mount back towards Rafael and drawn level with him. The men appeared to exchange some words before Santiago handed over something which looked like a white envelope. I wonder what it was.

***

San Rafael, Sunday 9th December 1984.

The days are passing so slowly. I still have another ten days to go before Rafael returns. I wish he would come back now. I long for his embrace, to feel his strong arms around me.

It's been torture having to go back to school. The other kids just looked at me in amazement. It had got out that I had run off with Rafael, the horse-whisperer. They looked at me in awe and respect in a way they never had before. They think I'm really "cool" but I'm just sad and disheartened. The "cool" adventure had ended with me having to return without Rafael and my father ill. There was nothing cool about it at all.

All Mama has said to me, in a harsh tone, was "This is all your fault," meaning, of course, what happened to Papa. I cannot pinpoint when it was that Mama's love for me diminished and this bitterness took its place. I had never really noticed it before. I just accepted that she was sad and mourning a loss I couldn't comprehend. But there has been a transformation, deep inside her, that has been triggered since I started seeing Rafael.

Flavia at least seems to understand me; she listened in wonder as I related my two days with Rafael out on the trail south.

"I would have gone as well," she'd confessed, "if I had been asked." I'd looked worried for a moment.

"What, with Rafael too?" I'd gasped, shocked by her revelation that she too had feelings for Rafael. She was my best friend, but I didn't want to share everything with her!

She giggled. "No, with Nacho!"

Nacho? I don't know how I hadn't seen it or why she hadn't confessed her feelings for my cousin before now. But I found myself smiling at the idea of my best friend with my cousin, both of whom I love dearly. For the first time in days, I felt happy.

***

San Rafael, Tuesday 18th December 1984.

Today is the day that Rafael is due to return. I have been waiting anxiously by my bedroom window all afternoon. I raced back from school as quickly as I could, positive that he would already be here waiting for me. But the house was normal. There was no extra car in the parking area. No additional horse in the stables.

Papa was brought home yesterday. He still couldn't move unaccompanied or talk clearly, but he was progressing. The doctors have said the recovery will be slow and that he may not fully recover, but he is a strong man and his chances are high.

I sat with him all yesterday afternoon, and read to him from one of the books I'd found in our library. I've always considered my father to be highly intelligent and educated, though it wasn't often he had time to read, being so busy looking after the family estate, so I thought he would appreciate me reading to him now. A bedroom had been set up for him on the ground floor, so that he didn't have to tackle the stairs yet. I was desperate to tell him that I'd only run because I'd heard about the plans to marry me to Santiago, but I didn't think he was strong enough to converse with me over something so important. So I remained silent except for my reading, gazing now and again out of the window, in the hope that Rafael would soon appear.

I believe I can hear a car coming now. I will stop writing. It must be Rafael.

***

San Rafael, Tuesday 25ʰ December 1984.

Another week has gone by. It's Christmas Day, but there is still no sign of Rafael. I have a horrible feeling something may have happened to him. But surely I would have been informed. Surely Nacho, or Rafael's mother Carmen, would have alerted me had there been an accident. But there is no news at all, and I don't know what to do. Mama hardly speaks to me, and Papa is like a vulnerable child to whom I cannot express my concern.

I desperately need to talk to someone. My only hope is Carmen. I will leave early on Saturday morning and ride to the Fernandez ranch. Perhaps she knows something. And it was time I was given some explanation as to what's going on with my parents anyway. She holds the keys to two doors, one of which has been locked for far too long.

***

San Rafael, Saturday 29th December 1984.

When I rode out this morning to the Fernandez ranch I expected to come back with answers. What I didn't expect was for those answers to turn my world upside down.

As I rode in through the main gate to the ranch I came across Carmen almost straight away. She was standing in the middle of the road leading to the house as if waiting for someone, and I imagine she was waiting for Rafael and probably missing him just as much as I was. Her face lit up on seeing me and she smiled at me warmly. It had been a while since anyone – apart from Papa – had genuinely shown pleasure on laying their eyes on me, and for that I was grateful and my tension eased. I wanted her to be my friend, despite the heartbreak she'd inflicted on my family. That is, the heartbreak that I believed she had inflicted, until I heard her story.

We settled down on the front porch, her beautiful honey-coloured eyes turned to me, drawing me in to their liquid pools as if hypnotising me, and

162

with a sad smile she told me the story. Many years ago, her husband Nicolas (Rafael's father) had been great friends with my father. They had been the best of friends, inseparable in everything they did, brothers in every sense. Then a young lady had fallen in love with Nicolas, and the inseparable friendship now had a new member. This lady was just as they were. She could ride like them, tackle the strong currents of the Diamanté River on horseback or foot with no fear, and would sleep under the starlit sky on the hard ground like any *gaucho*. She was one of them, and she belonged. She was renowned for her beauty and her gift with the horses. She could ride barefoot standing on the galloping horse's back, as wild as the Banguales who roam free in the Patagonia region. She was also renowned for her strong character and sharp temper. She was an impressive figure in every sense, and everyone loved her.

But it was because of her fiery temper that Rafael's father started to draw away from her. He loved her, but their arguments became more and more frequent and fierce. The friendship among all three became more and more strained. Nicolas was commissioned to ride down to Rio Negro with a small herd of cattle, and he did it alone. It was the first time that the friends separated. What no one expected was that a year later, Nicolas would come back – married, and his newly-wed wife with child.

The other lady was heartbroken, and out of spite she married the best friend. A few years later their child was born, a beautiful little girl they called Valentina. It was only when Carmen said my name that it struck me who this story was about and the significance it had.

"So it was my mother all the time!" I murmured in surprise as I realised that the torn letter that I had found was my mother's. I shook my head in bewilderment and stammered: "I had thought you were having an affair with my father. But all along it was my mother who was betraying the family."

"Yes and no," Carmen softly replied. "Your mother never got over her love for Nicolas, and although she tried to rekindle the old flame, my husband was in love with me. He had been honest with me. Your mother had sent him a letter to meet with him again, and he had shown me the letter. I was aware that your mother still loved him, and part of me has always felt sorry for her. But there was nothing that could break the love I shared with Nicolas. Despite your mother's insistence in trying to resurrect what had once been, there had been no affair. As for my husband, his love for her had died even before he met me. From the very moment we met and a new love grew. I was confident of this love."

Carmen paused. A tear trickled down her cheek as she talked about him, and I too felt my eyes fill with unshed tears. "The very morning of the accident," Carmen continued, "I had spoken with your mother in one of the town's squares, telling her to forget about Nicolas. He no longer loved her. She had a beautiful family to be proud of and after seventeen years there was no point in fighting to change the past. I didn't know why, after so long, she wanted Nicolas back in her life. She had to learn to let go of what could have been, because sometimes what could have been never happens. It is just a fantasy that we build on over time, distorting reality."

Carmen turned and smiled at me then. "If things had been different, you would never have been born, nor would my son Rafael. It's your turn now to make a beautiful life." She echoed words that Rafael himself had whispered to me. "What I never imagined is that my conversation with your mother would affect my husband so much. That very afternoon, under so much strain and concern over us, he didn't check the light aircraft properly before take-off, and he paid dearly for his distraction. The plane didn't have enough fuel to get him to his destination. A day doesn't go by that I wish for things to be different. For me to not have interfered as I did, demanding to speak with your mother and try and end her fixation with my husband. Because perhaps, then, things would be different. And now I have to live as I had tried to advise your mother. Not in the past, but to move forward, even though my heart remains buried with him..."

She broke off here, choking on the last words, and fumbled for a tissue to blot the tears that now flowed freely down her face.

I knew exactly how she felt. What would I do if her son never returned?

***

Rafael has phoned. But not me, his mother. He has been commissioned for another job. He's not coming back...

I don't even know how I'm writing these words. I can't believe it. I'm filled with heartbreak, disbelief and anger. How could he have gone off, when he promised me he would return? Is this new job more important than me? More important than us? I gave him everything and believed in him, and now he goes off as if I was nothing to him? His promise that he would return, blown by the wind and as futile as the dust which covers the tracks from here to Santa Isabel and beyond. One month ago I was in his arms, and now I am embraced by lies and broken promises.

I have taken off his ring. He will have to offer me a very good reason for delaying his return before I wear it again. But a part of me wants to believe in him. There must be a reason. Surely when he explains everything to me I will understand. I can only hope that that day will arrive soon and everything will be as it was before.

***

San Rafael, Sunday 3ʳᵈ February 1985.

I'm pregnant. There is no doubt. I've now missed two of my monthly periods, my breasts feel sore, and I'm constantly tired and nauseous. There has been no more news from Rafael. I want to forget about him, but he is on my mind all day long, from my waking hour to the darkest moments of the night. As dark as I am inside. I'm tortured with conflicting feelings. Bitterness at Rafael for his betrayal, though a part of me hopes there must be some kind of explanation.

I often find myself thinking back to the envelope that Santiago had handed over to Rafael the day they came to take me home. I have no way of finding out what was in the envelope, but I want to believe that that is the key to the change in my life. What had been inside? Was it money? Had my mother paid him off? Surely Rafael would not be influenced by money. I knew Rafael well enough to know that there were no riches in the world that would keep him from me. At least, I thought I knew Rafael, but perhaps I had never known him after all.

I have told my mother that I'm expecting. If I thought she would be shocked and surprised, I was wrong. She just nodded. She had a plan, she told me. She will send me away. I'm too exhausted and drained to fight this. Perhaps it's best that I go. I have nothing to keep me here now anyway.

"I will send you to Texas," she said. "We have distant relatives who live there. You will go before it starts to show. You will stay there, no one will ever know, not even your Papa. If he finds out about this, it will be the death of him. You don't want to be responsible for that, do you?"

I knew what her words meant. I wasn't to keep the child. Perhaps it would be for the best. Pretend that none of this has happened. But before I would agree to anything, I had one important question to ask Mama.

"What was in the envelope that Santiago gave to Rafael?" My voice had come out in a blank tone, with no emotion. My world had been turned upside down in such a way that I was exhausted. I had no strength left to fight, but I wanted to know. "Was it money? Did you pay him to leave me?"

My mother let out a harsh and bitter laugh.

"There was no need for money, Valentina. I tried to warn you. He left you as I knew he would. He's just how his father was. They are not men who you can keep. They are not men who will stay. They are men who will break your heart and leave."

***

San Rafael, Thursday 21th February 1985.

This is going to be my last entry in this diary. I have lost the desire to write. I no longer have anything I wish to express. There are no memories I want to save. Tomorrow I leave to stay with my relatives in Texas. My mother has convinced me that it will be for my own good and for that of the child. I'm to give it up, and I will.

There is no love in me. I'll never forgive any of them. My life has ended before it's even begun.

CHAPTER SEVENTEEN

CHANTELLE

I'm lost for words. I close the diary softly after reading the last entry twice. I feel so sad. I've also got a bloody stinking headache from the stress of it all. I'm surrounded by tissues, too. The tears started as soon as I started re-reading the diary, Valentina's beautiful electric blue wings, which had been broken before she'd learnt to use them.

Dolly, who obviously thought that the tissue-throwing was a new game, had excitedly chased after the first few I'd scrunched up and thrown on the floor. But after the first packet, she'd got over the excitement and had lain down again, ignoring me and the tissues from then on.

I grappled to stand, swaying like I'd just downed a pint or two of extra-strong cider (when usually half a pint of shandy does it for me). I slipped back down onto the sofa and from there I made it to floor level and crawled to the toilet. You cannot imagine the level of excitement and, may I add, confusion I caused Dolly as she observed my selected form of locomotion. She probably thought that for once this particular man's best friend had a full time play-partner, and was seemingly ecstatic by it to say the least. It did make getting to the toilet tricky as I had a leaping dog to dodge and her sandpaper tongue to parry, so by the time I actually found my way to the WC my nausea had passed and it was with relief that I was able to stand up straight, putting to an end this new game that Dolly had clearly thoroughly enjoyed. I wish I could say the same.

I felt torn in two. Robbie still hadn't answered my text. There wasn't much for it but to dial his number again.

The tone buzzed away and my heart quickened with each one. I had no idea what I was going to say, and if I really got tongue-tied I doubted Dolly would be much help, though she sat looking at me with adoring eyes, and that alone gave me some confidence. The line clicked.

"Chantelle?"

"Yes, it's me."

"Are you OK?"

"No."

"What's wrong?" (Apart from being pregnant and not knowing who the father is, and the man I love being thousands of miles away and rather off-hand, what more could possibly go wrong?)

"Will you come back?" I couldn't believe I was asking him this, my voice had come out sounding really whiny too. I cleared my throat. "I mean, I really need to talk with you. In person. Did you read my text?"

"What text? No."

Oh, for fuck's sake! Who on earth did I send the text to then? I felt like slumping to the floor once more – which, of course, would have taken me to "hero" status in Dolly's world.

"I've seen a text come in," Robbie said, "but I just thought it was a roaming text and didn't open it."

Top marks for Robbie's techo slothfulness! I was half-relieved, half-mad about it. At least I hadn't sent the text to some random bloke, confusing my love life all the more. If that was possible.

There was a moment of awkward silence which was broken by Dolly's sudden yapping. I could only imagine that she could pick up Robbie's voice over the line. I wasn't the only one missing him and showing it too.

"Is Dolly with you?"

"Yes." I suddenly strained my hearing. Had I just picked up a female voice in the background? What time was it over there? Was he sleeping with someone? I tried, unsuccessfully, not to panic.

"I just really need to talk to you in person," I repeated. "There is something really important I want to tell you." Not that I was sure what it was I exactly wanted to say that would sound more or seem more important than what I had already revealed in our previous conversation. I mean you couldn't really beat the magic words "I'm pregnant." Except perhaps if I'd said "I love you" but I couldn't bring myself to say them, at least not yet.

"I'll read your text as soon as I can," came his rapid reply. What the hell did that mean, *as soon as I can*? I was obviously at the bottom of the pecking order now, and how the crap had that happened? I strained my hearing once again. There was definitely a female voice murmuring in the background. A deep, throaty, husky voice that seductively whispered, down the line and into my ears, ironically louder than a deafening yell over a megaphone: "Roberto, *mi amor*, take me..." At least I'm pretty sure that's what I heard before the line crackled and I was left straining to pick up any other words over the interference.

My legs started to wobble. I had felt sick just moments before, and this additional shock was certainly not helping my queasy stomach. Dolly was going to be in for more fun and games as soon as I hung up.

"Sorry, have I interrupted something?" I asked in a panic, on hearing Robbie mutter something over the still crackling line. "I don't even know what the time is over there," I tried to explain in an apologetic voice that sounded on the verge of hysteria. For once I totally sympathised with Vivien Francis. My world had turned upside down in a second, and being pregnant had nothing to do with it. We both loved men who didn't love us back. It was as simple as that. Although not that simple at all was how it felt.

"I can't really talk right now, Chantelle," came Robbie's reply.

Silence. My mind was doing cartwheels. There seemed to be an endless list of possible things that Robbie could get up to with a husky-voiced Argentinian lady which would result in him not being able to converse with me. I tried to squeeze out an unperturbed "OK" but it just wasn't happening. And I certainly wasn't OK.

Robbie continued, "But you're right, we do need to talk. Can I call you tomorrow?"

I mumbled something which I hoped sounded like "Yes, whatever" because what I really wanted to say, or rather ask, was "What are you doing that's so important to stop you from talking to me now?"

With that, and with Robbie's words of "Talk tomorrow then" echoing in my head, the line clicked and I was left in silence again.

I was left momentarily stunned before I quickly turned to my phone again and Googled *Time zone in Argentina*. Argentina was four hours earlier than the UK, so 3am here would be 11pm over there. This additional information certainly didn't help matters. "Take me" said in a husky voice at 11pm didn't sound very chaste to me. It sounded more like Tango time.

I took a couple of deep breaths. I'd dealt with heartbreaking moments before in my life – losing my mother at a young age and then my father more recently. I could handle this. If Robbie had now decided that I no longer formed part of his future, it would be something that I would learn to accept. After all, he'd only come into my life a few months ago and I had lived happily enough without him before. But what I had learnt was that you have to take a chance in life. You have to take a chance on love and never give up. My parents had shown me that.

And it wasn't over yet, at least not for me. There was something deep inside, call it a gut feeling, call it intuition, that prompted me to believe that Robbie still had feelings for me. At least that's what I took to heart, and was thrilled to see that my optimism was still intact. I could play husky-voiced too if needed.

With that I went back to the sofa, queasiness momentarily cured. I still had one more letter to read, and I hoped that this letter would provide the answer to why Rafael never returned. Perhaps understanding the father, I would understand the son.

***

My dearest Roberto,

I hope that by the time you come across this final letter, you would have read the previous two letters: the one addressed to Mr Garcia asking him to translate my diary as well as this letter, and the letter you should have found at the start of the diary explaining to you who I am and how important the disclosure of this information is for me. I had no way of finding out what happened to you until my mother's death. But before I jump to that event, I want to explain to you what happened.

I was taken to stay in Texas, just three months pregnant with you. Your father Rafael never returned, my own father was in a delicate health condition and I believed it was for everyone's best interest if I stayed in Texas during the rest of the pregnancy and then return once more to San Rafael without you and pretend my pregnancy had never happened. I believed that I would be able to forget about you, but I was wrong. A day doesn't go by that I don't think of you.

You had a twin brother, but he'd died as a two-month-old baby. This is what was reported by the private detective who had been hired to find you. Your brother has been my Angel all these years, and has watched over me as I wish I had done with you – my sweet, beautiful baby who I was able to hold for just a moment. That moment has lasted an eternity. You will be thirty-one now, a grown man in every sense. I lost track of you the moment I gave you up, though I learnt from my mother, just before she passed away, that you were adopted by a British-American couple. The only thing to tie you with our family was a precious stone that has been in our family for generations: a diamond that for me would be worthless. There is no money in the world that could pay for my heartbreak. I would give my life just to see you one more time, which is why I believe I have gone on living all these years, in the hope that, one day I would hear of you and somehow be able to contact you, and share my story with you so that you would understand that if I had known what I know now, I would never, never have let you go.

My father passed away six years after his first stroke. He never fully recovered, and it was with a sad and heavy heart that I had to say goodbye to him also.

I refused to marry Santiago. Instead, I learnt all there was to know about running the family estate, which is what I've done since my father passed away. I never pursued my dream to become an actress, I never found anyone else to love, and I haven't seen your father Rafael since the day he left. I ride out every year on the 1st December to Salto de las Rosas. I sit by the tree where I spent that magical night so many years ago, and think every time about what happened, and wonder what could have been and why Rafael never came back.

I know I should forget about the past, I know that I should have moved on years ago, but I'm trapped. The first year on riding out to Salto de las Rosas, I went with the intention of taking my own life. I had nothing to live for. But something stopped me. I like to believe that your brother, my little Angel, had been watching over me, protecting me, though I longed to leave this world and join him in Heaven. But I've remained. Year after year I return

175

to Salto de las Rosas, There are thirty lines engraved into the tree's bark, a line for each year that has passed. I have never forgotten you, just as I have never forgotten Rafael. I hope that this letter reaches your hands and that on reading the diary you can understand that I did what I believed to be the best. I hope that you will forgive me. Perhaps with your forgiveness, I will have the heart to forgive my mother, and, perhaps your father also, even if I was never to see him again. In forgiveness I gain peace.

My mother, in an attempt to make up for the heartbreak she'd caused and the lies she'd told, had (unknown to me) spent several years employing a private detective to trace you. You are, after all, her grandchild. On her death she had left me the best gift she ever could. She had finally found you, and for that alone I have forgiven her and her terrible lies. When she sent me to Texas, she knew why Rafael hadn't returned, but never told me until she revealed the secret on her deathbed. When I finally found out the truth I didn't know whether to feel anguish or relief. We had all lived out our lives, the last thirty years, based on untruths that had been spun, like a spider's web, trapping us all.

Rafael never returned because the letter that had been handed to him by Santiago, all those years ago, was full of poisonous lies, which he chose to believe instead of trying to find out the truth. I will never forgive him for that, when it would have been clear to anyone who knew me that it was all a distortion of the reality.

But that is in the past now. All I can hope is that you believe me, that you understand my heartbreak, and that you find it in your heart to one day come and see me and let me hold you once more.

Your truly loving mother,
Valentina Mendoza.

CHAPTER EIGHTEEN

CHANTELLE

I must have fallen asleep; it was close to 4 am when I finished the letter, and I was shattered.

I woke feeling really sad. I'd had broken dreams of Valentina and Rafael, and of Robbie and Lionel who were babies in my dream. The images were mixed up with images of my own baby. I totally understood why Robbie had left so soon after reading the contents of the diary. I would have done the same. Sometimes you don't realise what you have until you lose it. And it's a shame that we often only appreciate things when it's too late. Too late to turn back, and too despairing to move forward.

I myself would give anything in the world to feel my own mother's warm, comforting arms around me once again. To tell her one more time that I love her. To fight for her when she was feeling weak. But you can't change the past, you can only learn and move forward. I have learnt that if you really love something, or someone, love alone is often not enough, you have to fight for what you want. You have to work hard to achieve your dreams – so whatever happened from now on, I would try my hardest to be the best me I could be, to offer the best future for my child that I could offer, and to win Robbie back (or at least give it my best shot). Not that I was quite sure how that was going to happen, considering he was on the other side of the Atlantic and perhaps in the arms of another woman.

My stomach rumbled. I glanced down at my watch. No wonder I was hungry; it was 5 pm. I had slept straight through the whole day. Dolly seemed to have disappeared too. And I didn't blame her, her bladder had probably been bursting. I expected to see a pool of pee on the kitchen floor. Luckily Dolly had held out, but it was with bounding relief that she sped past me as I opened the kitchen door to the garden.

I phoned Myfanwy as I put some bread in the toaster and activated the spaceship-looking coffee machine. I stepped back a pace and kept a safe distance from the coffee maker while it started to froth my milk, just in case take off was, as I believed, a possibility. The line clicked.

"Chantelle?" Myfanwy sounded a bit breathless. She'd probably sprinted to the phone or something, desperate to know my opinion of what I'd just read.

"I've finished."

"And...? Could you figure out why Rafael never went back?"

"Errr....no." I'd had my work cut out with just the simple reading of the Mendoza papers, mixed with trying to sort out my love life as well as having Dolly bounding around me every time I so much as lifted a finger. All things considered, I thought I'd done pretty well. *And Shit! I had to phone Freddy G!* I needed to find out if Lionel was OK. I had something extremely important to tell him too. Well, to be honest, three things. Fatherhood, bachelorhood and family-hood. Perhaps a bit too much information to take in all at once after a concussion. I'd have to space out relating the details, otherwise I risked causing Lionel permanent brain damage.

179

"I wonder why Rafael never went back?" Myfanwy continued sadly. "It would have all ended so differently."

"It would have done," I agreed. "You would have been given another child to adopt and I would never have met Robbie." I suddenly realised how fleeting the chances had been that I'd met Robbie in the first place. Perhaps he wasn't destined for me after all. It was just a fluke occurrence, and he had always been destined to be in Mendoza, the province where his biological family were from. It was their family name too. Robbie's passion for horses was obviously part of his genes also. It was clear his biological father's blood pulsed through his veins.

"What do you think happened?" I asked.

"I'm not sure, Chantelle. I read that diary when it first arrived just over a year ago. But I hid it from Robbie because I was scared to lose him. I was selfish and kept the information a secret. But the other day he came home looking so desolate about something, something that he was keeping to himself, that I realised that he was a grown man with his own life to live and his own problems to solve. Without me. I was being selfish by hiding his past from him. I had been blessed enough to have been given such a beautiful, loving child to look after, a boy that has grown into a handsome, caring man. It's now his time to live his life as he chooses. Even if he was to remain in Argentina, no one would ever be able to take away the thirty years I've had at his side, and for that alone I'm grateful."

Her voice caught at the end and I imagined her wiping away a tear or two, just as I was myself. Since I'd bumped into Sally just two days ago, crying had turned into my primary occupation. My hormones had really gone on the rampage. Usually I found it quite hard to cry. I'd cried so much when I was younger on losing my mother that I often believed I'd used up all my tears. But I could now safely confirm that the drought had come to an end and it was monsoon season.

"What are you going to do?" Myfanwy asked, bringing me back to the conversation and my rumbling stomach.

"Have some dinner. I haven't had anything to eat yet as I finished reading so late that I've actually spend all of today asleep."

"And then what will you do?"

Err...sleep some more? I mean, there wasn't much more to do in these parts anyway. Clubbing certainly wasn't an option. Weeding was the most energetic activity I could come up with right now, but I was far from feeling energetic.

"I mean," came Myfanwy's carefully level voice again, "will you go to Argentina too, and see if you can find out what happened? Support Robbie with this, he's probably feeling quite lost and lonely over there."

Not quite the impression I got when I last spoke with him. *"Robbie, mi amor, take me"* didn't sound very lost and lonely to me, but I thought it was best to keep this piece of information to myself. Myfanwy probably still thinks her son's a virgin, and I didn't want to be the one to take the blindfold off. That said, she'd get the shock of her life in nine months' time, as recalling my passionate night with Robbie things were back to square one: a 50/50 chance of fatherhood for each man. My mind had drifted, and it was a while before I registered what Myfanwy had actually asked me. Go to Argentina? Are you kidding? Me, let loose in South America with not an inkling of Spanish? I couldn't think of anything worse.

"Myfanwy, I don't speak Spanish."

"Nor does Robbie."

Well that doesn't seem to be an issue for him; he's already apparently found himself a native translator willing to work 24/7.

"You've got nothing to lose, Chantelle. Show Robbie how much he means to you by going after him and helping him. I know I'm being selfish by asking you to go. I would go myself if I thought it would make a difference, but I'm not enough to bring him back. Only you can do that." It all felt a bit surreal. I felt like I was playing out a scene from *Star Wars*.

The force is with you, Chantelle: follow your instinct and bring Robbie back...

"I don't think I've got it in me, Myfanwy," I mumbled, wanting to sound convincing. It would be mad of me to go, but I was actually feeling slightly hypnotised by the idea and Myfanwy's persistent soft murmuring.

"But you have, Chantelle. More than you realise. Believe in yourself and you will achieve great things."

Blimey! The force is definitely with Myfanwy. She'd obviously just crash-coursed with Yoda on coaching and mindfulnesses techniques. And got her money's worth, too, I realised, as I heard myself confidently reply,

"You're right, Myfanwy. You have to take a chance in life and in love. I will go, and try my hardest to bring him back."

"It is as it should be, Chantelle." With that the line went dead and I was stunned to silence for a moment trying to take in what the hell had just happened.

I couldn't believe I'd just agreed to go to Argentina. Crazy didn't come close, and in my stupor, it was a while before I realised I was surrounded by smoke, lots of choking smoke, and the kitchen was filled with a strong smell of burning. I quickly turned around to find the toaster alight with flames. I threw a tea towel on top of the fireball that had formed on the kitchen worktop. Bloody hell, I can't even make toast properly, how on earth would I get to San Rafael, in the province of Mendoza and bring Robbie back? I was going to need more than the backing of a legendary Master Jedi. Obi-Wan Kenobi was going to have his work cut out with his new recruit.

But there was nothing for it.

Argentina, here we come.

CHAPTER NINETEEN

CHANTELLE

Of course I couldn't leave just like that; there were things to do, flights to book, and I needed a to find myself a travel partner. I couldn't face this venture alone.

I ate a quick dinner, removing the burnt toast from the menu, and settled myself back down on the sofa. Dolly had resumed her position next to me, thumping her tail on the wooden floorboards, tongue hanging out, ready for action, whatever that may be. I picked up my phone and started searching for flights to Argentina. I had no idea if it would be best to fly to Buenos Aires and then get inland transport to cross over to the province of Mendoza. My mind was going at a thousand rpm. Without thinking twice I dialled Tammy's number.

"How's your Spanish?"

"Perfezionare il mio amico, semplicemente fantastico!"

That actually sounded more like Italian to me, but I wasn't going to be fussy.

"Good enough, Tammy! Get ready, we're going to Buenos Aires."

"Are we?" she replied, sounding a bit confused. "Is there a Buenos Aires in Spain too then?"

"Or perhaps Mendoza. It might be easier." I gushed out rapidly, not wanting to break my flow, not stopping to answer Tammy's question. "Yes, that would be better, fly straight to Mendoza and get a taxi or something to Valentina's house." I could hear Tammy voice in the background: "Who on earth is Valentina?" But I wasn't listening. I was miles away planning my reunion with Robbie and how I would somehow be the one to solve the mystery between his biological parents, and return home with him, content beyond words that everyone, including me, had finally found their happy ever after.

Of course, the greater mystery for me was finding out who really was the father of my future child. I had to phone Lionel too. And Vivien!! Shit! And why the hell hadn't Robbie phone *me* back yet?! Not that I really wanted to contemplate a detailed scenario of what Robbie was doing that was delaying his call to me.

Tammy had gone silent too, probably waiting for me to explain myself and my whacko plan. She was probably bracing herself for any hare-brained idea that I might come up with. I was blessed she knew me so well.

"Did Ray tell you that Robbie and Lionel are possibly twins, separated at birth?"

The notion still sounded so bizarre, hard to come to terms with, even for my mind which was pretty much game for any odd concept. It was such a huge coincidence.

"Ray told me," Tammy answered. "I've always said how awfully similar the two men are."

"Yes, well, they are twins. Robbie was adopted and so was Lionel. Their real mother tried to contact Robbie a couple of years ago, but Robbie's only recently been given a letter and diary that reveal all and I've just finished reading them. His biological family are from Argentina." (It clicked as I was saying this that it also explained why Robbie looked permanently tanned: I'd always thought that a little odd considering the British weather. Obviously he'd inherited his grandmother's Mapuche blood.) "His birth mother, Valentina, had to give up Robbie and Lionel at birth. Then she was told that one of the babies died, just two months old. But, guess what, after nearly thirty years the mother was given information that enabled her to trace what she thought was the one living twin. That's Robbie. He's flown to Argentina to see her."

"And what about Lionel?" Tammy asked.

"He's got concussion."

"What? From being told about his family?" Tammy sounded astonished by the possibility, when, really, this momentous discovery could well cause more than just a head trauma. I'm sure it would have done for me. Mind you, I had a certain facility to pass out under strain. It was amazing I hadn't done so yet.

"No! Sorry, Tammy, I've confused you. Lionel had an accident whilst shooting a stunt scene. He doesn't know anything yet. I have to tell him." And just as I said this, another wild, madcap plan started forming in my head. Could I possibly make it work?

***

I dialled and waited as the line connected and the tone blurred away with the now familiar buzz that you get when phoning abroad. "Come on, come on, answer the phone," I murmured. Dolly looked at me, head cocked to one side, ears pricked, seemingly knowing how important this phone call could be.

"Chantelle!" came a chirpy, happy voice down the line. I smiled. I was actually starting to grow really fond of this voice. "I'm so glad to hear you." *(Not that I'd actually been given a chance to say anything as yet.)* "I've had my phone with me all day, just waiting for your call." *(I know exactly how you feel, except the phone call I was desperately waiting for hadn't come through.)*

"Hi Vivien, how are you?" I replied, with genuine warmth in my voice. I'd had time to think things through and realised if Vivien and I had met under different circumstances, if we'd had been given a chance to get to know each other before Lionel got in the way, we might have become great friends from the start. As it was, the day that Vivien had tried to take her own life had been a turning point for both of us. Sometime things do happen for a reason and I was just glad that I'd been there to stop her drowning herself that stormy summer morning. As the waves crashed down around us a union was formed, stronger than those waves, something that would bind us.

Over time I began to understand Vivien, and by understanding her I also understood Lionel. He may have believed he loved me, but I wasn't so sure now that what he felt was love. He'd been misled by what Sally had told him, and on seeing me in that gangster film he hadn't listened to his own heart, but tried to carry out his fantasy with a stranger. I felt that deep down he did still love Vivien. He had been the first to her side when she was taken to the hospital after her attempted suicide. He went to her, not to me. He stayed with her while I waited alone in the cottage. Things had become clear to me now – and not just my feelings for Robbie. We had all been misguided, and now it was time to sort things out.

"I'm good, thanks, Chantelle. Missing you, but you already know that." She laughed, and I realised that her voice wasn't screechy at all (well, only a little bit), and her laugh was musical and beautiful.

"I've got good news and bad news for you, Vivien. Are you ready?"

"Should I sit down?" She sounded concerned.

"Well, as this could take a while to explain, it might be an idea."

With that, I unravelled the most astonishing plan that I had come up with yet. But with a sprinkling of my quixoticness and Vivien's alacrity, I did believe we had a good chance of pulling it off.

***

This time it was my phone that rang. I had been lounging on the sofa, watching a late evening film without really seeing it. The exhilaration of the last few hours and a night without proper sleep was taking its toll.

"Find," I said to Dolly who jumped up, letting out a string of excited barks as she looped around the coffee table a couple of times. She uncovered a lost sock (one of Robbie's I believe) and dropped it by my feet, content beyond words at her find. "Almost," I said, and patted her on the head as I moved the cushions that were strewn all over the sofa to try and uncover my asphyxiated (had it been a mouse) phone.

I had been longing for this phone call all day, but now seeing *Robbie* come up on the screen I was suddenly tongue-tied. Remembering what I'd promised myself the last time we spoke, I took a deep breath and answered the phone.

"Hello Robbie." I'd deepened my voice and it actually came out much huskier than I'd intended.

"Chantelle? Is that you?" I could hear confusion in his tone.

"Hi hun, yes. I've been waiting for your call, I'm feeling hot and a bit sweaty. I've had to turn the heating down and now I'm lying here stretched out trying to cool off…"

I paused, frantically searching for more lines I could shoot down the line to try and turn him on. I cleared my voice again trying to deepen the pitch even more.

"Dolly's here. Just two bitches together trying to cool off... together?!" That certainly didn't come out sounding quite how I'd intended. Err...think, think, think before you balls it up completely! "You know I was just having a dream about you, there was a lot heat and flames and firemen. I mean fire. Fire and water and smoke and sizzly things."

My voice petered out as I inwardly cringed. *What the hell!!* I don't think I could have cocked this up anymore! Sizzly things? For fuck's sake, where on earth had that sprung from?! I had wanted to sound steamy and smoking, but it hadn't quite come out to that effect, more like a burnt *Master Chef* dinner instead. My husky voice had been pretty impressive though. I didn't realise I had it in me.

Silence.

Perhaps I had impressed Robbie after all.

189

"Have you called the doctor Chantelle? You must be coming down with a fever or something. You sound terrible! Have you taken your temperature?"

I cleared my voice. It was probably best to pretend that I was getting a cold or something. Because, let's be honest, my plan, this one at least, hadn't worked quite as I'd intended.

"It could be the start of a cold, but I'm sure I'll be OK, thanks Robbie."

"OK Chantelle, you actually sound better already!"

Silence again. *Say something,* I mentally willed Robbie. Say something before I come out with something crazier than "sizzly things," because I was on the verge of telling him I loved him. No doctor could help me with that.

"I've been thinking," said Robbie slowly.

"Yes?" I prodded eagerly. Please let him be the first to say something endearing, to give me some sort of sign that he still has feelings for me. Any sign would do right now, I wasn't going to be fussy.

"That it might be an idea for me to stay here a little longer than I originally intended."

NO! This wasn't what I wanted to hear. This wasn't the sign I was looking for!

"No?" He sounded puzzled. I'd obviously spoken out loud.

"I mean, Ohh! Ohh! Really? Wow, I guess you're having a great time there. I mean, it's not surprising. It must be pretty amazing for you right now to meet your birth mother, see who she is, and learn her story in person. Spend time with her and she with you. I wish I could have been there when

190

Valentina saw you for the first time. It must have been really magical for both of you. I'm so happy for you Robbie. Really I am."

"I haven't met Valentina yet." *What! What are you waiting for man? Put the lady out of her misery for Christ's sake!* "She's away. Returns in a week or so apparently, that's why I can't leave just yet. I'm with Rafael."

"What! Rafael is there? But didn't he disappear before you were born?!"

Cor blimey, Valentina is going to be in for a real shocker when she returns. Someone should warn her!

"And we have so much in common, Chantelle. He's already taught me how to ride bareback without holster or reins. The other day we rounded up a whole herd of cattle..." I could hear Robbie going on and on about meeting his biological father. He sounded so happy and I was thrilled for him too, but the only thing that I could think of as his words started swimming in my head was that I was drowning.

I had lost him. There was no comparing me with what he was discovering there, on the other side of the world. He had flown there to find out more about his biological family, but what had really happened is that he had gone home, to where he belonged, whereas I'd been left behind with the lost luggage. And let's face it, it doesn't take a huge amount of imagination to envisage what a bummer that is.

CHAPTER TWENTY

CHANTELLE

I had lost Robbie, but I flew out regardless.

This wasn't about me any more. It was about doing what I thought best. Best for those whose cards had landed on my playing board. I had been dealt the Queen of Hearts and the Ace of Spades. The all-important cards were in my hands, and the fortune at stake had nothing to do with material wealth, but with the bringing together, or not, of a family that had crumbled long before I was born. Whose family line would now continue through me. The next generations of the Mendozas (the family, that is, not the whole province!), for good or for bad, was deep within me, growing, slowly but surely.

At least my bosom was getting bloody massive, it was only a question of time for my hour-glass figure to go pear-shaped. But as long as that was the only thing to go pear-shaped I could count my lucky stars, because there was a good chance that the shit could really hit the fan. And then what? I was about to rock up at San Rafael and I didn't have the slightest idea what I really hoped to achieve, but there was some unforeseen force pushing me forward. I had a plan, but would it be enough? I'd rolled the dice, but they hadn't stopped spinning yet and until they did, even when they did, anything was possible.

I turned to Tammy who was sitting next to me on the long-haul flight. I say sitting, but she was actually drooped to one side, neck looking like it would be seriously sore later, snoring loudly, keeping our fellow-passengers from snoring themselves. It had been a week since my telephone conversation with Robbie. I hadn't heard much from him since; just the odd text now and again which I tried my very hardest to ignore. I needed to protect my heart. I hadn't told him I was flying out. This wasn't about him any more. I was going for Valentina, for her grandchild, and for someone else.

Vivien, in the meantime, was developing our plan with extreme efficiency. I had underestimated her ingenuity, though thinking about it, she had been able to find me in the middle of rural England with nothing to guide her except her own intuition, so it should have come as no surprise that the task I'd given her to carry out was, for her, as easy as pie.

I'd had no direct contact with Lionel either, much as I felt bad about it. It was the only way for this crazy scheme to work. I hoped that one day he would forgive me and understand what I was doing and why. I had learnt through Freddy G that Lionel had recovered quicker than expected. Of course I knew the reason for this: Lionel now had Vivien at his side. Love is wondrous, even when we are blind to it.

It was love for my unborn child that was now driving me forward, and keeping me calm and collected despite my apprehension in what I had set out to achieve. In fixing the past I was setting myself free for my future. At least I jolly well hoped so, because if things did go tits-up (more than mine already were) then I would really be left in a fix.

Touch-down was smooth, immigration control, baggage reclaim and airport departure was passed in a blur. Morning sickness had disappeared with the entangled time zones, my body-clock obviously couldn't keep up and had opted to stop ticking for a while. I just hoped I had sorted myself out before it started again. It would do me no good to start retching on Valentina's front porch. It wasn't quite the first impression I wanted to make.

Tammy miraculously managed to sort out the car rental with a car and not another form of locomotion, which for a worried moment I thought might be the case when I kept hearing what sounded to me like "*autobus, autobus*" because "bus" in my language means something that is bright red, and more often than not two storeys high. Car rental sorted, Tammy slid the car keys over to me, winked and said, "I'll take on the language, you take on the roads." This was fine with me, though I'd completely forgotten to Google which side of the road I was meant to drive on and it slowly began to sink in that my crazy plan was probably battier than the car we had been given to drive.

As I climbed into the left hand side of the car and looked at the gear box to my right, I no longer needed Google to confirm that Argentina was one of the countries that drives on the right. We had a three-hour drive ahead of us, at least that's what the car's pre-installed SatNav told us. I guessed I would have figured out how to coordinate the car on the right side of the road by the time I got us to San Rafael. But even I knew that I was tempting fate to venture on this journey straight off a long-haul flight and so drove us to a nearby hotel where we booked in for the night. I needed time to acclimatise, time to adjust to being so close to finding out more about my child's family, and about the two men who, without either of them knowing it, had led me out here in the first place.

***

It wasn't until we left the hotel later on that evening, for dinner and a stroll around the area, that it really hit me we had arrived. The air that enveloped me was rich and warm, from British cooling autumn we had arrived to a semi-arid, continental spring. The streets were vibrant with colours, tall buildings stretched up along the wide broadway which was littered with trees, cars and people milling around. The Andes range outlined in the distance, a firm signature that this was a region of foothills and high plains. The Spanish-speaking voices floated over to me: sonorous, harmonious tones capturing the musical vitality that Argentina was famed for. Music and dance is an integral part of both traditional and contemporary life, which unites the people and functions as an important social tool for both national and regional identification. For me it quite clearly exposed my sadly lacking musical ear.

Tammy and I sat down in an open-air terrace overlooking one of the city's parks. Among the people milling around, I could make out music in the background, a live Tango performance taking place across the green, the faint breeze picking up the music and carrying it softly to where Tammy and I sat, embraced by the warm evening air. I had the hugest slab of beef steak on my plate, which I offered to Tammy and picked at the salad instead. I was too nervous to eat, let alone digest a kilo's worth of rump. Luckily Tammy's appetite hadn't been quashed, and I was relieved, as I really didn't like wasting food. As Tammy eagerly helped herself to a generous amount of the food on the table, she turned to me and asked, in a surprisingly relaxed tone considering how far we were from home (after all, this venture wasn't quite your average day trip to Brighton beach):

"So, I know we're here now. But could you just go over the plan again?" *(As if backing out was still an option?)* "Because, I'm sorry, but I'm still a bit confused. You say you haven't come out for Robbie. You love him, but you don't think it's a good idea to tell him, because he may then feel somehow obliged to return to England with you instead of following through with his dream, which, according to you, is to be a cowboy."

Tammy paused here, while I just nodded.

"You don't want to return to Lionel either, as, again according to you, despite him asking you to marry him in front of millions on live TV, he doesn't really love you. Apparently he loves someone else, though he isn't aware of it yet, and you, yourself, haven't actually discussed this with him in person, but instead with his ex-girlfriend."

Again Tammy paused and again I nodded.

"Sorry, darling," she continued as she downed her glass of Malbec and poured herself another, "I'm probably just being a bit dense here, sweetie, but in that case, what the hell are we doing here?"

Put that way, I did wonder myself.

"My mother." The words came out without me really thinking.

Tammy moved as if to say something, but seemed to think better of it and instead managed to wave the waiter over and order another bottle of red (or *tinto,* as I'd already learnt).

"I lost my mother before I really got to know her. I've spent a lifetime dreaming up someone who I talk to when I'm feeling low, who I ask advice to when I'm in trouble. Whose words I imagine whispered to me in the middle of the night and tell me that I'm going to be all right. I miss her so much, Tammy. I lost her before I had a chance to understand what it meant to say goodbye for ever. I can't even imagine what it must have been like for Valentina to say goodbye to her babies. I know that whatever I do, I'll never see my mother again, but for some strange reason, I just feel that if I can unite Valentina with her sons, especially with the one she believes died as a two-month-old baby, I will somehow be set free from the anguish I feel at having lost the most important person of my life at such a young age."

I paused to catch my breath, whilst Tammy reached out to softly squeeze my hand.

"Perhaps you believe deep down, if you fix this, if you somehow unravel why Rafael left, if you can reunite Lionel with his birth mother, your own baby's future will be secure?"

"Perhaps," I said. "Perhaps if everyone has their happy ever after, I will get mine too." I choked back a sob and Tammy leaned forward to brush away a tear that rolled down my cheek.

"I'm glad we've figured this out then," she said, as one of the waiters subtly laid a red rose down on the table.

"*Para las enamoradas,*" he said and winked at us before moving off.

"What did he say?" I asked Tammy.

"Oh, he just thinks we're in love," she laughed.

"He's right, I do love you Tammy," I declared, squeezing her hand back. "And what is it that we, or you, have just figured out?"

"That we're here for Robbie, of course. He's your happy ever after isn't he? It makes following through with your plan so much easier when we know what we are actually pursuing."

"Tammy, he's in love with someone else!" I exclaimed. "That husky-voiced woman."

"Yes, and you've said that about Lionel too. Except instead of a husky voice it's a squeaky-voiced woman. Chantelle, I do hope you've got a Plan B to fall back on if it turns out that both brothers are still in love with you."

"Oh," I said weakly. This possibility hadn't even entered my mind. "Surely not, Tammy. I don't think that's possible."

Or is it?

Chapter Twenty-One

VALENTINA

He's come back. How dare he come back and show his face here after all these years? I guess I was to blame too, I should never have revealed my secret to his mother, but I needed to share, not only my secret, but also the incredible discovery that had come to light when my mother passed away. I needed to confirm with someone that what had been revealed was true. And only Carmen held the answer. Only Carmen Gonzalez de Fernandez, to whom I hadn't spoken in years, could confirm my mother's twisted story.

But I never expected her to reveal the information to her son. It never even crossed my mind that they were still in contact, but of course they were. She was his mother, after all, but it was like a double betrayal, traumatising just to think that Rafael still spoke with his mother and had done so over all these years, but had never sent word to me.

Perhaps it was best, because as far as I was concerned he was dead. He died over thirty years ago. And I had mourned for him as any woman does a man she deeply loved. I had buried him in my heart and in my mind. Just as I'd also learnt to deal, at the same time, with the betrayal of a lover, because Rafael, by leaving me as he had done, had broken my heart, not once, but twice. I discovered many years ago that even when something has been shattered to pieces, you can still break it further, but never will the pieces fit back together again.

I would not accept his return now. He had taken too long. It was too late. I didn't even understand why he'd come back. It would have been better if he'd stayed away. What did he think he was going to achieve, except re-open a wound that had already scarred over? And why now? Because his mother had revealed the truth that had always been visible beneath a web of lies? Had he never figured it out for himself over all these years?

It had been my cousin Nacho, who had married my best friend Flavia, who had told me of Rafael's return. I remember his words clearly: *"Rafael is back."*

Just three, simple, harmless words, but it was like driving a dagger into my heart, the pain of knowing that Rafael was so close was more than physical, it unravelled a bitterness that still dwelt deep within me. My blood pulsed in anger, but what infuriated me more was that my own broken heart gave a flutter, like that of a young eaglet, desperate to leave the nest, but whose wings have been damaged.

I was so surprised by my own reaction that I knew I couldn't possibly afford to meet Rafael again. I didn't trust myself. I had learnt to live a life where sentiments or feelings no longer existed. I had created my own world, where I was untouchable. I had turned away from anyone who had offered a loving touch, or tried a passionate embrace. I watched the world go by as if behind a glass pane. Growing old in silent sadness.

***

But I did see him. It was a few months after his return, At the annual summer gathering, where all the neighbouring families turned out to celebrate our community, which had grown over the years. Production had steadily increased as the wine market expanded both nationally and internationally. I was proud to be a member of such a rich community. I had dressed with special care for this event, but for no one in particular. I knew that there was a chance Rafael would come. It's not that I didn't want him to see that I was still attractive, that men still sought me out for more than just simple companionship. I wanted him to see that, although deep down he had broken me, it did not show. I was my father's daughter. I had stepped into my father's shoes, and the business was now mine, run efficiently and fluently. I was proud of what I had achieved and I had done it alone. I was an equal with the surrounding winemakers. It was still a man's world, but I had made my place within it. I had made my vineyards the most productive, and above all I was respected.

I dressed with added care to reflect this. I may have been broken as a young girl, but that girl had grown powerful. I was strong. At least this is how I felt until I saw him enter the grounds.

There wasn't a man there that could outshine him. He had been gone for over thirty years, but everyone was happy to see him again. He had never been mentioned, at least not in my presence, but everyone knew who he was and greeted him with genuine warmth and enthusiasm. I had always

201

believed he was just a horse-whisperer, but there was so much more. There was a charisma about him that flowed out of his every pore and touched all those around. I watched, as if in slow motion, as he made his way to where I was sitting. Not once did he seem to look in my direction, but made his way closer to me as if guided by an invisible cord.

I thought I was confident enough to confront him, but with his every nearing step my heart fluttered, quicker and quicker. I wasn't sure if I could control my voice or my shaking hands. I was desperate to leave, push my chair back and escape into the cooling night. But as I moved to stand, his eyes sought out mine and we were locked together in a moment that left us both paralysed.

There are no words in this world to describe how a look held for no more than five seconds could last an eternity. It was as if the last thirty years of our lives flashed before us: what had been, what could have been, and what would never ever be. There had been an "us," but that "us" had remained frozen under the starlit sky of one summer, many years ago, and there was no turning back. With a thundering heart, I was the one who broke eye contact first. I pushed back my chair with force and escaped into the dark night, stumbling as I went.

I thought I was ready. I thought I could pretend that I no longer hurt, but I was hurting more than I was willing to admit, and the wall that I'd built up around me over all these years trembled, threatening to crumble. He was indeed the whisperer. Just one soft word blown in my direction was enough to alter everything, and I was furious beyond measure that my own heart was the one still clinging to what could never be.

***

This all happened several months ago. I've had no contact with him since then. If we find ourselves in the same social gathering, it is I who stands and leaves. I no longer care that people were starting to talk. And they do talk, because every Friday without fail, since our re-encounter at the summer festival, Rafael comes to the hacienda. He asks to speak with me, glances up to my bedroom window where I watch him from behind the silky curtains. Every Friday my staff politely inform him I'm unavailable. He does not insist or remain, but he does not tire either and returns every week. And my heart betrays me every time. I knew deep down that we needed to talk. That perhaps that was the only way to heal the wound that had been made so many years ago and had recently been opened once again.

I find myself dreaming, as I used to many years ago, about how it was to be held in his arms. About my babies, our babies, that I was only allowed to hold for one brief, fleeting moment. About how they felt whilst growing within me, their little kicks and fluttering movements. But I just couldn't face him, not yet. I had grown into a strong, independent woman. But the girl in me still longed to be held, and I had to teach her once again that it could not be.

I had just come away for a few days to Buenos Aires, a yearly trip to meet with some of our important clients. I wished to travel further, but often believed if I did, I may not return. I say business trip, and I tell everyone that that's what it is, but actually what I visit is an orphanage. An orphanage I co-founded fifteen years ago. The winery had started to do so well; the yearly profits were rising, and I had to satisfy my urge to help children who had been unlucky, to somehow invest in their future. I only wished I could do more.

I had just come back to the hotel from a busy day when my phone rang, I answered it without thinking. I didn't usually answer the phone if the caller ID comes up as unknown, but this time I did. It was one of those moments that you don't give importance to at the time, but then you're hit by a cannon ball, the force so strong that it knocks your breath away. Over thirty years had gone by, but the voice down the line hadn't changed and I would have recognised it anywhere.

"He's here," said the voice; tone vibrant, unmistakeable and unwavering. I wanted to slam the phone down, but found myself sinking to sit on the bed, my legs buckling under me, my head swimming.

"Who?"

"Our son."

***

I flew back the next morning on the first available flight. I must have been dreaming. Could it possibly be true? I didn't want to get my hopes up, after all these years. For one terrible moment I thought that it could be someone pretending to be my son, looking for an inheritance, and that it would be all lies. I could count with the fingers of one hand the names of the people who knew of my secret and I knew that none would betray me, but I had often imagined that someone might turn up after all these years and claim to be my son, in order to get their hands on my fortune. I didn't think I could take another deception.

I'd sent the diary and letters off so long ago that I had given up all hope that Roberto would ever receive them. The months following the sending of the translated texts were like torture. Every car that drove up the driveway could be him. Every telephone call was answered in hope. I had lived through months of waiting for Rafael to come back many years ago, but this was different. This love that I held in my heart was pure and untouchable. But the days went by and I received no news, no phone call, nothing.

I'd considered flying to England myself. I'd even bought a ticket. I went to the airport, but instead of embarking I remained and watched from the car park as the plane took off. I wished a million times that things could have been different, but you can't turn back the clock. I would be nothing but a stranger to the son who had survived. I could perhaps look into his eyes and know him to be my son, but who was I to him? No older than a child myself when I let him go. I had no right to interfere in his life now.

So I stayed at home and did what I did best. I hid my pain under my work and my business. But now, Rafael, of all people, tells me my remaining son has come home to me. I didn't dare believe that the world had stopped spinning against me and for once was turning in my favour.

As soon as I arrived back at Mendoza airport I hastened to recover my car and drove, as fast as I could, south towards San Rafael. Driving under such emotional conditions was probably not the wisest thing to do. I almost had an accident right on leaving the main road. I even had to overtake a car that was being driven on the left hand side of the road! I beeped furiously at the driver as I sped past. What the hell was she doing driving on the wrong side of the road?

CHAPTER TWENTY-TWO

CHANTELLE

God, that was a close call. I'd slipped onto the wrong side of the road. It wasn't really surprising surely, what with the open road and backdrop of mountains flashing past. I was absorbing the beautiful landscape that surrounded me when this crazy woman sped past in her flash silver jeep, shaking her fist and probably letting out a stream of obscenities at me on the way. But I wasn't going to let that worry me, I wouldn't have understood a word of it anyway. Fist–shaking, on the other hand, is a pretty universal language. I do believe she stuck up her middle finger at me too, but I couldn't be sure.

Tammy, in the meantime, looked aghast. She'd been texting Ray, and the swerve of the car as I positioned it back onto the right side of the road took her by surprise.

"Remind Ray to keep quiet about our whereabouts please, until we've actually seen Robbie that is. I don't want Robbie to know I'm here yet," I reminded Tammy, who I was discovering had the extraordinary ability of a co-driver. She could text, navigate, reading off our previously prepared route directions, whilst checking at the same time the car's built-in navigation system, fiddle around with the radio until we had a mix of tango, *quena* (Argentinian flute) and Reggaeton music, the perfect combination for headache initiation, and all of this without spewing. I did wonder how good Tammy, or myself for that matter, would be at any of the other principal co-driver's jobs, car maintenance on road sections or special stages often including the changing of wheels. I hoped to God that we wouldn't have to find out.

"Our secret is safe with Ray." Tammy flashed me a reassuring smile and fiddled once more with the radio knob.

"Isn't this just beautiful?" she sighed, leaning back as she wound down the car window. She held her arm outside the vehicle for a moment, playing with the warm air currents, her hand lifting and falling in a wave-like motion. I had a sudden vision of *Thelma and Louise*, but considering what a disastrous ending that film has, I thought it best to keep the image to myself.

I stole a glance at the hills to my right. I say hills as if talking about the Downs or something, near the Kent-Surrey boarder, often reaching heights of excess of two-hundred metres, and proud of the Downs as I am, even the highest point at Botley Hill at two-hundred and sixty-nine metres would look really pathetic against this backdrop. The Andes Mountains, as Tammy kindly recited after Googling about it on her iPhone, are the longest continental mountain range in the world. This range is about 7,000 kilometres long, about 200 to 700 kilometres wide, and with an average height of about 4,000 metres. The Andes extended from north to south through seven South American countries: Venezuela, Colombia, Ecuador, Peru, Bolivia, Argentina and Chile. Driving South to San Rafael, we were leaving behind the highest mountain outside Asia, the Aconcagua, at 6,961 metres. The mountain has a number of glaciers, continued Tammy, the most well-known is the north-eastern or Polish Glacier, as it's a common route of ascent.

Well, I'd take Mr Google's word for it. After almost hyperventilating the one and only time I cycled up Box Hill, a mere 224 metres high (though it certainly didn't feel "mere" at the time), I had no desire of taking on any of the seven summits of the world. My belly-button would soon have its own new summit to be proud of anyway, and that was more than enough for me.

It was a blissful drive south. A two-hour-and-fifty-four minute journey, according to Google Maps. Though I did wonder, after four-and-a-half hours and the petrol gauge alarmingly low, if hours and minutes had a different meaning in South America. I had only just about got the hang of driving on the right-hand side of the road; I didn't want to worry about time units and mathematical calculations too.

Tammy had dozed off after her geographical recital just as I was searching for a road sign to indicate our whereabouts. I didn't get a sign, but I did get about three-hundred cattle that just seemed to appear out of nowhere and slowly amble across the road, making me stop.

I manoeuvred the car to one side of the road and stopped the engine. I stepped out onto the dusty tarmac. The sun was high in the sky, reflecting harsh light around, the rays beating down at their midday peak, shortening the shadows around. The mooing of the cows filled the air, and they kicked up dust as they went. I started to wonder if the road sign I'd seen a while back was not the right turning I needed and now instead of heading south to San Rafael, I was heading into deep *gaucho* territory. As if on cue, I heard a shrill whooping sound coming from behind. If I hadn't known any better I would have sworn it was an Indian war cry and heading right in my direction. I now found myself and the rental car, swimming in a sea of four-legged, rather whiffy, mooing beasts. There wasn't much for it, because I really didn't have a choice, but to stand my ground and take a few selfies of the situation to Instagram later.

With a clatter of hooves I suddenly found myself face-to-face with a deeply-tanned, strongly-chiselled, masculine face. Smouldering eyes looked me over. Tammy, at this point, having been startled awake, was squeezing herself out of the car window. She had done this manoeuvre before, down by a river bed we had inadvertently driven into the day we met her now boyfriend Ray and his best friend Robbie – my Robbie (well, not really "*my*" Robbie, at least not any more, or perhaps ever). That first attempt at body coordination and hyper-mobility had ended with both Tammy and me covered in mud from head to foot. She had managed to get stuck in the car window and popped out like a champagne cork as I yanked her in an attempt to save her from the submerging car. We had both been bowled over and covered in gooey muck.

Despite the mud bath it had all ended quite positively, at least for Tammy and Ray. But I didn't think you should tempt fate twice.

"Keep still!" I cried out to Tammy over the roaring noise the cows were making. "You'll get trampled on."

"English?" came a startled, heavily-accented, voice from the *gaucho*, who now quickly moved his horse over to cover Tammy and protect her getting squashed and stampeded on. I have no idea why he had sounded startled to hear us speak in English. After all, I doubted any local would have got themselves in the mix we had, so it should have come as no surprise that we were Gringos. By this point Tammy was truly stuck, half-in-half-out of the car, and I observed, once again, how she could, under any circumstance, revert to her combined fluttering eyelashes, flushed cheek number. Damsel In Distress had been called into action, and she did not fail. Thinking about it, despite not being quite the superpower that I would personally strive for, I had to admit it got Tammy out of almost every possible awkward or hazardous situation.

"*Oh, gracias, Señor,*" came Tammy's pitiful voice as she allowed him to take hold of her hand and steady her as she slipped from the car window and somehow ended sitting behind him on his horse. I certainly wasn't going to take a picture of this manoeuvre and Instagram it. I couldn't afford to get myself in trouble with Ray. I needed him on my side in this venture. I'd told him I would look after Tammy, who was after all still recovering from her own concussion. I didn't think riding behind some good-looking Argentinian cowboy was quite the image that Ray would wish to see as proof of her recovery.

The last of the cattle moved on and the cowboy gave us a detailed explanation of how to get back en route to San Rafael and instructions of where the nearest petrol station could be found. I had been

211

gazing at him the whole while, but I wasn't really looking at him, rather imagining that this is what Robbie would be doing, riding out in the open plains, rounding up cattle as if it was second nature. But, of course, this vision of events was inside my head only, to the *gaucho* it must have seemed that I'd been looking at him all doe-eyed, and I felt terribly foolish when he blew me a kiss as he rode off.

"I think you've pulled there, Chantelle," came Tammy's saucy remark, breaking me out of my trance as she herself waved the cowboy off.

"Don't be daft, Tammy. You're the one that was *pulled* to sitting behind him on his horse!"

We both looked at each other, cracking up in laughter, no doubt causing Mr Cowboy to think, as he rode off, that we were giggling over him like two young girls with a new crush.

Two hours later and our peals of laughter had petered out. In fact, Tammy looked quite green by the time we arrived at San Rafael and made our way to the hotel I'd booked us into. I didn't feel too great either. What should have been just under a three-hour drive had turned into an almost seven-hour Dakar Rally. Tammy's co-driver skills had disintegrated in the last hour, making any off-road special sections off-limits to her queasy belly. As soon as we checked in we both collapsed on the bed and slept straight through the rest of the afternoon, evening and night.

CHAPTER TWENTY-THREE

VALENTINA

Nothing could prepare me for this moment. I had dreamt about it so many times over the years, but I never really believed that I would finally meet my son again. I still thought that it could be a trick, a hoax, someone looking for money. I had to trust my instinct. I was sure that, somehow, I would know if this man wasn't who he claimed to be.

I sat waiting for him in the library. Perhaps it wasn't the most homely room in the house, but I wanted the meeting to be private. I couldn't face meeting him on the porch and having everyone see my reaction. A reaction that could be a surprise even for me. How was I to act? Should I hug him? What should I tell him? Where to begin? I desperately hoped Rafael would have sufficient discretion to not accompany this man – our son? – at this first meeting. I didn't want anyone to intrude on a moment that was, for me, so private and intimate.

I had doubts over whether my son's reaction would be hostile. Surely not; surely if he was here, it's because he'd read the diary, he would know my story, he would have forgiven me?

I had arrived back at the estate at noon, after driving straight from the airport. He was due to arrive early afternoon. I was grateful for this, I didn't think I could take another night thinking about having him so close and not yet seeing him. He was due any minute now, and I found myself pacing about the fireplace in the library. I couldn't sit, though my legs felt weak. My hands and fingers tingled from the blood that was pulsing around my whole body. I could feel slight perspiration forming on my forehead as I nervously walked around. Every now and then I would pause and strain my ears. Was that a car I just heard pulling up on the gravel path? The grandfather clock chimed 2 pm, a distant, echoing, gong in the background. Any time now.

I tried to calm myself, but it was impossible. I had been waiting a lifetime for this moment. I had also grown tough because of the things I'd been forced to bear. Tougher than I perhaps realised. Or so I thought, until the library door opened and he walked in.

The room began to spin. I leaned heavily on a fireplace armchair. I couldn't trust my legs, I didn't trust my voice, but my heart knew without a shadow of a doubt that the young man before me, who slowly entered the room, was my son. His look held mine in an unwavering gaze, a shy smile lit up his face and his brilliant blue eyes shone like the sky on a clear summer's day. I wanted to run to him and hold him, but my legs shook and I remained rooted to the ground.

It was as if I had been taken back in time. Before me was a young version of my father, but with Rafael's colouring and Rafael's smile. I sent a silent prayer of thanks to God, or whatever force it was that had sent my son back to me. Miracles did exist. Mine had just walked back into my life.

The young man walked towards me in strong, confident strides. He stopped before me for just a moment.

"Mother?"

I tried to speak, but my voice was caught and no sound came out. I feebly nodded my head and before I knew it I was wrapped in a strong, powerful embrace, where words were of insignificance under such a universal, loving gesture.

I really didn't want to cry but I found tears streaming down my face and it was a while before I gathered myself together and was able to speak.

"Thank you," I said in my stilted English. "Thank you coming, you imagine not what see you means to me. To know that you grown, such great, handsome man."

To which he simply replied: "Thank you for giving me my life."

***

We spend the whole afternoon talking. My English is very basic, but sufficient to communicate in a modest way. Roberto, or Robbie as he says everyone calls him, made a solid attempt to speak Spanish, and I have to say he was quite proficient at it.

He tells me about his life in England, his adoptive mother Myfanwy, who I have to admit sounds like a lovely lady whom he dearly loves, and I couldn't be more happy knowing that he has been well looked after.

He loves horses. I laugh out loud at this. Of course he does, he is half Fernandez half Mendoza, there aren't two families in the world that love horses more. He talks and talks and talks and I just find myself hypnotised by him. I can't quite believe he's here. This beautiful man in front of me; my son. He doesn't seem to be aware of the impact he has made on me and just goes on talking, in the most natural way, as if we had known each other for years.

I take in his strong muscular arms and wiry fingers, a reflection of his love for the outdoors and physical labour. His thick, dark hair which falls across his face when he leans forward. His perfectly-chiselled face, his strong jaw and Roman nose. Could he be more perfect? And then he turns to me an offers me that shy smile of his, his brilliant blue eyes crinkle slightly reflecting two pools of light out of his tanned face, and I just can't believe that there is a part of me responsible for this amazing person before me. Because apart from his looks, the way he speaks, the softness in his tone, the elegance in the way he holds himself portrays a side to him that is caring, respectful and kind. I am just spellbound. I'm aware that his adoptive mother has played a great part of shaping this side of his persona, and I inwardly thank her for being such a wonderful mother and for turning him into such a gentleman.

It seems that Robbie had arrived a few days ago and by chance had bumped into Rafael who had ridden over as he always does every Friday. There would have been no doubt in either of the men's minds that they were father and son, the similarity is quite startling. It had taken Rafael a couple of days to locate me, as my loyal staff would not reveal my whereabouts. It was my cousin Nacho who in the end gave way, his daughter has also met Robbie and it seems they have become quite good friends. In fact they have arranged to ride together tomorrow, out to Valle Grande. Rafael will go with them and I would love to go too, but I can't, not yet. I needed to talk to Rafael first.

The time had come to face the facts. I could no longer ignore his presence. For our son, I would confront the ghosts of my past.

***

The following morning at day break, Robbie set off with Milena, Nacho's daughter, they were to meet Rafael on the way. I had insisted that Robbie stay at the hacienda while he remained in the area. I haven't dared to ask when he plans on returning to England. I will pretend, for the next few days at least, that he will stay forever.

I decided to remain at the house, whilst the others have gone out riding. I settled on the front porch as I finished my breakfast, taking in the glory of the landscape around me. I will never tire of this view, of the rocky mountain range about me, white peaks which can be seen from afar, a contrast to the rich green, cultivated vineyards that lay closer.

I sighed in peace. It's been a long time since I felt so tranquil. I was glad that I had the remainder of the day to myself. I needed time to assimilate the fact that Robbie was here, that Rafael had returned. I breathed in deeply, taking in the smell of the rich soil, damp with the early morning dew which threw a blanket of stillness around, except for the birds who chirped with their early morning song. It was a moment I hoped to cherish forever, because, for the first time in years, I felt happy.

As I put my feet up on the veranda's fence, I heard the distant hum of a car or some sort of vehicle approaching. I wasn't expecting anyone and peered out to see who it could be. As the car approached slowly, I had an inkling that I recognised it somehow. But it didn't belong to anyone I knew, yet as the driver parked it to one side of the grounds and emerged there seemed to be something familiar about her. I should have gone indoors and have one of my house staff attend this lady, but curiosity got the better of me and I remained observing her.

One of my guard dogs ran up to her, and instead of growling as it would have done with any other stranger, it jumped around her in joy. The tall young lady bent down, cuddling my dog in a loving, fond way. There was no rush in her actions, she looked totally relaxed and shared a moment of play with the dog, who seemed happy and remained at her heels. The passenger door opened and another young lady emerged. Petite and pretty, had she been alone I would say she was quite comely, but she was totally overshadowed by her friend, who I found I was mesmerised by.

The tall girl made her way over to her friend, who didn't seem to want to leave the safety of the car because of the dog. It took a moment before both girls walked together towards me and the hacienda, the tall girl stopped from time to time to look around, seemingly delighted by her surroundings. Another of my guard dogs ran to her and, again, this dog seemed happy in her presence. She almost tripped up over them and laughed out loud at her clumsiness and I found myself smiling back at her antics.

Who on earth was this awkward but totally fascinating young lady? And it clicked: this was the lady who I overtook yesterday, driving on the wrong side of the road. But as she neared I realised that this wasn't why I felt I recognised her. There was something else, but I just couldn't put my finger on it. The early morning breeze picked up her dark, curly hair, swirling it gently before pushing back off her face, revealing her high cheekbones and a slender oval face. She was still not aware that I was watching her. There was something so familiar, my heart quickened. It couldn't be, surely? I felt blood pulsing in my temples. I was confused. I had given birth to two boys, I had held them both for that one brief moment many years ago. One had died. So who was this young lady before me? Who looked so much like her, like *la Bruja*? The similarity was remarkable. Was my mind, my memories playing tricks on me? I'd had twin boys. There had been no baby girl. Or had there?

I suddenly felt a bit faint. The pressure of the last couple of days taking its toll. Wounds healed long ago had been opened again and the emotion was high. The girl suddenly seemed to be aware of my presence, and turned to me. I was caught up in her liquid, honey-coloured eyes. Eyes I'd seen before.

She smiled, radiating beauty and charm, though seemingly unaware of the impact she was having on me.

"Valentina?" she asked in a soft voice. With that my mind blurred and I slipped to the floor.

CHAPTER TWENTY-FOUR

CHANTELLE

"Err…Tammy…" I said in a flap, "I think she's fainted on us."

This made announcing my presence all that more complicated. "Quick, hold her legs up," I said as I moved over and slapped her cheeks slightly. This was not how I had imagined my first encounter with Robbie and Lionel's birth mother would be like. There was no doubt it was her: the smokey grey eyes, the ash blonde hair, and their faces, Robbie's and Lionel's, mirrored in hers.

"Do you think she's recognised me?" I asked, "because she looks very much like the lady who overtook us yesterday and beeped furiously at me for being on the wrong side of the road."

"She wouldn't faint for that though, surely?" Tammy was now puffing a bit from the exertion of holding Valentina's legs up.

"Do you think I should slap her a bit harder?"

I hoped to God she wouldn't stop breathing. Mouth-to-mouth with my future child's grandmother certainly wasn't on my bucket list.

"How about some water?" Tammy suggested.

Personally I fancied something a bit stronger.

"What? And just chuck it at her?" I asked in surprise.

"Yeah, I would have thought that that should do the trick."

The dogs at this point were barking like crazy. Lying at floor level was obviously a universal game for all dog breeds worldwide. They both looked excited beyond measure. Not thinking about it twice, I picked up the jug of water that was on the veranda table and chucked it all over Valentina.

I held my breath for a moment in hushed trepidation before I let out a sigh of relief as Valentina stirred.

"You're right Tammy. It does do the trick."

"Thank goodness for that! I was just improvising. I didn't really expect it to work!" She plopped Valentina's legs down.

Personally I just hoped that Valentina wouldn't be too mad at me. I certainly wasn't making the best first impression. Yesterday I almost caused her to have a car accident, and today I'd managed to make her beautiful cream blouse go all transparent. Gently I held onto Valentina's hands and guided her up to a sitting position.

She looked at me all confused, as I took in again the resemblance between her and her son (or should I say sons). The same form of the mouth, the slightly upward slant of the eyes and gently arched eyebrows – though Valentina's eye colour was a silvery grey, darker than both Robbie's and Lionel's.

I had to be jolly careful how I phrased my conversation with Valentina. If this had been her reaction on just seeing little old me, I couldn't even imagine what the outcome could be when I told her about Lionel, let alone about her future grandchild.

Settled once again on the veranda swing, I was relieved to see that Valentina seemed to be getting her colour back. Tammy politely asked Valentina if she was feeling better or if we needed to call for help. At least that's what I think she said. A moment or two passed with no reaction from Valentina, and I was seriously starting to question Tammy's linguistic skills, then Valentina replied, in English, a very heavily accented voice, that she was feeling better, then asked us who we were and how she could help us.

"I'm Robbie's friend," I explained, speaking slowly. I imagined that by now they would have met. I waited to see her reaction.

"Robbie's friend? Girlfriend?"

"Almost."

That seemed to puzzle her, but then again I was just as puzzled by my relationship with her son.

"But I'm not here for Robbie," I went on to explain, or rather confuse her still further. "I'm here because I've read your diary and letters." She started to look shocked and a bit pissed-off to be honest, they were extremely private letters after all, not something to be share with anyone, certainly not with a complete stranger who drives on the wrong side of the road and chucks water all over the place at the first given opportunity. So I quickly added, "Let me explain. Robbie didn't give me the diary, someone else did. Someone who loves Robbie very much. Someone who cares for him and only wants what's best for him, but also misses him terribly. And this person felt that if I was to read your diary, I could perhaps help Robbie, help him understand what happened so that he could be free to return if

222

and when he's ready." Not quite how Myfanwy phrased it. I believe her words were *Find out the truth and bring him back...* Myfanwy had sent me with the backing of the Force. I'd even picked up two Chewbaccas already, two walking carpets, which now lay at my feet.

Slowly Valentina's looks seemed to soften as she comprehended what I was saying. "His other mother?" she whispered. "Myfanwy?"

I nodded.

"But if you not here for Robbie? Why you here?"

"Has Robbie not told you?"

"Told what?" Valentina's look of puzzlement returned added with what seemed to be a slight look of apprehension. Personally, I couldn't actually believe that Robbie hadn't told Valentina about Lionel, that there was another brother who was very much alive. Why was Robbie holding back on this information and keeping it a secret? Lionel had every right to know about his birth mother, and Valentina had every right to be informed that the other son didn't die. That he was a world-famous movie superstar might come as an additional, unexpected surprise too.

"You say in your diary that you had another son. Why do you believe he died?'" I asked.

Valentina looked at me as if seeing me for the first time. Her penetrating gaze seemed to reach deep within me, which was quite unsettling. She then scooped up my hands in hers and held them as she peered into my face and held my gaze. I was now the one starting to feel anxious. What was she doing? Frankly speaking, she looked ashy pale

223

again, as if she'd just seen a ghost, and I didn't think that this was a positive sign, I didn't need her flaking out on me again.

She let go of my hands and cupped my face.

"Err... Tammy... help..." I softly hissed under my breath. This was getting awkward and I didn't want to be rude to our hostess. But what on earth was she doing?

"You look much like her," Valentina murmured, still holding my face.

"Like who?" I breathed out in bewilderment. Believe me, this is not how I had envisioned the conversation going. Who the fuck was she talking about?

"Like grandmother yours."

"What?" I broke away from her touch and stepped backwards, startled. "You knew my grandmother?"

I was impressed. I'd only met both my grandmothers a few times myself. My Italian grandmother had passed away not long after my mother, the shock and sadness of losing her daughter too much for her. And Valentina couldn't possibly be referring to my British grandmother; my dad's mum was an English Rose in every sense, a reflection of our surname. But despite the name, my colouring was a contrast to her pale, translucent complexion and clear eyes. I had flowered into a much more exotic flower, or so I was always told.

"*Perdoné.*" Valentina apologised on observing my startled reaction, pressing one of her hands to her right temple. She looked a bit flushed and shaken and momentarily closed her eyes, while I stole a quick, disconcerted glance at Tammy, but she just

224

shrugged back, obviously just as confused as I was. "It be days very emotional, I be mistaken." Valentina spoke again after a moment's silence.

"That's quite all right, Valentina," I said. "It must have come as quite a shock on seeing Robbie again. And I realise you probably need time to adjust to having him around." *Talking of around, where was he?* "But I do need to tell you something urgently, something that is extremely important." I was thinking about trying to break the news to her softly, about phrasing it all correctly so that it would all come as less of a shock. But I couldn't really see the point. There's nothing like being upfront and direct. *Out with it, girl,* as my dad (God bless him) would have said. But perhaps I should have warned her somehow, because my candid words of "Your other son is alive, he's an extremely famous actor and will be arriving any minute now," actually made it sound like I was making the whole thing up and it was just all part of a terribly, tacky TV reality show.

If I thought that Valentina would faint again from the additional information I had just passed on to her, I was wrong. She actually looked at me quite sternly as she said, "I forgive you, you young, but cannot someone's house arrive, tell lies, expect people to believe. Why believe you?" She tried to remain stern, but her voice shook and she crumbled in grief.

This reaction left me totally befuddled; I would have actually preferred it if she had fainted again. I had hoped to bring her happiness, but she didn't believe me. She had received so much heartbreak over so many years I guess it was normal for her to be distrusting.

225

"Explain me," she continued. "Sorry, you name?"

"Chantelle," I answered, just barely a whisper.

"Explain me Chantelle, why believe you?"

I breathed in deeply. Words weren't going to be enough to convince her. I reached into my handbag and removed a silk handkerchief, then slowly unwrapped the soft material to reveal a beautiful jewellery box. With shaking hands I opened it and there glinting in the morning's rays were the most beautifully cut diamond chandelier earrings – a gift Lionel had given to me the night of the cast party. We had just finished shooting his latest film where I had body-doubled, and he had given them to me to wear at the party. This had confirmed to Viven that she had indeed lost the man of her dreams, and it was the following morning that she had tried to take her life. It was also the day I saved her. I had tried to return the jewels and gave them to Gabby, but Gabby (without me knowing) had put them back inside my suitcase.

"How you get earrings?" Valentina asked, searching my face. I knew she believed me now. A unique set of diamonds had been sent with the boys, the set separated the day the babies were separated. It was the only thing to tie them to each other and to the Mendoza family. These jewels had been in the family for generations, and had been passed down to each son. By a miracle of events, I had seen both halves of the matching set. I had met both sons and for some reason, unknown to me, I was the one that had to try and bring the family members back together again. It was an awful lot of pressure to be under, especially as there was still a good chance it

226

could all go to pot – and then who would get the blame?

"Lionel, your other son, gave them to me."

She looked at me truly astonished. I wasn't sure if this was because she knew, with this level of proof, that I couldn't possibly be lying (which meant that there was, indeed, another son alive), or because she was wondering why on earth this son had been given *me* such a precious family heirloom. I had actually wondered the same thing myself.

There was a moment of stillness and silence. Valentina shakily stood, but her legs gave way and she slumped down again, her hand on her heart. She looked from me to the jewels again. She opened her mouth as if to speak, but nothing came out. And, if I'm honest, she looked rather peaky too, a mix of ashy pale and seasick green. It was just a question of time before she faded on me again, and I'd run out of water. Slapping her around the face a little harder would be my only option. I braced myself for action.

"Whoops!" I said out loud on seeing Valentina fall back, eyes closed. "Here we go again Tammy," I said out loud as I quickly positioned myself before Valentina. I had been aware that fainting again had been a possibility, though it was the last thing I needed. I was just about to take Valentina firmly by the shoulders and give her a good shake when she opened her eyes, giving me the shock of my life, and then, much to my alarm she started laughing, loud hysterical laughter, and I really didn't know how to respond. I guessed a good slap to snap her out of it would work too.

Surely with the noise she was making, someone would appear from the house to check she was OK.

Although in most cases laughing is taken as a positive sign, I wasn't too sure this hysterical outburst was that good for Valentina's health. It was only a question of time before she started choking or stopped breathing all together from lack of proper oxygen flow. The worst thing about it was that it was utterly contagious and it wasn't long before Tammy was also in fits of laughter.

"Tammy!" I exclaimed crossly, "Don't you start too!" But it was too late. There were tears streaming down her face as both women before me hung on to each other as if they had known each other for years, were the best of mates, and had just come in from a pub crawl. Much to my dismay they even shared a word or two in Spanish, which got me totally flummoxed.

It was then that my phone went off and I left them to one side in helpless stitches as I answered the call.

"Hi Vivien," I said, and I never thought the day would come when I was actually relieved that it was Vivien calling me and that she was in fact more coherent and in-control than anyone else around me. At least that's what I had thought before I heard her breathless voice:

"Hi Chantelle. Things are getting a bit out of control."

"Ok," I said, trying to keep calm, surely nothing could be more out of control than Tammy and her new mate Valentina, who were still cackling about in the background. "But do you think you'll manage to convince Lionel to fly out?"

"Oh yes," she breathed down the line. "It's not so much Lionel, it's—" But before she could continue I interrupted.

"Vivien, it's fine, as long as you can get your booty overhear with Lionel, I can handle anything else. Don't worry, you're doing great. So when do you think you'll arrive?"

"The day after tomorrow, perhaps the following latest."

"Top job Vivien! You're a star! If you can, just text me before you arrive. If not, don't worry – I'll be here waiting for you! You're a real beaut Vivien. I couldn't do this without you!"

"Err, yes," came Vivien's not so convincing reply, but I wasn't going to worry about any additional complications. I had enough on my hands with trying to get Tammy and Valentina under control. As long as Lionel arrived soon, I could sort things out. The pieces were slowly falling into place.

***

Valentina finally calmed down, and Tammy had almost settled; a silly giggle would still escape now and again from her lips and I had to keep sending her stern glances. Not that she really paid any attention to me; a stern glance from one of the dogs seemed to be more effective.

Valentina had now taken in that her other son was alive and was due to arrive in the next few days. She had gone limp after the emotional outburst. It was just as well she wasn't quite with it. It avoided all those awkward questions such as *How did you meet my sons? How did you find out?* The answer to the first question would be: I met Robbie whilst covered in mud, and I met Lionel whilst filming sex scenes. (Lionel obviously doesn't come out terribly well in this account, and frankly nor do I.) And I thought it best to keep this information to myself. And how did I find out? Because of the diamonds I'd seen, because both men are so alike, because both had been adopted at two months old, because of the diary I had recently read, and because both had made my heart beat in a way that I hadn't known possible.

We had remained on the hacienda porch, a couple of Valentina's staff had appeared moments earlier, concerned by the noise that had been kicked up. Tammy and I were received with startled looks, but to me that was normal. Since hitting a semi-stardom status of my own, I always seemed to get the odd look and I didn't think much about it.

The staff, following Valentina's instructions (at least what I imagined to be instructions, as it was all said in rapid Spanish), brought out trays and trays of mouth-watering delicatessens, and an abundant mid-morning brunch was laid out on the veranda table. Argentinians have a reputation for their love of eating, and Valentina's larder was obviously stocked to feed an army. There was so much to choose from: pancake filled with sweet paste, *dulce de leche,* shortbread cookies, *alfajores* sandwiched together with chocolate, cheese with quince paste, *dulce de membrillo*. There were even sandwiches de miga: delicate sandwiches made with crustless buttered white bread, very thinly sliced cured meat, cheese and lettuce. And to drink *mate* and freshly-brewed coffee. The nutty, toasted aroma filled the air, and I felt like I was in paradise. It lasted for about a minute, until the mixed concoction of such strong coffee and rich, sweet foods, started to play havoc with my trumped-up taste buds and I started to feel really, really sick.

"Toilet?" I managed to ask, seriously worried that I was about make my own, personal contribution to the breakfast table. Valentina guided me, and despite my really queasy stomach and the fact that I couldn't even stand up straight, I was able to take in the exquisitely-furnished hall, with a wide curved staircase leading to the first floor, with portraits on the walls. One stood out more than the rest. It was of a handsome man who looked almost alive. The artist had done a remarkable job: the eyes seemed to twinkle with life and amusement, the dark blond hair fell forward across his handsome face, with a cow-lick to one side making the hair curve a little. This had to be Gabriel, Valentina's father. There was quite a similarity between father and daughter. It was even reflected in Robbie and Lionel. There was another portrait alongside. A beautiful lady, with an indigenous aura about her. Soft brown skin, raven hair and black eyes. Despite it being a portrait, the eyes didn't look soulless or lifeless in this painting either. Instead, they were like two pristine onyx stones with a flare and light of their own, slightly hazed behind a sheen of sorrow.

I hoped now that Maria Perez de Mendoza had found her peace.

I was left in the bathroom to myself and retched a few times, though nothing came up. I hoped to God Valentina wasn't on the other side of the door listening. I wasn't too sure how I could explain this morning sickness for anything else than what it was, and I wasn't sure how much more hysterical laughter her body could take. I splashed my face with cold water and leaned against the sink, closed my eyes briefly and breathed slowly. The nausea seemed to be passing. Thankfully my morning sickness bouts weren't too frequent and I could semi-control them. I was just about to open the door and step outside when I heard two voices.

"*Ella es igual a la Bruja!*"

"*Igual, igual. La Bruja de joven, Dios santo, será su nieta?*"

The voices faded. I recognized the word *nieta.* If my GCSE Spanish classes didn't fail me, it meant granddaughter. But *bruja*? "She is the same as the *bruja*?" they'd said. I wasn't sure about that. I tried to think, I was sure I remembered the Kings' maid Sav say something about *"bruja"* when referring to her grandmother, the day I asked her to get the pregnancy tests for me. What was it she'd said?

As soon as I got outside I whispered to Tammy, "What does *bruja* mean?" But Valentina heard me, and sharply turned to look at me and then towards the house entrance again.

"Why are you asking after *la Bruja*? The witch?"

That was it! Witch! But why on earth were people going on about witches now?

"I was just wondering what the word meant, you know, just trying to pick up a bit of local lingo."

Valentina looked at me blankly.

"Local lingo?" she repeated. Now it was her turn to ask for linguistic translation. But the translation was left to one side as I was suddenly distracted by a distant figure that appeared on the horizon.

A shaft of light seemed to shine down on the lone rider who was galloping towards us, like a vision, the light blurring everything around. Instinctively I stood, mesmerized by the approaching figure. The well-built physic, the tanned skin, the union between horse and horseman. There was only one person who could ride like that and make my heart flutter.

I moved around the veranda table as if hypnotised, and before I knew it I was down the steps and running towards Robbie. I could hear an intake of breath behind me as Valentina asked in a startled voice, *"Where going you?"* But I didn't care, this was Robbie – and though I had convinced myself that I wasn't here for him, I knew there was no fooling my heart. I desperately needed to talk to him, to be embraced by his strong arms. I could hear myself calling out his name. *"Robbie, Robbie, oh Robbie,"* my voice wavered with emotion that caught in my throat, but I kept running, blind now to the tears that were streaming down my face. I had lost all sense of self-control and was probably making a real spectacle of myself, but I didn't care. I just needed to reach Robbie as soon as I could.

As the galloping horse and rider approached I could see through my blurred vision that the horse was slowing to a canter and then to a trot. I remained rooted to the spot in the middle of the driveway, my legs weak with emotion. But I did think to myself as I wiped my tears away to try and get a better look: *Gosh, hasn't Robbie's hair grown awfully long in the last few weeks.*

But I didn't give it a second thought; my arms were up above my head and I was furiously waving at him now.

"Robbie, Robbie!" I called out again, but just as the words were out, my voice faltered and petered out. *Is that a goatee he's grown too?* I wasn't too sure it suited him to be honest; he looked very odd. My outstretched arms slumped as the horse neared and I suddenly realised that I had been shouting and waving like a moon-struck calf to a complete and utter stranger. *Shit! This wasn't Robbie!!*

And I couldn't make a quick exit and pretend to be making my way somewhere else, as I was still stuck in the middle of the driveway. The rider had just jumped down from his horse, inches from me, with a look of concern and confusion on his face. To be honest, he looked just as startled at seeing me as I did him. But where his expression just reflected puzzlement, mine must have also reflected embarrassment. I felt like a complete and utter plonker.

"Hola," he said and leaned forward to kiss me, and despite my reflexes making me quickly step back. I wasn't quick enough. His arm went around my back and held me; one quick kiss on my right cheek and then my left, a long hug, a pat on my back and to finish with a quick, complete, body scan (I felt like I was going through customs again).

I was aware that this was how Argentinians greeted everyone, but I was a bit put out under the gaze and close proximity of a person who obviously had to be none other than Rafael! At least he hadn't fainted on me as Valentina had, though there was a definite look of confusion and intrigue in his look as

234

his eyes held mine. And me? If I could have disappeared I would have done. I felt terribly foolish, but there was nothing for it but to put on my best smile and say "*Hola*" back.

I had imagined Rafael in my mind, and the man that stood before me reflected this image quite accurately. Slightly older, but I could see the charm, the confidence, the startling eyes, one a deep green and the other an intense blue. Eyes that held me, and read me as if reading an open book. There was an aura about him so powerful that it enveloped me like a blanket, covering up my vulnerability and wiping away my earlier awkwardness. I was lost for words (not that I could say much more that *Hola* in Spanish anyway, but that was beside the point). I could have spilled out my inner woes and sorrows to this man and know that I would be accepted for who I was, and that he would bring out the best in me and, more importantly, teach me to do this for myself.

But in the meantime, we just strolled side-by-side back to the house, in complete harmony, with the horse peacefully trailing behind.

***

Where was Valentina? She'd vanished on seeing Rafael arrive. I also twigged that, though being twice my age, she obviously had better eyesight than I did and that I probably needed to wear spectacles instead of making one of myself. But my main concern was: why was Rafael here? (Apart from trying to woo Valentina back, of course.) Valentina had told me he had gone with Robbie and her niece on some excursion, so now, much to my dismay, Robbie and his new ladyfriend had been left unchaperoned and wouldn't return until tomorrow. I could feel my morning sickness (combined with conventional nausea) return at lightning speed at the very thought of those two alone together for twenty-four hours.

Rafael seemed about to go, when I told him, with the aid of Tammy's translation skills, to sit and wait. I was determined to start sorting things out. *"You're interfering lass. If you play with fire, you'll only get burnt,"* as my father would have sternly pointed out. Quite right, I thought, but this wasn't going to deter me at this moment. I'd got a thing for hot, sizzly things anyway, as I'd already discovered. And, besides, it was too late. I'd flown to the other side of the world to interfere, and I certainly wasn't wasting my airfare.

I went indoors alone. I passed once again the family portraits which seemed to be guiding me and found myself going up the stairs. I had no idea which way to turn, but kept silent so see if I could hear anything. All was quiet on the upper landing, but there was one door that was slightly ajar, and following my gut instinct (not that my gut was that in-tune of late) I headed over to the door and knocked.

Silence.

"Valentina?" I called out softly as I nudged the door open a little further and peered in.

She was sitting on the bed looking out of the window. Her proud profile was silhouetted against the sunbeams that filtered through the partially-drawn, soft gauzy curtains: curtains that acted as a veil hiding her broken heart, hiding her pain from

236

the outside world. I calculated that she must be about forty-eight now. I imagined that Valentina had always been beautiful, and age had only enhanced her beauty, emphasising her slender bone structure, her petite physique, a disguise to her strength of character. I had only been with her for a morning, but that was time enough to know that she was a formidable woman. She had not been broken by her heartache, but instead had learned and grown stronger. She was someone you found yourself admiring rather than pitying. She had taken what life had thrown at her and survived. Now life had turned things around, and (whether she was aware of it or not) the future of many lay in her hands.

"You know you need to face him at some point, Valentina. You need to talk with him – for your own good as well as that of your sons."

"I want not to. He many years ago left. Too late, why another chance give him? I speak about our sons, but I want him not in my life any more." She said this with conviction, I was sure she had thought about it carefully, but there was a tone in her voice that indicated otherwise, the way she gave a soft sigh on speaking her thoughts out loud. And there was something else, too.

"You say that, and yet you still wear his ring around your neck on a silver chain..." I broke off here as she turned to look at me with a flushed face. Her hand instinctively went to her neck and fingered the ring that glinted and hung there.

"There is a time to be proud, there is a time to be angry, just as there is also a time to forgive, to forget, and to love again..." Don't ask me where I was getting this inspirational talk from. It must have been the hormones making me all wordly-wise, soppy, sensitive – and wordy!

"Why this so important to you? Why doing you this?" There was genuine curiosity in her voice as she looked back at me as if trying to scan me for more information. Was there really more to me than met the eye? A crazy gringo who had just rocked up out of the blue, bringing a whirlwind of life-changing information. I suddenly felt older and wiser than my years (which was a first!), and the fact that someone else seemed to see this in me too was quite astounding.

Though I just looked back at her, I wished I could answer, but it wasn't the right time, not yet. And what I most worried about was that if things didn't work out, the right time would never come. For the first time since I started this mad venture to bring everyone their Happy Ever After I started to have doubts, despite having Valentina look at me as if I knew what I was doing, because quite frankly I didn't. The jumble of events was quite alarming.

For a start, Robbie had gone off with some new lady friend and had no idea I was here interfering. And I had a feeling he wasn't going to be too thrilled about it.

Secondly, I still had to face Lionel. I had no idea what Lionel's reaction would be, but there was a good chance he wasn't going to be over the moon about things.

And finally, why the hell was everyone looking at me as if they'd just seen a ghost?

CHAPTER TWENTY-FIVE

VALENTINA

The girls had left, I heard their car drive off, with a promise that they would be back soon. I had insisted that they return and stay in my house whilst they remained in the area. The tall girl was obviously someone very special to both my sons, and for some reason, I needed her close. She knew my sons better than I did, but there was something else. There was something terribly familiar about her. Or perhaps it was just that she was enveloped in a magical aura that seemed to captivate all around her. I had only met one other person capable of this. And this person was sitting downstairs waiting for me.

I could delay no longer. It was time to confront the ghosts of the past and speak with Rafael.

With a heartbeat that belied my calm exterior, I descended the stairs and made my way outside once more. It was still mid-spring and today the air was cool, comforting me, cooling my burning interior.

Rafael rose as soon as he saw me. He was older, but the way he looked at me was just the same as all those years ago. Nothing had changed, at least perhaps for him, but I knew that my eyes were cold. I had tucked my precious ring necklace deep inside my blouse. I had almost taken it off before descending the stairs, but, as far as I was concerned, the ring was given to me by another man, not the one who stood before me now. His penetrating familiar gaze aside, I really didn't know him. Perhaps I never had.

I didn't know where to begin. The anger I had felt many years ago had been buried, though perhaps it may have done me some good to shout and scream and hit out at him. I preferred to show a side of me that Rafael wouldn't be ready for. A side to me that had emerged over the years. A self-control and coldness that even his magic couldn't touch. It was unbreakable.

"Please make yourself at home Rafael. Tell me, what can I do for you today?" I spoke first, words as distant as if attending to one of the neighbouring landowners who I really didn't have time for, a curt smile on my lips.

If I thought he would be discomforted by my coldness, he didn't show it.

"Thank you for receiving me, Valentina," he said, as I suppressed any emotion that I could feel building-up on hearing my name float from his lips.

There was a moment of silence as we both seemed to battle internally with what we both really wanted to say. For my part, I longed to tell him to leave and never come back, but that would reveal that I still hurt and couldn't forget. I was too proud for that. Plus, whatever he had done, he was the father of our sons and I didn't want Robbie or Lionel to have to deal with our own sad, deeply unhappy past. I didn't want anything to break the magic of their return.

I motioned for him to sit, and keeping a distance I sat also. Everything had gone silent as if we were caught in time; the birds had hushed and the hum of the tractors working the land had fallen silent. There

240

was no noise from inside the house. Everyone and everything had hushed. How important were we, to cause such stillness and anticipation?

The horse whisperer had returned. Anything was possible.

It was Rafael who broke this haunting silence. "We need to talk, Valentina." He said my name slowly, softly, as if aware that every time he said it, there was a possibility of breaking down, stone-by-stone, the wall I'd built around me. But it wasn't a wall. I had built a fortress; there was no way in.

I remained silent, my eyes on the mountains before me, the white peaks in the distance touching the sky. I had freed myself from his overwhelming magic. It had taken me years and there was no way I was going to let him pull me under his spell again. I remained outwardly calm as I turned to him and nodded, permitting him to continue. I would listen to him. I would listen to his side of the story. I owed it to my sons and to myself. Perhaps then, and only then, I could truly move forward.

Without taking his eyes off me, as if searching for any sign that could give me away, he began. His voice was low but clear.

"There isn't a day that goes by that I don't regret with my whole being that I didn't return as I had promised. I have spent the last thirty-three years wishing to turn back time. I should have known better. I should have found out the truth sooner. But by the time I did, it was too late. I came back once; your father had just passed away and I saw you from a distance. The most beautiful girl in the world had grown into the most breathtaking woman I had ever seen, will ever see... but I was too ashamed to make my presence known to you. I couldn't face looking into your eyes, as I do now, and see reflected there the coldness that is so visible. I couldn't face knowing that I had truly lost you. My naïvety, my stupidity, drove me far from the most important person in my world. All I can ask of you now is that, with time, you learn to forgive me, and to believe me that I never wanted to hurt you, I never wanted to lose you, but at the time it's what I believed I had to do. To save you, to save myself. You must understand that. I fell into a trap and believed the lies. I should have listened to my heart. I should have followed my instinct. You must believe that. I know I've returned too late. I have no place in your life now, but I just want you to know that I have returned to stay. Even if I can't be part of your life, I want to spend the rest of my years as close to you as possible. I've missed so much of you, and I don't want to miss any more, even if it's just observing you grow old from a distance. I can't bear to be away from you any more. You are no longer the young girl I left behind, just as I'm no longer the Rafael who left you. But my heart still belongs to you, and I would do anything in the world to prove it to you."

He broke off here; a tear slowly trickled down his face, and I had to fight the urge to wipe it away. There was no shame in his honesty, in his tears. His gaze never left mine, his eyes a doorway to his soul. And I did believe him. But the wall I had built over the years was strong. There was no way into the fortress. But as he held my gaze I realised that he knew this, just as I could also see he likewise knew that all he had to do was help me find the way out.

Rafael left moments later. I was emotionally drained. So much had happened in the last few days that I couldn't keep up. I couldn't quite believe that this was all real. It felt so much like a dream – and if it was a dream, I had to admit I hoped never to wake up. Could I possibly find happiness and peace after all this time? Life had taught me simply to survive, to go through the motions of living without feeling. I wasn't ready for anything else. I didn't dare hope for anything more.

I remained sitting on the veranda in a trance. When Rafael had left, he moved as if to give me a hug or embrace me in his strong, powerful arms, but had obviously thought better of it on seeing me back away. I had promised to listen to him, to his side of the story, but I had promised no more. Besides, if what he had said was true, that he just wanted to be close to me and no more, I could not refuse him this. He was free to live as he wished, but he certainly couldn't expect some softly-spoken words to change how I felt, how I had learnt to live. So he had left in silence.

I had not uttered a word. There was nothing for me to add, at least not yet. I needed time to adjust to this new situation, and a part of me didn't want any change in my life. I controlled everything around me.

At least I thought I did, until a few days ago. I was beginning to understand that life would continue to teach me things whether I wished to learn or not.

***

Early the following day the girl Chantelle and her friend came back. She bounded up the veranda stairs with an energy and eagerness I had not felt in years, the dogs playfully chasing after her. She radiated charm and a positiveness which was contagious. I believed she was nervous on seeing Robbie again, just as I was. He would arrive at any moment, and I was feeding off her excitement.

Then the following day I would meet Lionel? I couldn't quite believe it. I had Googled him, and, just as the last week didn't feel real, seeing the famous superstar on the internet which was just flooded with information and photos about him made everything seem all the more surreal. How could the private detective hired by my mother not have been able to trace this second son? He was a superstar! Why had there been lies told about him dying in his early months? Was it to hide his past? To maintain it as secret to everyone, making him more of a mystery to his fans? Could it be a whole marketing strategy? Or perhaps his adoptive parents (who, according to what I'd read on the internet, were one of the wealthiest families in LA) had, for their own selfish reasons, paid to keep their son's past a secret from all? It didn't make sense. All my mother had been able to tell me was that she had only been able to trace one of my sons. The other had died. Or so she had been told. And I believed her. There was no need for her to lie to me on her deathbed, and it was evident in her final days that her last wish was to amend her mistakes. She had wanted to find him just as much as I had. So who had separated the two of them, and why? These were questions that I felt would remain unanswered, but I really didn't care right now. All that mattered was that both sons had survived, had grown up healthy, strong and happy, and that I had been given this chance to see them again.

It wasn't long before we heard horses along the drive and I could sense Chantelle tense up next to me. I stole a glance over at both girls. The friend Tammy had taken hold of Chantelle's hand as if to calm her somehow. I stole a glance at Chantelle. Her face was slightly flushed, but in a way that was becoming. She really was beautiful and I wondered to what extent she was just friends with my son or sons, because it was strange that she had met both of them and seemed to have a certain influence on both.

As the riders neared I could hear her breathing becoming more rapid. She moved to stand, then sat again, her friend Tammy whispered something in her ear, which I was unable to catch. And then there was a gasp from both girls which drew my attention back to the riders who had slowed to an easy walk as they moved up the gravel driveway to the parking area. Milena, daughter of my cousin Nacho and my best friend Flavia, had reached out and softly laid a hand on Robbie's arm as both merrily laughed out loud at something that had been said. There was an intimacy between both young riders that I hadn't observed before, and now took in with great detail.

Milena was glowing; her auburn hair cascaded down her back in soft waves, her petite silhouette outlined as the mid-morning sun shone down on her from behind. She looked totally mesmerised by Robbie who drew his mount to a halt and athletically leaped to the ground before helping Milena dismount. Milena kept her hands on Robbie's shoulders a moment longer than necessary, and it was actually Robbie who moved first to break away from her touch. They still weren't aware that we were watching them, and if it hadn't been for Chantelle at my side, who I could feel getting more and more fretful witnessing the scene, I would have wished for Robbie to have put his arm around Milena or touched her in an endearing way. But I knew that right now would not be a good moment.

The couple now let the horses loose in the field near the house and moved towards us. Again, Milena's rich, husky laugh filled the air and she seductively shook her hair off her shoulders as she moved a step ahead of Robbie, showing him her petite but curvaceous figure from behind. I suddenly felt slightly anxious observing the young couple, and Chantelle, next to me, just seemed totally paralysed by what we were all seeing. She had turned ghostly white, her exotic-looking skin totally drained now of all colour. Tammy whispered to her again, still holding tight on to her hand.

Robbie and Milena neared and it was now that they turned to look at us. Milena reflected puzzlement and Robbie, on seeing Chantelle, just stopped in his tracks. There was a fleeting look of astonishment. And did I also catch a glimpse of something more? The next instant, his faced turned to thunder. He stormed up the steps, grabbed Chantelle's hand and pulled her away from us hissing, but loud enough for all of us to hear:

"What the hell are you doing here?"

CHAPTER TWENTY-SIX

CHANTELLE

What the hell was I doing here?

This certainly wasn't the welcome I was expecting. The guard dogs had been more thrilled to see me, and they had been trained to kill.

"Chantelle, are you nuts?" Robbie continued, not letting go of my arm now as he roughly took me to one side. If what he was going to tell me in private was meant to avoid a scene, he'd already managed to get everyone's attention with his outburst. I knew there was a chance he had starting seeing another woman, I wasn't blind to the fact that Valentina's niece was totally smitten by him and he probably had feelings for her, but did that justify him going ballistic now? *Jesus!* And I thought I knew him, but the Robbie I knew certainly wasn't this grump who stood before me.

"Let go of me!" I exclaimed crossly as I pulled my arm away from his grasp. "What the hell has got into you?"

"You're pregnant!" He hissed back. He was just inches from me. His blue eyes flashed in anger, and once again he placed his hand on my arm, but this time his touch was tender, a contrast to the fire in his eyes.

"Yes, that's what the four pregnancy tests have confirmed."

"You're not safe here! You're putting your baby at risk."

What did he mean? But my blood pressure was certainly at risk under this sudden tension. I'd never seen Robbie like this before.

"There is a risk of the Zika virus here."

I looked at him, aghast at the sudden realization that I was putting our (?) child at risk. I felt faint and almost swooned – though not out of desire! I could hear Robbie's voice as he continued, but I felt distant, miles away, as if I'd just had an out-of-body experience from the shock of it all.

"That's your problem, Chantelle. You don't think. You just act and leave the consequences for everyone else to sort out after you…"

"What, here in Argentina? Isn't it Brazil and Colombia, tropical areas, not like the dry areas and high altitude of the Andes Range? Those mosquitoes can't survive at altitude." I could hear my voice waver and peter out in confusion as I spoke. It didn't even feel as though the words were coming out of my own mouth. Was this all for real? I wasn't sure if I was trying to convince him or myself.

My legs suddenly felt weak, and I was actually glad now that he was gripping me hard again as I would have collapsed to the floor for sure.

"All my vaccinations are up to date, Robbie," I continued, my voice sounding very feeble. Was I really putting my baby at risk? But it was true. I hadn't really checked. I hadn't consulted my GP before flying.

Robbie broke my thoughts. "There isn't a vaccination for Zika. Chantelle, what on earth were you thinking?"

"I… I… I just needed to come," my voice faltered as I spoke. "I just needed to sort this all out.

248

I needed to see you, to explain. Of course I wouldn't have come out if I thought I was putting my baby at risk."

I really needed to sit down. I was lucky I hadn't fainted or thrown up everywhere, which in my current state was another distinct possibility.

"I want you on the next plane home," Robbie declared. But I wasn't really taking in what he was saying.

"I… I… What?? Next plane home? Robbie I'm here now, there are healthy babies born in Argentina every day. I can't go just yet."

"Why?"

"Lionel is on his way."

"*What!!* For fuck's sake, Chantelle. So this is all about Lionel then!"

"Robbie!" I exclaimed in shock. I didn't recognise this man before me. What had happened to the selfless man I'd met in England? "What has got into you?" I was fighting the urge to shake him now. Shake some bloody sense into the man who was acting like a child. A good spank might have done some good, had it been an option. "This isn't just about you, you know. Why haven't you told Valentina about Lionel?" I was still puzzled about this. "Were you going to keep it from her for ever? That her other son is still alive? I can't believe how selfish you're being about this. Lionel and Valentina have every right to know. Anyway, I've told Valentina – and for your information, Lionel is arriving tomorrow!"

I spat out the last words, and with that turned on my heel and ran into the house.

***

I threw myself on the bed as soon as I got to the room I'd been given to share with Tammy, and the tears just gushed out. When I flew out I knew I had a good chance that things may not go quite according to plan. But I hadn't counted on it going totally skew-whiff. Could I really have ballsed this up any more? I was putting my baby at risk.

And I still had Lionel to face tomorrow.

Shit! I wasn't too sure if I had the strength to confront him now. What had I really been thinking when I flew out? That I was going to be the Fairy Godmother to everyone, wave my magic wand and make everyone happy? I felt totally foolish, but worst of all I now seriously worried about the possible health risks to my unborn child. I buried my head under the soft feather pillows.

It wasn't long before there was a soft rap on the bedroom door and Tammy came in.

"I overheard everything Robbie said. Well, we all did, actually. It was a bit hard not to. At least you've been saved from telling Valentina she's going to be a granny soon."

"What!!" *Christ, could things get any worse?* "But… but... I never said who the father could be."

"Well Valentina seems over the moon by the idea. I guess it doesn't really matter to her who the father is. Not sure I can say the same for Milena. Poor girl looks heartbroken over Robbie."

"She can have him!" I spat out "He's such a dickhead! I can't believe how selfish he's being about this whole thing. He should have told Valentina about Lionel. It was the least he could do.

I don't understand him and I certainly don't need him. I can do this by myself. But Tammy, do you think I'm putting my baby at risk with this Zika virus? I'll never forgive myself."

"Look, Chantelle, I don't know. I'm no expert. I'm no doctor, but Valentina has told me to tell you that you shouldn't worry too much. Confirmed cases of Zika infection here in Argentina are minimal, and even less at altitude areas. She's given me this mosquito repellent just in case. It's safe for you to use." She paused while she handed me the spray and I fumigated myself from top to bottom as if I were going to go through some sort of quarantine control test. "But I think Robbie's right in that perhaps we should go home soon. Perhaps next week, once you've sorted things out with Lionel."

"I'm such a fool, Tammy," I sighed. I felt like a fucking idiot at any rate, and I just cringed thinking about the emotional mess I was causing to myself and to all those around.

Tammy came to sit by my side and put her arm around me.

"Hey, you are the best friend anyone could want. I really admire the way you get out there and fight for what you think is best. You don't sit back and watch life go by; you are out there every breathing moment chasing your dreams, following your heart. You are the most beautiful person I have ever met, inside and out, and I'm proud to call you my best friend. I didn't even think to check about possible pregnancy health risks. Anyway, you're here now. Lionel will be here tomorrow. You finish what you've set out to do, and if people can't see for themselves how brave you are, how generous you're being, then don't waste time on them. But if it makes you feel any better, Robbie would be crazy to let you go, and I only think he's really mad at you because he cares for you. He's worried about you. And I'm sure he's got a totally understandable explanation as to why he hadn't told Valentina about Lionel."

She paused, and as if on cue there was another rap on the door. I tried to compose myself expecting Valentina to come in, which is probably who and what I needed – some hysterical laughter might do me some good. But it was Robbie who peered round the door. He looked somewhat calmer, but as our eyes locked and my heart did a little backflip despite my anger at him for his rough reception, his own eyes were still cold and he offered no smile. He pushed opened the door a little further and gently placed some white netting on the floor, then retreated, saying to me as he closed the door, "Use this."

Tammy got up and brought the white netting to me before disappearing into the en suite bathroom for a moment. I shook out the netting. It was a little itchy for my liking, and I couldn't quite make out which way was up, but I wasn't going to fuss about that too much. Anything to keep the mosquitoes away. Five minutes later the netting was around me and I was starting to feel quite hot. That's when Tammy appeared from the bathroom and stopped in her tracks on seeing me.

"What the hell are you doing?"

"What do you think I'm doing? I'm protecting myself from the mosquitoes. Though I can't seem to figure out which way around this bloody thing goes!"

252

"Chantelle!" she exclaimed, unsuccessfully stifling a giggle, "that's meant to go around your bed, not around you. You look like an Egyptian mummy!" She burst out laughing. "Sorry!" she added apologetically, on seeing my serious face. I really didn't feel like laughing, but I had to admit I was relieved that the netting wasn't an item of clothing, and that Tammy had been able to point it out to me before I made a catwalk appearance with it on. I had got the impression that Valentina thought quite highly of me, and I didn't want to ruin this perception just yet!

***

"We'll be arriving in about half an hour."

Vivien had not failed me. Her text came through quite early the following morning. I left Tammy sleeping and ran to tell Valentina, but I couldn't find her. I walked out of the house, down the driveway. The morning was fresh, a slight balmy warmth on the early breeze. I slowly strolled down the private road. I was quite nervous about seeing Lionel.

In the last few days he had sent me several texts to which I had replied in a very standoffish manner. I didn't want to totally ignore him, but I had to start making it obvious that something was amiss. I had to give Vivien a fighting chance to win him over if my plan was to work, and for this to happen I had to take a back seat. I had madly thought that if Vivien was the one to run to Lionel's side after his car accident, if she was the one to inform him that his biological family had been traced, if she was the one to be with him through all these ups and downs,

Lionel's feelings for her would be rekindled. I needed him to fall back in love with her and forget about what Sally had told him about me, that he would only be happy with a certain Chantelle Rose. I was the name, but I wasn't the one for him.

Yes, there was a child, and I would have to talk to him about this, but the first step was to play Cupid with Lionel and Vivien and just hope that he would forgive me. I relied quite heavily on the fact that as I was the one who had been able to find out about his biological mother and pass this information on to Vivien, he would, at least, be thankful to me for this. At least I bloody hoped so, otherwise I would be escaping to the UK on the next available flight!

Just as I stood by the driveway waiting for Lionel and Vivien to arrive, looking in the meanwhile across the open countryside towards the mountain range in front of me, I heard someone approach from behind and turned hoping it would be Valentina. But it was Robbie who stood there. My heart leaped, but I was still so mad that he had spoken to me so roughly the day before that I didn't know what to say. I had flown to the other side of the world for him. I had been ready to declare my feelings for him. I had remembered the night we had spent together and had envisioned a future with him. But he hadn't waited as he'd promised, and the future I now envisioned belonged to my unborn baby only. There was no Lionel and no Robbie. There was Dolly and a whole load of weeding, but that was pretty much it.

I remained silent and turned my gaze to look back out to the mountains.

"I hope you know what you're doing, Chantelle," came his stern and serious voice next to me.

"What do you mean by that?" I asked. Though personally, of course, I didn't know what the hell I was doing! Honestly, did he think I had planned to get pregnant? I certainly hadn't planned to fall in love with the wrong brother. I hadn't planned on putting my heart out there for it to get broken. I hadn't planned to risk the health of my unborn baby. If he believed I could plan all this on purpose, I must have reached a new level of manipulative skill that I didn't know existed.

"Lionel is a huge superstar, Chantelle. Do you know the possible media hype this story will get? Did you think that Valentina would want her past and her life to be broadcast across the globe? The press are going to have a field day when this story gets out."

Err... No. I hadn't really thought about it.

I started to feel a bit queasy at the thought of these quiet surroundings swamped by paparazzi trying to get a shot of Valentina, but at the same time I had seen the way Valentina had looked at Robbie, her son, and I had seen her reaction on hearing that her other son, Lionel, was still alive. She was the happiest woman on the planet.

"Do you think she really cares?" I replied. There was more anger in my voice than doubt. I believed I was right. That I was doing what was best. "I've read the diary. Valentina has spent her whole life missing you. Searching for you. Do you really think she gives a shit whether the whole world finds out or not? You and Lionel are her world, that's all she cares about now. She'll know how to deal with it. She's dealt with so much already, this will be a walk in park for her. The hype will die down and there will be another story to tell. That's what happens. If you think a snatched photo will ruin her life, you're very much mistaken. Her life was ruined thirty-three years ago, and now, finally, it's coming back together. You've been selfish not telling her yourself." I was still so mad that I was really drumming home that the one who had been wrong with this was him, not me. "It's not like you, Robbie. Why?"

I turned to him now. I was desperate to see the Robbie I knew, not this stranger who had received me yesterday as cold and distant as the snowy mountain peaks on the horizon.

He turned to look towards the mountains himself as he answered, but his voice had softened.

"Of course I was going to tell Valentina. I was just waiting for the right time. I just needed a few days to adjust to the situation myself. And yes you're right, I was being selfish, because for just a few days, I wanted to feel special and unique. For once I wanted it to be about me, not about Lionel, who has everything."

"Jesus, Robbie, you are so childish. Of course you're unique and special. Just ask Myfanwy. Just ask all your friends back home. Ray, Tammy, anyone!"

Just ask me, I wanted to say, but my words were caught in my mouth before they came out as we both turned towards the sky on hearing a distant hum. There was a black spot in the sky that was getting alarmingly close, then I saw rotating helicopter

256

blades cutting through the air making a thunderous noise as they slapped against the air currents. As the helicopter lowered I found myself squinting as dust particles were blown in our direction and all around. The aircraft lowered, hovering over the open field, where the horses were now running wild in fright.

As the helicopter made a safe touchdown, the engine died and the blades stilled, I was aware of four big black jeeps making their way towards us at alarming speed, kicking up dust as they sped across the country lane parallel to the horse field in front of us. They swerved into the private track the led to the house and stopped at the far end. I looked back towards the helicopter and could see what looked to me like Lionel and Vivien disembark from the aircraft. Well at least they were together I thought. But why so many jeeps? I obviously wasn't going to speak my thoughts out loud, but bloody hell; if I didn't know differently, this looked like a take from some action film when the goodies had escaped, but the baddies were hot on their trail. Robbie and I had fallen silent and watched as the scene unravelled before us.

Lionel and Vivien had now reached the jeeps. There was suddenly a mass of people at the end of the drive as everyone clambered out of the vehicles. My eyesight wasn't great, but unless I was very much mistaken I could make out a crew with cameras, and Lionel and Vivien seemed to be having their make-up touched up. There were people with clip-boards, others frantically talking on their phones. I could make out Freddy G's stout frame as he walked over to Lionel, and *Holy shit, was that Gabby?* My throat went dry. I hadn't given credit to

Vivien when she said things were getting slightly out of control, but it looked like a whole circus had just rocked up. This wasn't the quiet but emotion-filled long-lost-mother-at-last-meets-long-lost-son family scenario I had fondly imagined. Fuck me!

"I think I'll just leave you to it then." Robbie turned and stormed off.

Thanks for nothing! I wanted to shout to his retreating back but I couldn't actually get any words out, stunned as I was to silence on seeing how many people had just descended on Valentina's property. I was starting to admit that perhaps I hadn't handled the situation quite as efficiently as I had thought.

Was Lionel planning on filming this re-encounter? I couldn't quite believe it. Surely he didn't need the money? Having said that, his helicopter and the monster-sized yacht that he had marooned in the middle of the Pacific were quite high-maintenance toys; a bit of extra cash would probably always come in handy.

I had to stop this. And before I had a chance to really think things through, I found myself running down the driveway. Of course, in hindsight, this is the complete opposite of how I should have approached Lionel, as on seeing me he just dropped everything and ran towards me too. Despite my fast-moving legs, everything seemed to be happening in slow motion. I could pick up Vivien's startled face on seeing Lionel take off towards me. Gabby also turned to look at me, but more in trepidation than anything else, and two of the film crew swung their cameras towards us. Then there was Lionel, who looked so ecstatic running towards me. Of course, I had no idea how much of his eagerness to reach me was all a show to put on in front of the cameras, but I'm sure my face, instead of looking all lovey-dovey as it perhaps should have done, was more masked with indignation and annoyance and there were no drama classes in the world that could help me hide my facial expressions.

Before I knew it Lionel had me in his arms and was swinging me around. I pressed my hands against his strong chest trying to give me some space. I could hardly breathe after my manic sprint down the drive together with his embrace which crushed my ribs. I was also vividly aware that I had two cameras focused on me and most probably Vivien and Robbie were looking on. I couldn't afford this reunion to get any more cherubic; otherwise all my efforts to play Cupid with Lionel and Vivien would go to pot.

"Lionel," I gasped, really struggling to catch my breath. How best to phrase this? "*I'm pregnant, but I don't love you any more, and anyway it might not be yours*" would knock the message home pretty efficiently, but I certainly didn't want that to be caught on camera in a potential viral video. "How's your head?" But Lionel just cupped my face in his hands and looked deep into my eyes.

"Thank you," he whispered softly. And for a moment, with his eyes fixed on me and his arms around me, my world seemed to stop spinning and it was just him and me, and for one eternal second I forgot where I was, who I was and who we were – and for that one second I did wish things to be different, to be far away from where we were now.

But life wasn't like that. This was Lionel before me, not Robbie. Lionel who belonged to a world so different from mine. He was here to meet his biological mum for the first time, and we were already swamped by cameras, media, press, agents, make-up artists. It was a world where I would never fit in and where I would never really know if things were for real or just a show put on in front of the crowd. He needed someone who understood him and his world. That person was right behind us, no doubt looking on in slight stupefaction – and I didn't blame her.

"We need to talk," was all I could say. "But first you need to meet your biological mother, and you have to tell everyone, except perhaps Vivien, that they have to stay behind. You can't go in with your film crew. It's not right."

He gave a chuckle, and spoke to me as if I was still a child.

"Of course, babe. They're only here for back-up."

Back-up? I must have looked astonished. Usually people call on the police force or the army for back up, not a film crew. Mind, Gabby, who had also turned up with Lionel's team, had quite a lethal instinct.

"If this story leaks to the press," Lionel went on, "I need to have my team to get the images first. That way, I publish the story first, control how it appears, and everyone else backs off because it's no longer unique news."

"Right," I said. It didn't feel quite right, but I wasn't going to argue. "So are you ready?"

I looked him in the eye. Was this just going to be a game for him?

I could see an excitement reflected in his eyes that I hoped had nothing to do with this being a potential viral story if it was to leak. So his next words took me totally by surprise.

"I think this is the first time in my life I don't feel ready. I've tried to trace my biological family for years. I've used private detectives. I've done DNA tests to discover my ethnic background. I've chased endless clues and always come to a dead end. When I met Robbie in the UK I didn't actually believe we could be related. I just thought it was a massive coincidence. But it looks like the coincidence is you, honey. You have found us. You have brought us here. I really don't know what to say."

Nor did I, to be honest, but I wasn't going to philosophise about it right now. I could well end up talking about which came first, the chicken or the egg, and, frankly, there really wasn't time.

"Let's go and find your birth mother then, shall we?" I said as chirpily as possible, and I motioned to Vivien to join us. "I think it's a good idea if Vivien comes too."

But Lionel didn't seem to hear me, he had turned to face the main house and I think it was the first time that he actually looked a bit anxious. A pivotal moment for him, no doubt. I just hoped Valentina would keep her laughter to herself, at least for the first few minutes. I just didn't think Lionel would understand the joke. Or anyone else, for that matter, apart from Tammy of course.

Vivien made her way up to us and we embraced each other as if we had been the best of friends since nursery days.

"Thanks," I softly whispered into her ear, as I was well aware that without her help I would never have got Lionel here so efficiently. A bit too efficiently, perhaps, considering his whole crew had rocked up too. I gave her hand a quick squeeze as I strategically moved her between Lionel and myself, so that as we walked to the house, it was Vivien who stood beside Lionel. He would be close to Vivien, not me, when he came face-to-face with his birth mother for the first time. This was going to be a memory that would be engraved in his head and his heart for the rest of his life, and I wanted the woman of his life to be at his side.

And that woman wasn't me.

CHAPTER TWENTY-SEVEN

VALENTINA

I watched as the three figures in the distance approached. I had run outside on hearing the roaring helicopter and had seen Robbie, who hadn't been aware of me, storm past in what appeared to be great annoyance. I could vaguely make out several cars that had been parked at the far end of the drive. A group of people remained there in the distance as the three people approached: Chantelle on the left, a tall blonde woman in the middle, and on the right a man who had to be Lionel. There was a huge similarity between Lionel and Robbie. They were the same height, the same build, the same colouring.

I couldn't believe that my other son had survived. This man had the same mixture of my father and Rafael as Robbie had, but with an added something that made him move with such confidence and assurance that was perhaps on the verge of arrogance. He had left the helicopter in the middle of my fields as if it was his own private landing ground. I didn't really think such an extravagant entrance was quite so necessary anyway, but this son was a world-famous superstar. He was used to making an entrance everywhere he went. Perhaps it was something he needed to underline his world celebrity status. Though this was not necessary for me. All I had wanted was to see my sons again. They had no need to prove anything to me. All I cared about was that both sons would understand me and forgive me. That's all that really mattered and that they were well and happy.

I remained on the veranda as the three young people approached. Then in unison the two ladies dropped back and it was only Lionel who moved forward, confidently taking the veranda stairs two at a time until he was facing me, just a metre away. He paused for a moment, looking a bit unsure of what to say, how to react. Here was someone who lived playing out roles, acting out other people's lives, pretending to be everyone and anyone but himself. But this was his own story. There were no cameras, just raw feelings.

I could see his confidence melt away before me, his self-assurance crumbled, and my heart went out to him. I opened my arms and he fell into them and sobbed as any child would looking for comfort in his mother's arms.

"I've been looking for you all my life," he wept. "And now I've finally found you."

And I knew exactly how he felt.

***

No one could find Chantelle. After my emotional re-encounter with Lionel I was introduced to his pretty lady friend Vivien, his adoptive sister Gabby, his agent and great friend Freddy G (I believe that was his name). I was suddenly surrounded by all these people that it was hard to keep track of who was who.

Robbie appeared once again and it was obvious that there was a great appreciation and comradeship between the two men. Everything felt too good to be true. And before I knew it they were organising a homecoming party. Of course I was so happy to have my family together that I was more than ready to agree, and it was a while before we realised that both Chantelle and her friend Tammy were missing.

We searched everywhere. Robbie tried phoning her, but there was no answer. Their rental car was still parked in the parking area and it was a mystery where they had disappeared to. I sent my house staff to cover the grounds, but there was no sign of them anywhere. It was then that I received the phone call. I looked down at the caller ID.

I shouldn't have been surprised; things didn't just fall into place like this without a touch of magic. There had to be a greater force that was bringing all this together. Now, with a beating heart, I started to feel that perhaps what everyone had said all these years was true: that "*the Bruja*" really did have magical powers. That she could bring about and foresee events. But I had never believed the rumours were true, because if they were, why had she never warned me all those years ago?

I answered the phone.

"Valentina?" Her voice was still young, despite her now advanced age. She was still vibrant, she could still captivate anyone with her smile. Her eyes still shone bright, eyes that I had seen in a younger face just recently. "Your young guests are with me, the two young girls, I just thought I'd let you know, so you don't worry." She paused for a moment. "I think I need to tell the tall girl the truth. She needs to know so that the spell of the past is broken. She is why they have returned. You must have seen it too, the resemblance. Rafael recognised it, which is why he has brought her to me today."

I remained silent. The *Bruja* had spoken, and there was little point in arguing with her.

"Carmen," I replied after a moment of silence, "they are your grandsons. Rafael is your son. I trust in you to do what you think is best."

Besides, I was curious. Who was Chantelle Rose, this young lady who had bewitched my sons?

CHAPTER TWENTY-EIGHT

CHANTELLE

The phone clicked in the hallway and I could hear Carmen making her way back to Tammy and me.

It had been such a bizarre morning. First Robbie, who had got me angry at his selfishness in not telling Valentina about Lionel. Then Lionel, who had rocked up in the most flamboyant manner possible. At least the reunion with his mother had not been filmed in the end, and then Rafael had turned up out of the blue and pretty much kidnapped me and Tammy. I had felt the need to go for a walk, Tammy had joined me, but we had just rounded the main house to take a gravel path that led to another part of Valentina's grounds when Rafael appeared and told me (well, Tammy, who translated) that we had to go with him, that it was urgent. So there I was getting into a stranger's car, in a distant land, to be driven off into unknown terrain, without my mobile, without telling anyone where I was or who I was with, and, obviously, not setting a high example of prudence in the process.

A while later, in what I could only describe as very awkward silence, we arrived at what had to be the Fernandez Ranch. It looked just as I had imagined it. The horse corral to the left of the grounds, the rungs of the wooden fence shone with fresh varnish, the main house, beautiful, though not quite as grand as Valentina's, just beyond. I was relieved when Rafael parked the car and we were able to get out. I wasn't too sure why we had been brought to his family home, or what it was that was so urgent. And if he thought he'd get me on the back of some wild mustang, he was very much mistaken.

It was then that she appeared. I could only imagine that it was his mother, but as she approached there was something so familiar about her I started to feel a bit faint. Her dark hair, now streaked with grey, was held back in a loose plait, and there were curls that escaped making her look younger than her years. Her olive-brown skin, somewhat wrinkled now, still reflected a beautiful face and she had an elegance and agility when she moved towards us which echoed years of active, outdoor life. She was almost as tall as me, but what really startled me was when she moved closer and my eyes locked with hers, it was as if I was seeing an older version of myself. Her honey-coloured eyes, with the same gold flecks reflected in my own, stared back at me and as she held out her hand to hold mine, an electrical charge ran through us, so strong that we both jumped back. There was a physical crackle, which probably added an extra frizzle to my already unruly hair.

"Welcome," she said. If I had been impressed with Valentina's English, Carmen's English accent was flawless. I must have looked startled. "My family moved to Europe for several years when I was a young girl. I spent two years in Dartmouth." She pronounced the Queen's English better than I did (not that that was much to boast about to be honest, given my South London accent). "But you

268

don't look very British to me. At least, despite your name, you don't look like a typical English Rose."

I wondered how she knew my surname? Nothing like a quick search in Google to do your homework, I guessed, but answered: "Well, my mum was Italian."

"That explains it," she murmured. And I thought she was referring to my dark looks, but she went on "From Catania?"

"Yes!" I was surprised. There are well over a hundred main cities in Italy.

Carmen continued, "My grandfather was from Catania, in Sicily. He moved here to Argentina when he was a young man. Perhaps we're family?"

She chuckled as she said this, but her look was serious. Personally I must have looked dumbstruck and as the image of my own grandmother flashed before me (her gentle smile, her soft curly brown hair which always smelt of jasmine, her golden-coloured eyes), it sunk in why Carmen looked so familiar. There was a strong resemblance between both women. I inwardly panicked for a second. What would that make Robbie and Lionel to me? Some sort of distant cousins? As long as they were as distant as kissing cousins, I guessed it really didn't matter.

With that, Carmen took us inside and we were made comfortable in her sitting room. She excused herself for a moment and I heard her saying a few words on the telephone before returning.

"Tammy," I whispered to my friend, "This is getting really weird."

"Tell me about it," she said, looking out of huge unblinking eyes. "Looks like you're family!" There was a slight tilt, in her voice and I could see she was fighting back a giggle that was bubbling up inside.

"Tammy!" I hissed. "Don't start!" It would do no good to fall into fits of laughter whilst we waiting for our hostess to return. The only person I knew who would understand this type of hysteria was Valentina, and she wasn't here to explain it.

Talking of Valentina, I suddenly thought about Rafael, who had disappeared. He'd probably gone back to her house. He still hadn't met his other son Lionel yet, my possibly distant cousin? I felt a bit queasy; was this all some sort of supernatural trick? Who was behind all of this? I had been put in both men's paths and through one of them I had found out who their biological family was. I didn't believe in ghosts, but I was starting to feel a bit spooked. But before I could pursue this line of thought, Carmen returned and sat down before us.

"I've been waiting for you," she began, looking me straight in the eye. "I had a vision a long time ago." What, like Fatima? Or a more Patheos vision? I was tempted to phone Sally and let her deal with this: I had a feeling these ladies would get on like a house on fire. As long as Carmen didn't get out a Ouija board I guessed I should be OK. I tried to settle myself.

"You know they call me *La Bruja*? The witch? Though I don't really have any special powers. Now and again I'll have a vision and it's so strong that I know what I'm seeing is true. It's not something I choose or can make come about at will. But it happens. I had envisioned my husband before I had ever met him."

Well, I thought, trying to put things in perspective, nothing special there, we all envision meeting Mr. Right before he turns up, don't we? And some keep waiting eternally for the vision to materialise too.

"I saw my husband's plane accident before it happened. I tried everything in my power to prevent it. I even went to meet with Maria, Valentina's mother, to try and put a halt to her crazy obsession with my husband in the hope that it would prevent the accident, but to no avail. I could see everything happening but I had no power to change things. I knew that my son would leave me, that he would leave Valentina too, but there was nothing I could do. I have learnt that life has its course and we cannot interfere. We can only ride the journey as best as fate allows us. Life is like a wild mustang. Sometimes to ride it the journey is smooth, but more often than not, the journey is wild and dangerous. But always beautiful."

She paused here. There were no tears under her shadow of sadness, but the veil she internally carried was still there. Though if she continued with her metaphoric language, it was only a question of time before she lost me completely, and Tammy, bless her, could only translate from Spanish.

Carmen continued: "Two years ago, Valentina came to me with a story that her mother had spun years ago, more than a story it was a web of lies that had been so deeply woven that no sphere of light could penetrate. It was dark and evil." She broke off and laughed, a sad musical sound. "And they called me the witch. But the real witch died just over two years ago. Then, the very same day Valentina came

271

to tell me the story, the secret, I saw you. You were sitting on a stool, in a red dress or some sort of red outfit. For a moment I believed I was seeing a vision of my granddaughter, and that, perhaps, Valentina had got it wrong and that one of her babies was a girl: a beautiful baby who had flowered into a breathtaking woman. But I know now you are here for another reason. You are why the boys have returned. Through you they have found their roots. Peace is returning."

Personally, I didn't feel very peaceful. To be honest I felt a bit freaked out and somewhat lost. I thought Myfanwy has sent me with the backing of the Force, but it was pretty strong with Carmen too.

"You need to know the truth," she continued, "so that finally the spell that's holding Valentina from Rafael is broken and everyone finds their happiness."

I wasn't going to argue with Carmen, but in truth, all that Valentina and Rafael needed to do was sit down and have a bloody good chat, perhaps with a bottle of wine or two. There was no spell, just misunderstanding and heartbreak. But Carmen continued, and I remained silent so as not to break her flow.

"There was a letter. Maria had written it. She was desperate still to hurt me. I had lost my husband, but that wasn't enough for her. She had to drive my son away too, despite the heartbreak it would cause to her own daughter. She didn't care, she was poisoned by anger and resentfulness, and nothing else mattered but revenge. She had always believed that I had stolen Nicolas. But he never left her for me. It was her own poisonous self that had driven him away, long before he met me. But she had never accepted it. It had driven her crazy over the years and it was a very sick lady who gave Santiago that letter to hand over to my son all those years ago. If only I had envisioned the letter and had been able to stop it, everything would have been so different."

Carmen paused here, the heartbreak and sorrow still evident on her face. I was rooted to the chair, I was curious to know what happened, but surely there was someone else, more responsible, to share this information with? And what the hell did she think I would do with it? She was the witch, not me. I didn't even have the power, or common sense if you like, to foresee the possible health risk I was exposing my unborn child to, let alone break a thirty-three-year old spell.

Carmen's eyes glazed over as she slipped back into the past for a moment before turning to me with a soft smile.

"The letter said that Valentina's father was Nicolas – the father, too, of young Rafael!"

***

Well, that certainly explained things. Rafael had obviously freaked out. And I didn't blame him either. Those poisonous words had blinded him to the obvious truth. You only had to look at Valentina once to see that she was the spitting image of her father Gabriel. I had observed it for myself from just a portrait, but Rafael had fallen for the lies, and when he realised that he had fallen into Maria's trap, he must have felt that it was all too late to try to put right all the damage that this had caused.

I was grateful to Carmen for the information and to have had part of the mystery resolved, but I had no idea how best to use this information or what it was that Carmen thought I was capable of achieving. What I did know was that I needed to talk to Lionel, and then I would be free to go home. There was little or no point in me remaining here much longer. My priority was my unborn child, and I was starting to feel quite drained by all the current events. I needed to sleep and rest, not to chase after ghosts and break love spells. I had enough on my plate as it was trying to act as Cupid with Vivien and Lionel.

And my Cupid's arrow had obviously gone a bit skew-whiff, as on arriving back at Valentina's house, I was met by a panicky Vivien who gushed out all teary-voiced on seeing me: "He doesn't love me."

I could only imagine that she was talking about Lionel. At least I hoped she was: it would do my plans no good if she was to fall for Freddy G, who, short and dumpy though he was, had quite a reputation as a Don Juan. I needed Vivien to still have feeling for Lionel if my plan was to work.

"Of course he does, Vivien," I replied, a confidence in my tone to mask my own doubts. Was I really going to be able to pull this off?

And as if on cue Lionel, appeared and confidently strolled towards us. Out of the corner of my eye I could see Tammy gently taking Vivien by the arm, steering her away whilst saying, "He does love you, Vivien, but let them just talk for a moment together."

Believe me, I thought, when I spew out everything to Lionel (and there was a good chance

274

that it may be in the literal context with my queasy tummy), not only will I ruin his $1000, hand-made, Martin Dingman shoes, but his heart too.

***

We settled on a garden swing seat that we found a little way away from the main house, in a grass area that was surprisingly green and soft for this arid climate. There were exotic flowers growing around the borders and the scent of the Lady of the Night was strong.

Lionel turned to me, his brilliant dark-green eyes flashed in the late afternoon sun as he took hold of my hands in his. He paused for a moment as it was obvious he saw that his engagement ring was not where it should be. He passed one of his fingers over where the diamond should have been.

"You gonna tell me what's up?" He let out a soft, sad sigh as he held my gaze. It was ironic, really, that he was the one showing me much more tenderness than Robbie. His concern was evident on his face, and there was a part of me that momentarily panicked. Perhaps, by telling him that our engagement, love affair, everything, was over, I was about to make the biggest mistake of my life.

But there was no turning back. He had to know what had happened between Robbie and me. I couldn't keep it from him; I couldn't live with a lie like that. He deserved to know. But, in all honesty, this wasn't just about Robbie or about me. Lionel needed someone who understood his world. Someone who had lived and breathed it, like he had, from a young age. Someone who could deal with the press, the fans, all the manic Hollywood stuff. That person was, without a doubt, Vivien. But before I could get a word out and explain this, to my total and utter mortification I suddenly felt really nauseous. My dangling nerves, internal hormonal riot, the strong scent of the Lady of the Night making a deadly mixed with Lionel's cologne was all too much. And before I knew it, the lunch that Carmen had so carefully prepared came back up.

Lionel quickly but gently held my hair back, concern in his voice as he softly asked, "Are you OK? Something you've eaten?"

"No, I'm pregnant."

There, the words were out. That was one thing less to fret about. He knew the first part of the story now.

"What!" came his startled and unbelieving voice. "How did that happen?"

Oh my God! I thought. Was I really going to have to explain the birds and the bees to Lionel?

"Well…" I began, a silly giggle escaping as I wiped my mouth with a tissue that Lionel handed to me, as he stared at me with a look of total and utter disbelief. "That's what happens sometimes when you have sex."

Lionel jerked in the garden seat, which rocked under his weight, looking before him in shock. After a few minutes of total and utter silence, his stillness and lack of communication actually started to scare me.

"Lionel?" I softly whispered, trying to urge some sort of response from him that was more than this strange silence. I wasn't too sure how I'd expected him to react, but I wasn't expecting a silence like a forgotten melody.

A moment later Lionel stood up, a bit stooped to be honest, and he looked in pain, as if I'd just kicked him in the balls or something. And I guess in a way I had, because it explained his sad look as he turned to me and spoke in an icy voice that sent a shiver down my back.

"Chantelle, I can't have children."

And with that he stormed off.

CHAPTER TWENTY-NINE

VALENTINA

I could make out Lionel who slumped past in the distance, he was hunched and looked in pain. I had seen him talking to Chantelle. What on earth was that girl doing to make both my sons so enraged? First Robbie and now Lionel! Could it be true what I'd thought I'd overheard Robbie say the other day, that she was pregnant? Surely this news should bring happiness, not distress and pain. Though I couldn't exactly say I was happy when I found out I was pregnant all those years ago. But what had happened to Chantelle? I found myself walking towards the Italian garden where Chantelle was still sitting. I could hear her softly crying as I approached. She quickly wiped her eyes on seeing me, in an unsuccessful attempt to hide her tears.

"Sometimes good to cry," I offered, in an attempt to make her feel a little better. I should know: I spent years crying until I thought there were no tears left. It's funny how you can survive, even when you feel as if you've gone to hell and back. "I know not why you upset, but if makes you feel better I thank you. I found Robbie, you found Lionel. He not be here if was not for you and I would never have know that he alive still. I know not why he angry now. But if it not for you he would never have found me." I paused here; I wish my English was better, but I think I had expressed myself correctly.

Chantelle turned to me and offered me a sweet smile. She really was beautiful, so much like Carmen. Was there a connection? What had Carmen seen to believe that Chantelle was the one to break the spell of unhappiness that had bound us all for so many years? It was astonishing that Chantelle had met both sons, but coincidences happen. Could there be more?

"Pregnant?" I asked, as I softly placed a hand on her stomach. I surprised myself by making such a direct inquiry. I had no right to interfere in this young girl's life and ask such a delicate question, but it just came out without me really thinking. "Father?" I went on to ask, before I could stop myself.

"I wasn't too sure," she replied. "But Lionel has just told me that he can't have children."

She blushed a deep crimson as soon as she spoke, because though it was just a short sentence, it told a story of a thousand words. She had obviously had an intimate relationship with both men. I didn't envy her delicate situation.

"I had already decided that even if the child was Lionel's I couldn't live my life in a world where I just don't fit in. You know, Lionel's not really in really in love with me anyway, it's just the idea of me, something he was told when he was a very young man. But I didn't want this to be the way he found out that I'd been unfaithful to him. What a bloody mess." Chantelle sighed. Her shoulders drooped, and more tears escaped her golden eyes and trickled slowly down her face as she continued.

"I should be happy. In a way this is what I wanted. I wanted the father to be Robbie, because that's who I love, but he's changed these last few weeks and I've lost him. He belongs here. He's discovered a part of him that was missing, and I'm not going to be the one to take it away from him."

She paused, and though she looked at me, I sensed it was Robbie she was seeing in her mind. Robbie, the first of my sons to return. A young man who was steadfast and serious. He hadn't told me about Lionel, but I knew he had his reasons. And it was obvious, at least to me, that his heart belonged to this young lady who sat next to me. It was obvious by his concern over her, which he had masked with anger, and by the way he looked at her with burning desire. I had known that look once, a long time ago.

Chantelle continued: "I'll return to the UK on the next available flight. It's time for me to go. Lionel has arrived, and that's what I'd had really planned for: to reunite you with your second son and for him to find his roots too. I hope at least for this, in time, he will forgive me."

"He will," I quietly offered. "Please promise me one thing. Whatever happens, keep child, enjoy every moment with baby. I never had chance to do that. Do for me, look after grandchild mine." I paused for a moment before tentatively adding "And let me visit?"

"Of course," Chantelle replied. A soft smile played on her lips as she turned to me, and I opened my arms and embraced her in a warm, motherly hug. She sobbed into my shoulder and we sat there for a while in soothing silence. "But promise me one thing too," she added. "Give Rafael one more chance."

And it was if her Cupid's arrow struck to the very core of my heart.

**

As if on cue Rafael appeared, and before I knew it Chantelle had slipped away.

"May I?" he asked politely, and on my nod he sat down beside me on the garden swing-seat. I stared before me, willing myself not to look at him. I was feeling so emotional that to steal a glance at his handsome face and catch his gaze on me would open too many doors, break down too much of my wall, and I wasn't ready yet for that.

"Do you know who she is?" he asked me softly.

I shook my head. "Do you?"

I was glad that the conversation wasn't going to be about us. I still needed time to find myself, my true feelings, before I could deal with my past. These last few days had been so emotional that I didn't want to make the mistake of opening my heart up again for the wrong reasons. I couldn't risk it.

"It looks as if there may be a connection between her and my mother. They both have family from Catania in Sicily. My mother believes she's been sent to break the sorrow of the past. I've never really believed my mother's fortune-telling myths. But perhaps my mother's right. *Our* sons have returned, after all, and she's here too."

As he stressed the word "our" he turned to look at me; I could feel his gaze on me, willing me to look at him too. I resisted for a moment. My whole past, with all its sorrow and pain, flashed before me in an instant. But as I sat there, I realised that the future didn't have to be the same.

More importantly, I didn't want it to be the same. I didn't want to be alone any more. I wanted my world filled with happiness, with love, with laughter. My family had returned; there was no turning back now. Nothing would ever be the same. I had been given this opportunity to finally meet my sons. The future was bright and I wanted someone to share it with. And the only person I had ever wanted to share my life with was sitting just an arm-length away.

I took a deep breath before I turned to look at him and as our eyes met and locked there was a crack of thunder and before we knew it, torrential rain came down, but neither of us moved.

"Could you blame me for not returning, Valentina, when I was told what I was told?"

"You should have known it was a lie, Rafael. You should have come back and figured out the truth for yourself instead of running away."

There, the words were out. But there had been no anger in my voice, just sorrow.

"You're right," he said. His voice was clear, but just as sorrowful as my own heart. "And I regret my mistake every breathing hour of the day. I don't know what I can do to make it up to you, but I'll spend the rest of my life trying." He paused, and I could hear Chantelle's voice in my head as she'd whispered, just a moment ago, *"Give Rafael one more chance."* But it wasn't that easy. When you've gone almost your whole life protecting yourself, when you've learnt to live alone, when at last you've found inner peace, how do you start again with all that risk it involved, with emotions you never expected to feel again? For a moment I hesitated. Could it possibly be worth it?

But then Rafael reached forward and softly tilted my chin towards him and our eyes locked once again. And as much as I tried to fight it, I knew that for him it could be worth it. His gaze then lowered to the base of my neck, and without seemingly thinking, his hand went to the chain that hung around my neck. He tentatively lifted it, and his ring fell onto his palm. A ring that I had kept hidden, always tucked under my clothing, for the last thirty-three years. He slowly unclasped the silver chain and the necklace fell loose into his hand, then slipped the ring from the silver chain until it fell once again onto his palm. But this time it was free from the chain that had kept it locked away, just as my heart had been kept locked away all these years with its own invisible chain: an invisible chain that I could feel was about to break.

Rafael's look was one of amazement, no doubt at seeing his ring again. And, as if in slow motion, he fingered it and re-read the engraving on the inside, words that he had said many times, a lifetime ago.

And whispering those very words, "*My world begins and ends with you*", he took my hand in his and slipped the ring back on to my wedding finger, where it should always have been all these years. We remained silent for a moment. I hadn't been able to refuse the gesture. I hadn't been able to withdraw my hand from his touch. To live this moment again after so many years answered my question: that yes, change and risk are both worth it.

Rafael was the first to break away. He slowly stood; we were both soaking wet and I was aware that my blouse had gone transparent under the torrential rain, but his gaze was on my face. He held out his hands to me and helped me to my feet, then said, with a soft smile on his lips, "You'd better get indoors and change. You'll catch your death of cold."

I just nodded and turned to move back to the house, but before I left I faced him once more.

"Rafael, the boys want to organise a party this Saturday, I think it's a good idea. A homecoming party. I just plan to invite family and a few honoured neighbours. I would really like you to come too."

"Of course, thank you." He hesitated for a brief moment before adding, "Valentina, will you please reserve a dance for me?"

And I knew, as I was sure he did too, that once I fell into his arms I would never leave them.

CHAPTER THIRTY

CHANTELLE

As soon as I saw Rafael appear I thought it best to slip away. There was so much chemistry between Rafael and Valentina I really didn't want to be hanging around them and cramping their style. I certainly didn't want to witness, first-hand, a passionate snog between them. And it was only a question of time, because whatever Valentina tried to convince herself of, it was obvious, at least to me, that they were still in love with each other.

I found myself wandering alongside the horse field opposite the house, frantically going over my conversation with Lionel, when it started pissing down. Not just your normal London drizzle, which is what I was used to, but torrential rain that lashed down aggressively, and within seconds I was soaked to the bone. But I had no desire to go back to the house and so ran to a nearby tree and sat down, protecting myself from the rain under the tree's thick evergreen canopy.

From Lionel's reaction I very much doubted he was lying about not being able to have children. He was a bloody good actor, but the look of complete shock at hearing my words about being pregnant couldn't have been improvised. I had really hurt him and it just goes to show how badly I'd messed up my whole relationship with both men. I really knew nothing about either of them. I had agreed to marry Lionel and I didn't even know his basic clobber. If I had really loved him I would have married him anyway, even if I had known he couldn't have children. That wasn't an issue for me. It was everything else.

I sat in silence for a moment. All I could hear was the splatter of falling rain around me, so when I heard a familiar voice right behind me whisper my name, I involuntarily screamed out loud – only to have my mouth covered in a vice-like grip. But there was no daunting me, and I bit down hard on the hand, drawing blood.

"For fuck's sake!" We both said the words out loud together, and had it been anyone else standing there I would have found the situation quite funny. But Gabby was as scary as hell and there was nothing remotely funny about her.

I braced myself to sprint to the house, though I knew she was much faster than me. Faster, stronger, leaner and meaner. That was Gabby. And she scared the life out of me. Though as I looked back at her, standing my ground, because I had already sussed that it would do me no good at all to run with this fighting machine hot on my tail, I glimpsed a look of sorrow, weakness and pity in her eyes. There was nothing lean and mean about the way she stood. Instead, she looked hunched and broken.

I just stared at her. If looks could kill, she'd be done for. I would never forgive her for her mad scheming to keep Lionel and me together. All because she had fallen for what Sally had told her so many years ago, that until Lionel had met the lady of his dreams (a so-called Chantelle Rose), she wouldn't find her own happiness. Well, it just goes to show that it was all just a load of mumbo-jumbo,

286

because Lionel *had* met me, I wasn't the lady of his dreams, and Gabby had never looked worse. In fact, if Gabby hadn't interfered as she had, I probably would have gone ahead and married Lionel, because at that point Robbie hadn't sunk so deeply into my heart. What a bloody mess.

But though I wanted to scream all this at her, I thought it best to remain quiet and see first what she had to say. She was the one that had slunk up on me, so I would let her initiate the tête-à-tête, and then, depending on what she said, I would decide on whether or not to clout her round the ear. Not that realistically I would ever have a chance at overpowering Gabby in hand-to-hand combat, but all the same subtly glanced about to see if I could spy a bit of broken branch or loose stone that could, as a last resort, be used as ammunition.

What I didn't expect was her to slump down to the ground, cross–legged, and start mumbling out some sort of benediction. I wasn't too sure if my safety in her presence depended on me joining in in this odd ritual, or if I could nimbly move away without her noticing.

I took a step back, away from her, and automatically her mumbling stopped. Fuck me! I thought she was scary before, but this was really starting to freak me out. She patted the ground next to her, beckoning me to sit beside her. And for an insane moment I almost did. Luckily I came to my senses and stood my ground. Presumably, on seeing that I wasn't going to get comfy next to her, and I certainly wasn't going to recite a blessing in her honour, she let out in a low murmur: a few words, but for the life of me I couldn't hear what the hell she was saying.

Then she stated very clearly: "I really love him."

What! Who the hell was she going on about? Surely not Lionel!! And really I didn't think I was quite the right person to be sharing such an intimate detail with, because, let's be honest, I didn't give a toss who Gabby loved. All I cared about was that she was as far away from me as possible. And with that thought in mind, I was just about to slink off again when she continued, "Every time I think I've finally woven my way into his heart, something happens to drive him away. Every single time." She sighed, deflated and sad.

Perhaps you scare the shit out of whoever you're going on about, I thought, feeling sorry for whoever it was. But I remained silent, trying to suss out the potential danger. Being in Gabby's firing range, I had to acknowledge this was one tricky situation.

"Did I ever tell you how sorry I am?" she said. "Sorry to have messed up so much, and taken things that step further than I should have. I never meant to hurt you."

I should have felt relief on hearing her words, not only a confession about her heartbreak (which to be frank was more than enough for me), but also about her manipulative actions. But I could feel myself getting more and more worked up as I remembered all the things she had done. Someone needed to remain calm, and I thought it best, for my own personal safety, if that someone was me.

"I have led my whole life waiting for the man of my life to tell me he loves me, and I just keep waiting." Her voice petered out.

This wasn't the Gabby I knew, who told you to your face how it was and what was going down whether you liked it or not. The Gabby who had knocked me into shape in the roughest manner possible with no compassion. The Gabby who had sent the Kings' driver to scare me away from my pastoral dreams in rural England, with no consideration of my feelings or of the possible danger she could and did inflict on me. If it hadn't been for her, I certainly wouldn't have got myself into the mess I was in now, and would most probably have returned to Lionel as his fiancée.

But then I wouldn't have this precious life growing inside me.

I paused for a moment in my thoughts. *Does this mean I actually have to thank Gabby?*

"Can you do it for me?" she asked.

"What? Thank you?" Now I was feeling really confused.

"Thank me? Why? No!" She let out a gruff laugh, though personally I didn't find the situation remotely funny. I was still trying to figure out if Gabby was harmless or not.

"Tell Freddy G."

"Tell him what?" *That you've collapsed under a tree in the pelting rain whilst you talk nonsense?* Personally, I would keep that information to myself.

"That I love him."

"What!"

And this is when Valentina's hysterical, contagious laughter caught up with me. And as

289

much as I tried to control myself I could feel my shoulders begin to shake in hopeless mirth, and a giggle bubble up inside until it erupted from my lips in a loud snort. I was aware that cackling out loud was the very last thing I should be doing at such a delicate time, not just because of Gabby's love-struck revelation, but because I was feeling terrible about Lionel. But I just couldn't help myself.

It was a while before I could compose myself and give Gabby an apologetic smile. If ever the saying that opposites attract was true, for Gabby it was spot-on. For all her sly, crazy, psychotic behaviour, I also had to admit there was a side to her that emanated sophistication, elegance and breeding. She was part of the select few that could rub shoulders with royalty and not feel intimidated. And Freddy G! Well he'd be capable of downing his Piña Colada in front of royalty and high-five them on the way to the WC. They were worlds apart in every possible way. Gabby was class, and Freddy G was a loud, unruly baboon.

To be fair, though, he did have boundless energy and could charm birds out of trees in his roly-poly way. I just couldn't see that this could be a match made in heaven, but here was Gabby looking lost and lovesick. And she was calling on me for help, which just went to show how desperate she was if she believed I could be of any use. I actually started to feel sorry for her.

I should have held my ground and told her to piss off (after all, she'd almost killed Tammy with her psychotic scheming), but I found myself sitting down next to her. I was starting to feel a little queasy again too, so I thought sitting was my best option in any case.

"If you love him, just tell him."

Wise words, although easier said than done. But really, life was too short for anything else. In fact it was too short to waste time hating anyone and I could feel my abhorrence toward Gabby start to melt. It wasn't right of her to try to frighten me away from England, but I also knew deep down that she would never have intended to hurt me. I even believed she respected me and held me in high esteem. I had survived her boot camp and actually passed with flying colours. For that alone I knew I'd earned her respect.

"But what if he doesn't love me back?"

"Then it's up to you to decide if he's worth fighting for or not. But perhaps what you really need to ask is: what if he does love you back? Because if he does, right now you're wasting time. And life's too short to waste time, because once it's gone we can never recover it."

Gabby looked at me, her emerald-green eyes reflecting a look of promise and expectation. And it hit me, as we sat there for a moment in silence, that this was bloody good practice for when my future baby hits his or her teens and needs a bit of worldly advice. I hoped that I'd be there to give it, that I'd be the one my kid confided in, and that he or she would have more common sense than the person sitting beside me right now.

"Is it true Lionel can't have children?" The question was out before I could stop myself.

"He's told you?"

I nodded.

"Nobody knows. It is one of the few secrets we were able to keep from the press when he fell ill. Not that he's ever felt a need to keep it secret; he's always been quite open about how he would adopt anyway. He got mumps when he was in his early teens, one of the extremely rare cases that got complicated and caused him infertility. I'm sorry, did he not tell you before?"

I shook my head.

"He should have done, of course. After all, he did propose to you. I think the only non-family person who knows is Vivien."

"I think he still loves her, you know, despite this fixation with me."

I paused. Gabby's response to this was going to be crucial. I'm sure if she believed it too, she would tell me. She was always brutally frank.

"Possibly," came her reply. "You know, she's actually a really nice gal. She didn't take the break-up well at all, and set out to dislike you from the very start." *I had kind of figured that out for myself.* "But from what I can see, it looks like you're friends now?" It was said as a question rather than statement.

"Yes. I misunderstood Vivien at first, but we're getting on fine now. In fact if it wasn't for her, perhaps Lionel would not be here now." I paused for a second before I continued. I'd had another crazy idea.

"I need your help." Gabby owed me big time, and I didn't think I had anything to lose by involving her in this love triangle. "Lionel is an amazing guy in every sense, he really is. He would be a dream come true for most girls. For most except me. There is a part of me that loves the part of him that has nothing to do with his celebrity status. I've been lucky enough to get to know this part of him, but I can't keep him from who he is. I'm not the right person for him, and the thing is I think deep down he knows this, but for some crazy reason he's still clinging on to what the fortune teller told him so many years ago. It's not real, though. But Vivien *is* real, and she still loves him. You have to help me get them together."

Gabby looked at me astonished, I wasn't too sure if she was wondering how the hell could she help me play Cupid when she couldn't even figure out her own love life (which was true, and perhaps what I was saying was actually a very bad idea), or how it was that I had changed my feelings so completely in such a short space of time. What on earth had happened?

But before she could answer, we were disturbed by the rustle of leaves behind us and someone cursing in French. Whoever it was, tripped up over the web of branches on the ground. A huge multi-coloured umbrella appeared first, followed by the roly-poly figure of Freddy G beneath it.

"Poochy! There you are! I've been looking all over for you. You're soaked. What were you thinking, darling?"

And before he could spy me, I took off leaving them alone together, and ran through the relentless rain back towards the house.

Poochy??? Bloody hell. He was smitten and she couldn't see it! Someone's in for a romp tonight!

***

I escaped to the bedroom I was sharing with Tammy. As I'd bounded up the veranda stairs I spied Robbie and Milena standing close together on the far side, looking all smoochy and rather love-struck and my heart strings gave a pang. Bloody hell, this was worse than being on *Love Island*. Love sparks were flying all around and I was the odd one out. I trudged up the stairs to the bedroom feeling totally deflated. Playing Cupid wasn't half as much fun as I'd expected. Time to book my flight home.

With that thought in mind I opened the bedroom door, to find Vivien and Tammy with curling tongs in their hair (where the hell did they get curling tongs from?) and spongy looking toe-nail separators in their feet. The smell of fresh nail varnish hit me strongly as Vivien and Tammy both peered towards me out of multicoloured clay faces.

"I'm brightening," said Tammy whose face was yellow.

"And I'm moisturising," added Vivien whose face was fluorescent pink. On the floor was a bottle of fizz and two champagne flutes filled to the brim. I felt as if I'd just walked in on Tai's make-over scene from *Clueless.*

"Here," said Vivien, moving towards me. "I've still got one more." And before I knew it I had a green face. *Great for closing enlarged pores*, I read, taking the now empty green tube from Vivien's hands. *And acne treatment*. Not quite as glamorous as *brightening* or *moisturising*.

"Here," said Vivien once again. "Have some champagne while I do your nails."

"Oh, I can't."

"Why not? It's just a little glass, harmless!" She giggled as the 'harmless' champagne that she'd already drunk started to work its wonder in her system, leaving her weak with hopeless laughter.

"She's pregnant," called out Tammy, as she herself flopped to the floor under a spell of tipsy giggles.

If there was ever an antidote for drunkenness, for Vivien those words were it. Despite the fluorescent pink mask, I could physically see her face drain of all colour as she turned to me.

"Pregnant?" she whispered, as her legs wobbled beneath her. "But, but... Lionel can't have children, at least... that's what he's always told me..." Her voice petered out with a hiccup as she collapsed on the bed behind her.

There was a moment of total silence. Even Vivien's hiccups had been shocked out of her system before Tammy gasped in awe:

"I say, that's awfully lucky, isn't it, Chantelle? I mean, that makes Robbie the father then, doesn't it?"

***

Vivien was still staring at me in shock (probably trying to figure out how on earth I'd managed to sleep with another guy whilst I was engaged to her beloved Lionel), when there was a knock on the door. I moved to answer but just as I reached the door I could distinctly hear Robbie's voice. *Shit*! I didn't want him seeing me with a bogie-green face mask on. It wasn't exactly my most glamorous look. Without giving it a second thought I ran into the bathroom and whispered to Tammy as I closed the door: "Can you open it please? I think it's Robbie."

I pressed my ear to the door as I heard Tammy say, "Hi Robbie."

There was a low murmur from Robbie before I heard him quite clearly say, "Is Chantelle here? I need to speak to her."

"Err... no."

"No? But it's chucking down with rain outside and she'll get ill out there. I have to find her."

"Yes, right. What I mean is she's not here, here, but in the bathroom."

"Is she OK?" I could hear concern in his voice. This was the Robbie I knew, and my heart gave a little tumble as I pressed my ear further against the door. I was probably smearing the door with gooey face-mask, but hearing his words was more important to me. I could clean up the mess later.

"I think she's being sick," continued Tammy, giving extra unnecessary detail, but she was on a roll; the champagne had loosened her tongue and there was no stopping her now. "You know, morning sickness and all. She really is quite bad. But she's tough is our Chantelle, doesn't let on how terrible she's feeling. Looks frightfully awful too. Quite green."

"Green?" Robbie sounded confused. "I think we need to call for a doctor or something." His voice sounded closer, as the words floated over to where I was hiding. Then there was a rap on the door right where my ear was pressed, leaving my eardrum buzzing. I instinctively took a step back.

"Chantelle?" I could hear Robbie call out. "Are you OK?"

I unsuccessful tried to make a retching sound. But, to be honest I sounded more like a startled cat. At least on my second attempt I managed to sound a bit more human than a cat bringing up a hair-ball.

"Can I come in?"

Are you kidding me?

"Err... I'm okay," I said as I rushed to the wash-basin and ran warm water in a mad attempt to scrape off the green goo that was plastered all over my face. To my horror there were even clumps in my hair. Great! Now it looked as if I'd managed to puke backwards on myself, if that was physically possible. But before I could fathom out the physics of it (enough to give me a headache even on a good day), there was another knock. As if in slow motion, I could see the door-knob turn and the door slowly inch open.

"Please can I come in?"

I quickly splashed my face with the very lukewarm water trying desperately to clear the clay off my face before Robbie got any closer. I could see him out of the corner of my eye, despite the water dripping down my face. I was only partially done before I could feel Robbie's hands tenderly take hold of my hair and hold it back. He then reached for one of the bathroom towels and tentatively held it towards me.

I took the towel from his hands and pressed it to my face. I didn't dare look in the mirror and just hoped to God that I didn't look too green to cause alarm.

"Here," he said as he now reached for a tissue and tenderly wiped away what he probably thought

297

was snot that had stuck to my nose or something. I mean, if this wasn't love, what was?

"Feeling better?"

I looked at him doe-eyed. This is the Robbie I'd fallen in love with: tender, caring, considerate and kind. A side that he had closed off to me these last few weeks and I had no idea why. I just nodded, fighting the urge to fall into his arms. I longed to feel them around me. But I held back as he continued speaking:

"Shall I get Valentina to call for a doctor? When do you plan to go back to England, anyway?"

So this was what it was all about. Trying to find out when I was going home, so that I didn't cramp his style with Milena! I surprised myself by my own wicked chain of thought, but my emotional state was wired rather fine right now, and Robbie trying to get rid of me was the only thing I could think of. That and craving peanut butter and tuna pate sandwiches, of course, cravings I thankfully hadn't felt since the first day I suspected I was pregnant.

"First thing Monday morning." It was a complete lie, I hadn't booked yet, but I was going back as soon as possible. I needed space. It was time I put my baby first. And with that I pushed him out of the bathroom. "I'm sure you and Milena will both be relieved to know that I'll be gone very soon." With that I forcefully closed the door in his confused face before he could get another word out.

"We need to talk," I heard his muffled voice behind the closed door.

"Not now," I sobbed out as tears filled up and trickled down my face and to my horror I saw my reflection in the mirror. I still had electric green eyebrows (no wonder Robbie looked confused), and my hair was full of clumps of green clay. Just fucking great!

***

He stepped away, even though his heart told him to stay. He turned to go, although his arms yearned to hold her once again. He ached to discover the truth, but was scared of what he would find.
How did he ever think he could forget her?

CHAPTER THIRTY-ONE

VALENTINA

It's been a strange couple of days. A great tension between Chantelle and both my sons. In fact Chantelle has pretty much kept to her room the whole time, avoiding mealtimes. She has promised me that she will come to the party tonight. It has just started, but I'm not so sure. All the guests are here, but she is nowhere to be seen. She says she will return to England soon and I will miss her, more than she can imagine. For some reason I feel that my family has returned because of her and I will be eternally grateful to her for it. And not only that, but my family will continue to grow through her.

She has promised me that she will keep me informed on how the baby grows and has invited me to stay with her once the baby is born. She has no mother or father after all. Her only condition has been that I must go with Rafael. I laughed when she said this.

"How can you be so sure that Rafael will want to come with me?" I asked her.

"Because he loves you," was her simple reply, "and you still love him."

And she was right. I had never stopped loving Rafael, but it was hard to make a place for him now when I had lived for so many years without him. He seems to know this, too, and has kept a cordial distance these days. He has visited several times, and together we have shown the boys the farm lands, on horseback and also up in Lionel's helicopter. It was only when seeing it from the sky, with the spectacular view of the green vineyards which stretched for miles, with the backdrop of mountains in the distance, that I was aware that my land peaked on the northern side and actually touched the Fernandez Ranch. I had never appreciated the union of soils before, but more incredibly the spot was marked with a giant spiral, an enormous shape made out of stone blocks which stood out even from the privileged birds-eye view high in the sky.

It would have taken months or perhaps years to have achieved this magnificent, perfectly symmetrical image. I was reminded of our ancestors who rode the plains before us, free from material ties, from the chains of modern life.

I instinctively turned to look at Rafael who sat next to me, his deep gaze on me. A modern man in conventional dress, but still primitive at heart. A man who belonged to the wilderness around, untameable, and yet all I could read from his eyes was that he longed to stay. His heart belonged here with me, in this land that had brought us together, a land that knew no boundaries. There was no doubt that he was behind this work of art. The roar in the helicopter was too loud for me to ask him, but he nodded his head as if reading my mind and he reached out and covered my hand with his own warm palm. Rough skin against my smooth fingers.

Instinctively I jerked my hand to break away. I hadn't wanted to, but it was inevitable, it's what I had done to everyone who had come close to me over the last thirty-three years. But Rafael wasn't just anyone. He gently pressed his hand on mine again, his fingers wound through mine. Just this simple, innocent touch was enough to warm me from the tips of my toes to my flushed cheeks and I turned to look out of the cockpit again in an attempt to hide my visible emotion from his searching eyes. But my hand remained in his, our fingers entwined as they should have always been, and I was the one who pressed back and squeezed our fingers closer. I hadn't felt so happy in such a long time. If this was a dream, I hoped never to wake. Life was giving me this second chance, and I knew that only a fool would close the door to such good fortune. If I had learnt anything over these years, it was that I was no fool.

The fiesta had begun and Rafael was with me: he stood proudly by my side greeting our guests as if they were just that: "our" guests. We still hadn't had time to talk properly, even to be alone. The last few days had been chaotic organising the party and spending as much time as possible with Lionel and Robbie before they left. Lionel would be going first thing in the morning. His scheduled was overflowing and his obligations piling up. Robbie hadn't said when he would leave, and I half-hoped he would stay, but what would happen to Chantelle? It seemed clear, at least to me, that she loved both men in her own way, but whatever relationship she had had with them no longer existed.

When I questioned Chantelle about this, she simply replied that Lionel belonged to a world where she would never fit in, and Robbie had just discovered his place in this world, a place light-years from her or where she calls home. There was no going back, only forward. She had accomplished what she had set out to achieve: a reunion of lost sons, of lost brothers, of lost lovers. Part of her journey in life had ended here. It was as if there was a part of her that had found peace in these arid plains, and would forever remain resting entwined between the rocky mountains and the flat lowlands.

"Believe me," she had said, "my journey has not ended but will continue, perhaps not how I expected, but in its own special way. I have a baby to put first now, and I will embrace this new journey. I will live every moment in memory of my mother, who died too young, and for you, who lost so young. I'm happy to embrace motherhood with open arms. I don't need Lionel or Robbie to tell me that I'm unique, that I'm special, that I'm loved. I've learnt that for myself."

It was a very convinced and confident Chantelle who said these words. So why is it that when she looks at Robbie I can see her confidence crumble, her heart openly break, before my very eyes?

***

My thoughts were broken as Rafael turned to me. We had just finished the dinner and the tables had been cleared, the musicians had struck up a tune, and he gently took me by the hand and led me to the centre of the dance floor. A blanket of silence fell over our guests as they all hushed and turned to watch us. It was a slow tango and as the notes floated over to us in the warm evening breeze and I fell into Rafael's arms I was relieved that my body moved rhythmically under his gentle leading. I hadn't danced in many years, let alone in the arms of

303

someone who made me feel so much with such a simple touch. I was aware that everyone was watching, but all I saw was Rafael's eyes as he gracefully held me close and we moved as one. It was a beautiful dance and with his warm hand in mine, his firm arm supporting me, I knew, at last, that the only fortress I wanted to surround me and support me for the rest of my days was that offered by his arms, by his body. I had no need for anything more. He had successfully opened the door that led to my heart, and I had stepped out again into the bright sunlight after years of darkness. The warmth that fell over me was wondrous.

As the music died and the piece came to an end, there was a thunderous roar of applause from our guests. Everyone here tonight were my closest friends and family. They had been waiting eagerly for this reunion and it was with genuine warmth that they congratulated us. But despite the noise, I could hear Rafael who whispered to me as he tenderly brushed a strand of hair back off my face.

"My darling Valentina, I'd said that I would be happy to spend the rest of my life just to watch you from afar, but now that I have you in my arms again I don't want to let go. I want to be at your side for the rest of my life. I want to be the first person you say 'Good morning' to and last person to whom you say 'Goodnight.' But I'll understand if you wish it differently, and I will respect your decision."

Before I could stop myself, or even think beyond here and now, I whispered to him, "The only person I have ever wanted in my life is standing in front of me right now, and I will never want it to be any different."

Words that danced out over the silvery night, and I knew I would never regret them.

CHAPTER THIRTY-TWO

CHANTELLE

I watched from the bedroom window as Valentina and Rafael danced together. Such a beautiful, elegant couple. They were made for each other, so it was about bloody time they got their act together. Such a shame, though, that life had dealt them such a sorrowful hand when they were so young. Things would have been so different.

I, for one, certainly wouldn't be here now.

And why me? Why had Rafael's mother envisioned me? Were we distant family? Some questions would perhaps remain unanswered, though it warmed me to think that perhaps there was a greater force that had brought me out here. Despite having lost Robbie to the great outdoors (and Milena), and given up Lionel to the flashing starlit world where he belongs (with Vivien), there was a part of me that felt great inner peace. I couldn't quite explain it. I guess the pregnancy hormones had something to do with it. At any rate, something was chilling me out, I hadn't touched a drop of alcohol in weeks!

I was startled out of my train of thoughts by a sudden knock on the door. A voice called out my name: a voice I would recognise anywhere. My heart squeezed in anticipation and I moved quickly to open the door. I hadn't wanted to leave without clearing up what had happened, and I was glad that he was going to give me that chance.

Lionel stood there before me, looking so handsome in his evening suit, a perfect cut for his well-built frame, his dark hair shone in the evening light and his green eyes flashed. Hell, Vivien was one lucky lady! She knew him better than anyone, accepting him for who he was and what he represented. I felt a brief pang of – what? sorrow? regret? jealousy? that I would never know him as well as she did. I didn't deserve him.

"Can I come in?"

"Of course." I moved to one side to let him enter, and suddenly felt really nervous. What was he going to say? Blimey! It was getting a bit awkward, too, I though as I suddenly found myself sitting next to him on the bed. I hoped to God Vivien didn't suddenly walk in on us. It doesn't matter how innocent it was, sitting on a bed next to Lionel would not come across at all well.

"I know it was childish of me to believe, over all these years, that until I met a so-called Chantelle Rose I would never be truly happy."

Personally I've always thought so myself, but I was glad that it was Lionel, not me, who was stating the obvious.

"But for some reason I kept hanging on to what I was told. But you know what? That crazy lady, that complete loon of a fortune-teller, was right." He softly chuckled, though I wasn't so sure Sally would find it all that funny to hear his description of her.

He continued, his voice now serious. "I have been trying to trace my biological family for as long as I can remember. I needed to know who my biological parents were, where I was from. Not because I wasn't happy; I've been extremely lucky to

307

have the adoptive parents I have, to have been given their generous, unconditional love. But there was a part of me that was missing, and now it's come home. And though I'm still hurting that you fell so quickly into another man's arms…"

(Y*es, can't quite believe it myself.*)

"… that you could believe I would be capable of hurting you…"

(Y*es, another cock-up on my part.*)

"… I also know that if it wasn't for you I would not be here now. I would never have found out the truth. So though it's not quite what I believed all these years, it was true that until I met you I would never find true happiness."

He paused here for a second and softly placed his hand on my knee. I was surprised to find that though I felt his warmth through the thin fabric of my dress, the electrical charge that would have swept through me from just a tender touch just a few months ago was gone. It was a brotherly gesture, and as I looked into his eyes I knew the feeling was mutual, there were no sparks as we looked at each other, just respect and friendship.

"I just wanted you to know that I did love you though. I do still love you, but it's a different love now."

(*I sighed with relief. I'm glad he clarified this last bit about the level of his "love". I was starting to panic that I'd got his brotherly look all wrong.*)

"I will leave tomorrow, but I would like to remain in touch, you are a special woman and only a fool would want to lose you forever. You may not be my wife as I always imagined, but you will be my best friend. What do you say to that?"

This is, of course, when my chilled-out pregnancy hormones turned into the emotional tear-drenching hormones, and before I knew it I had tears streaming down my face. He was such a bloody wonderful guy. It was also time, I realised, to return his engagement ring. I moved to where I had placed it for safe keeping, before returning to sit next to him, once again, on the bed.

"Vivien is one lucky lady," I whispered, and handed back to him the beautiful, and bloody enormous, diamond ring. With that Lionel took me in his arms to give me a big brotherly hug. While held in his strong embrace, my eyes picked up a movement by the partially-open bedroom door. Was I mistaken, or had I just seen a shadow fall back?

"Tammy?" I called out. But there was no answer.

"Come on," said Lionel, oblivious to my somewhat anxious look. "Let's go and join the party."

***

Child of his mother,
Son of his father,
Blood of his brother,
Lover of his lover.

***

We walked out into the warm, balmy evening and I led Lionel over to where Vivien stood with Tammy. As if in slow motion Vivien turned to look at us. Her golden locks fell down her petite shoulders in perfect shimmering waves. Her face lit up on seeing Lionel, radiating a beauty I had never before appreciated so vividly: her perfect oval face, her flawless complexion (with a little helping hand from the moisturising face mask and perhaps a few other cosmetic tricks), her huge sparkling baby-blue eyes and a smile that was utterly breathtaking.

I nudged Lionel and said, "I think someone is waiting to dance," and with that I winked at Vivien as Lionel took her by the hand and led her to the dance floor.

What a perfect night for romance, the air was richly perfumed with Lady of the Night and lavender. The stars shone bright all around, silver dancing lights in the night sky. As I looked about I spied Gabby dancing with Freddy G (well, towering over him to be exact), Valentina still held close in Rafael's arms, and now Lionel and Vivien. I contently sighed as I turned to Tammy and said, "My job here is done, it's time to go home."

Tammy linked her arm through mine. "You know sweetie, I'm really proud of you. I'll give it to you, you've pulled this off. I'm not sure how, but you've done a bloody good job. You didn't spike their drinks with some dodgy love potion Sally gave you, did you?"

I laughed. "I wish! I'd have used it all up on Robbie if that had been the case though. Talking of Robbie, where is he?"

Tammy shrugged, and it was then that my eyes fell on Milena. She was dancing in the shadows on the far side of the dance floor. Her arms were wrapped around a tall, well-built young man, and my heart froze. I couldn't quite make out if it was Robbie or not, he looked very familiar. The tall frame, the dark hair, the powerful arms. But would

310

Robbie really turn up to the party in *gaucho* clothes and cowboy boots? God he really had found his roots in the Pampas. And bloody hell, he'd picked up the tango really fast, too. He was leading Milena with such confidence, legs circling up and out. Five steps with a swivel, circle, lift.

"Is that... that...?" I could hear Tammy stutter next to me in stupefaction as she too spied the *Strictly Come Dancing* couple. And I had to admit I would have given them top marks, too.

"Looks like it," I muttered sadly.

"It is, isn't it? God they make a really good-looking couple, too!"

"Thanks, Tammy!"

"Look how they move! I would never have thought he would have it in him! Fancy that, rather lush, too!"

"Cheers, Tam."

"If he moves like that on the dance floor, can you imagine what he must be like in bed? I wish Ray could move like that."

"Have you finished?"

"Well, I say! Fancy that! And what a coincidence! I never thought we would see him again, but it's him isn't it? The cowboy that we bumped into when we got lost on the drive down?"

"What?" I peered closer. So that's why he looked so familiar.

So where the hell was Robbie?

CHAPTER THIRTY-THREE

VALENTINA

They've gone, all of them. The house is quiet once more.

I woke this morning and was startled to find my bed empty, too. For a moment I felt that it had all been a dream, but as I spread my hand over to where Rafael had slept, I could still feel his warmth on the sheets.

I hugged his pillow to me, breathing in his aroma, and I sighed, a childish smile on my lips as I remembered the previous passionate night in his arms – the same as every night since the party we'd held in Lionel's and Robbie's honour. "I have a surprise for you," he had whispered to me as we had lain together covered only by the shimmering moonlight which had filtered through the bedroom window and fallen around us. Now it was early morning, and I could hear noises outside and went to the window to peer out.

I caught my breath. Could it be? I grabbed my dressing gown and ran down the stairs. My breath caught as I stepped outside to get a better look. There before me was Dancer. There was no doubt about it. She was old now, but even in her advanced age she stood proudly and softly neighed, it seemed in recognition, as I called out her name and ran to her. My arms went around her neck and tears filled

312

my eyes. My mother had sold her all those years ago as a punishment for running away with Rafael. But she never knew, as I was to now discover, that the "horse whisperer" had found out, and was the one who had bought her and had kept her all these years.

Dancer had been a gift from my father, a beautiful, precious gift. Life had also given me priceless gifts: my two babies who had now grown into two wonderful men. And without a doubt one of the most beautiful things that life had returned to me was this handsome, amazing man who stood before me now. They call him the "horse whisperer," but to me he was so much more. He was my soulmate, the father of my sons, and the keeper of my heart. He had been able to lead me out of the fortress that I had built up around myself over the years. The drawbridge had been lowered, and I was never going back inside. This is where I wanted to be: outside enjoying all life had to offer me for the rest of my days. Because there are no regrets in life, just lessons learnt.

CHAPTER THIRTY-FOUR

CHANTELLE

I sat in the midwife's office for my second check-up. I couldn't quite believe that it had only been three weeks since my last one. I had just arrived back from Argentina and was actually lucky I hadn't missed my appointment. I don't think after my previous disastrous check-up, it would do me any good to start skipping appointments.

I sat in a bit of a daze as the midwife went through the procedure. I was still suffering from jet lag, so I guess it came as no surprise when she tried to clear up the father's name that I didn't come out with a conventional reply. I had no idea why the father's identity was so important to the National Health Service anyway, or perhaps it was just the midwife being downright nosey. But the facts were that Lionel couldn't have children and Robbie had just buggered off and had never confirmed our passionate night together anyway, leaving me thinking that perhaps I had just dreamt the whole thing up. I hadn't been able to find Robbie the night of the party or the following day, and his telephone was once again off limits. So on the midwife's insistence on knowing who the father was, I gave my most honest reply: "The Holy Spirit, apparently."

There was a moment of silence, then a quick intake of breath (my own, because I anticipated being told off for such blasphemy), but amazingly the midwife didn't even raise an eyebrow but actually turned to the computer screen and tapped away at the keyboards, leaving me desperately anxious and more than a little curious to know who the hell she'd actually named as the father.

But I wasn't going to worry about that right now. I was meeting Sally as soon as I had finished with the routine check-up. I had some urgent questions for her which unsettled me far more than what the National Health Service thought about my sleeping partners – or miraculous lack of them.

I was going to mention to the midwife that I'd just come back from Argentina, but for the moment remained quiet. I was keeping the baby no matter what, and, anyway, there was something that Rafael's mother, Carmen, had said to me at the party that made me believe that the baby was growing healthily. She had told me that she'd seen the child, a beautiful baby, healthy and strong. She refused to tell me if it was going to be a boy or a girl, but she did say that it had the most incredible eyes, as blue as the sky on a summer's day – and there was only one person I knew whose blue eyes could light up my day like the sun's rays. It was with a sinking heart, though, that I had a feeling I would never see them – or him – again.

***

"You look just glowing, pet. Absolutely radiant, pregnancy suits you my flower," were Sally's words on seeing me as she enveloped me in her motherly hug. Perfumed notes rich with lavender embraced me, and I was whisked once again back to my childhood: the daily walks on Wimbledon Common, the happy chatter of people lolling on the soft green grass, children squealing in delight as they dipped their feet in the pond, bees humming in the background, and the distant bark of a dog amongst the noise. Wimbledon will always be special. It was the only place that really brought back memories of my mother, and for that alone it will be my most sacred place in the world.

"You seem more at peace m'duck, you radiate tranquillity. I'm so happy for you pet."

Well, if she was going to compare me to the last time we met up, when I spent the greater part of the time in floods of tears, I guess I had improved immensely. The tranquillity, however, was just another symptom of being jet-lagged. Frankly I didn't know if it was day or night. But I needed to know if Sally really could foresee events, or was it just intuition? Was there magic behind her words, or was she just very good at reading people: a therapist who hid behind tarot cards? A bit daft, really, because she wasn't getting half her money's worth per session. I mean, a visit to a professional therapist could cost an arm and a leg, not just a fiver, which is what Sally said she charged for palm reading.

"So tell me, pet, you wanted to ask me something?"

We paused here for a moment as the waitress placed our order down on the coffee table. We were sitting in a cafe off the High Street in Wimbledon Village as I had a longing to return to where I'd spent my childhood. I didn't know what I was expecting to find here, but it was refreshing and calming strolling up the hill from the train station. Well, it was refreshing until about half way up, then it turned rather exhausting, and I don't know why on earth I hadn't caught the number 93 bus up the hill instead. But the brisk autumn air cleared my mind with each step I took, and by the end of it, though I was puffing and feeling a little queasy, I was glad for the walk and I had a feeling that I would get the answers I was looking for.

So now I turned to Sally and asked, "Was there a reason you babysat me? Was there something intimate and special you shared with my mother?" Perhaps I should have phrased that a little differently; it sounded as if I was probing to find out if they were lovers or something, and if that was the case I certainly didn't want to know about it.

Sally sighed and looked away for a moment, her eyes glazed over and though she seemed to be just looking across to the other side of the street. It was obvious she was miles away, whisked back in time, to a younger self perhaps, a young woman with the world at her feet and endless possibilities stretching before her.

"I met your mother at an arts and crafts festival. I had just learnt to read tarot cards and was doing readings. I remember your mother suddenly appearing by my table, her rich laugh seemed to fill the hall as she sat down in front of me. I had been mesmerised by her dark looks and flashing smile. Your father was with her and had said 'I don't believe in this, but go ahead and see what the future holds in store, as long as I form part of it I'm happy.' 'Just watch' she'd teased. I remember her words so clearly as if it was yesterday. I shuffled the cards, cut them and lay them out, then reached for the first one to turn it over. '*The Sun*,' she said, before I showed

317

the card, and it was. I reached for the second card. '*The Lovers*,' she called out, before my fingers even reached the card. '*The Star*,' she correctly called out with the third. And so it went on. It was just a game for her, but it was just incredible the way she could foretell the cards. Your father was shocked. So was I. But she didn't give it any importance at all. I was fascinated, I needed to learn more from her. We became friends and she showed me everything she knew so that I could develop my skill."

I sat spellbound listening to Sally. *So it was true, there were people who could foresee events?*

"Chantelle, everything I know about fortune telling came from your mother. The difference was that I work from intuition, where she worked from magic. She had the gift..."

I felt really faint. I could hear Sally anxiously ask, though I felt miles away, "Are you OK, pet? You've gone as white as a sheet."

And it flashed before me: the image of him, so clear, as at the same time a current ran through my whole body. I was at the cottage, Dolly was with me. I was down by the old oak tree that stood in the middle of the garden at the back of the house. It was dusk, and the evening air was starting to chill me. "You can keep a secret, can't you?" I'd just said to the collie dog who grinned back at me, her tongue lolled to one side, tail wagged frantically. "I'll take that as a yes." And that was when she started to bark, excited yaps, but instead of remaining with me she took off towards the cottage entrance, after some rabbit or something no doubt. But as I turned to look to see where she had gone, a shadow fell over the kitchen door.

318

And there he stood.

"Chantelle, sweetie, are you OK?" I could hear Sally's insistent calling bringing me back to the present. Her warm hand on mine, gently squeezing it. "You look like you've seen a ghost, pet. Sorry; I didn't want to upset you with this talk about your mother. Let's talk about something else, shall we? Have your tea before it gets cold and here have a scone, it will do you good. Shall I butter it for you?" Only a Brit would butter an already rich, sweet pasty and load it with jam, too. Build up the body fat to get you through the winter months, I guess.

"I know she was from a place called Catania in Sicily, but did she tell you anything more about her family? It's just that since she passed away I lost touch with my relatives there. I was so young, and Dad had such a hard time coming to terms with her loss, we just drifted from them. Perhaps it's time to re-build old bridges." I spoke more to myself than to Sally, but she seemed to understand.

"That's what your mother used to say, that it was time to re-build old bridges. She was always going on about how one day she wanted to go to Argentina. Some of her family had moved there, a great-great-uncle or something, if I remember correctly. She was always saying how she wanted to renew lost family ties."

"What?" I just stared at Sally, open-mouthed.

"That a great-great-uncle of hers had moved to Argentina."

"No, the second thing you said, that she always wanted to renew lost family ties." I did a quick calculation in my head, amazed that I could actually think straight and calculate anything more complex than one-plus-one in the giddy mental state I was in right now. A great-great-uncle of my mother could be Carmen's father? The generation gap was exact. That meant that my great-great-great-uncle would be Robbie's and Lionel's great-great-grandfather. Oh My God! We *are* related. I was sure. It was my mother with her magical powers bringing us together as she had always wanted. Carmen had the gift too.

It was too much to take in, I didn't know whether to dance on the table or sob my heart out.

"We're related!" I exclaimed out loud.

"I don't think so m'duck! I'm from the Midlands! A far cry from Catania."

And with that I scooped Sally into an energetic hug.

"Thank you, thank you, thank you," I cried. I said it to Sally, but I just hoped that my mother could hear me too.

***

It was dusk and I was feeling a bit of a chill as the evening rays started to disappear. A cool blanket was settling around, the leaves lay crisp on the cold floor, frost would cover them tonight. I was down by the oak tree, the old tree that proudly stood in the middle of the cottage garden, near the octagonal greenhouse. Dolly was with me, watching with inquisitive eyes as I carved several initials into the bark.

V & L. These initials were already there. I had mistaken them for C & R, but it was clear that this carving had been done by Vivien when she had stayed here. She had got her Lionel back in the end,

320

just as we had planned. She'd send me a couple of texts thanking me for all my help, when really it was me that had to thank her for loving Lionel as he deserved.

I now added other initials too:

V & R (Valentina and Rafael)
T & R (Tammy and Ray)
G & F (Gabby and Freddy G.)

Everyone was so bloody lovey-dovey and had their happy ending. Everyone except me, by the looks of it. I sighed, then turned to Dolly.

"You can keep a secret can't you?"

She barked back excitedly.

"I'll take that as a yes!" And with that, I carved:
C & R

Considering that Robbie didn't want anything to do with me any more, perhaps I shouldn't have carved that in the bark. I glanced at the initials again, well, I could always pretend that I'd carved my own first and last name initials into the tree. I am Chantelle Rose after all. But why I would carve my own name in a heart would be a bit more awkward to explain.

Dolly, still at my heels looking at me with inquisitive eyes, suddenly started barking excitedly, jumping up at me, wagging her tail at warp speed.

"It's OK," I said as I reached forward to pat her head. But she was gone, racing back to the cottage entrance with an enthusiasm usually saved only for rabbits. As I watched her run, my heart quickened. I'd seen this before. I'd been here before, in another time, but now it was for real. There was a noise from the side passage that ran down the left-hand side of the cottage, and a silhouette appeared: the figure of a person who had haunted my dreams since my return. My heartbeat quickened. Could it be him? I didn't dare move. I didn't want to break this spell. Perhaps it was all just an optical illusion – the evening shadows playing tricks on my overheated imagination.

The shadow fell across the kitchen door and then turned back towards to me. My throat felt dry. It was just as well that I didn't feel threatened because there wasn't a hope in hell that I could call for help. My voice had just been swallowed by the shock of seeing him again.

"Chantelle?"

He called out, he must have picked up on my silhouette in the shadows of the oak tree. But my legs wouldn't obey my desire to run to him, I actually desperately needed to sit. I leaned back against the trunk of the solid tree behind me, my heart level with my most recent engraving. *C & R*. Why had he come back? He had found his new home, his new family, his new calling on the other side of the Atlantic. There was nothing here for him, so why had he returned?

I remained rooted to the spot as he approached, though my heart felt as if I'd just run a marathon, and just kept quickening with each step he took towards me. I knew that I had misinterpreted his relationship with Milena and that there was and had been nothing between them. Milena had recently broken up with her boyfriend (the good-looking Argentinian cowboy that had guided Tammy and me back to San Rafael after our little detour into the sticks), and it seemed Robbie had been a shoulder to cry on, but no more. There had been no *"Roberto, mi amor, take me..."* (as I thought I'd heard on the telephone); rather *"Roberto, tell me more about England."* I got all this information from Valentina the day after the party, when it became quite clear that the young Argentinian couple had re-kindled their passion. Milena, apparently, had always been fascinated by Europe, in particular the UK, and Robbie had been like an open book for her to learn more. It had been Valentina who had invited the young man to the party. It had been her initiative to play Cupid with them. "I can match-make too," she had said, smiling at me. But Robbie had disappeared, and much as I desperately tried to find him, his whereabouts were a mystery to all.

But here he was now. Just inches from me, and I actually found myself fighting the urge to hit out at him. He had acted so childishly in Argentina. Not telling Valentina about Lionel, then telling me off for going to Argentina in the first place, not showing up at the party, and then leaving without saying goodbye to anyone. Christ, I had no need for another childish fool in my life. The baby that was growing inside was going to be more than enough, and I hoped to God less foolish. So it was in this frame of mind that I pushed past him and said, "What the hell are you doing here?"

Not quite the welcoming he was expecting, I was sure, except for Dolly's homecoming. She had been so ecstatic to see him again that I think she even peed.

He grabbed my arm as I tried to move past.

"Because you are the most annoying, stubborn, rebellious, headstrong, reckless woman I've ever met, and I love you."

What?

He drew me close, his eyes had deepened to dark sapphire, flashing desire as he looked at me (it was either that or he was still incredibly pissed off at me for interfering the way I had).

"And that's meant to make me feel better?" I retorted, my voice level a contrast to my mind, and my heart, which had accelerated beyond control. *Did he just say he loved me?* It didn't help that that I was also distracted by his warm hand that now moved down my arm and slipped behind my waist, pulling me close to him.

"Because you are the most amazing woman I have ever met: fearless, lion-hearted and simply beautiful. Only a fool would allow you to walk away without fighting for you first."

"But you did let me go, you just disappeared without a trace." If that was his way of fighting for me, I hoped to God I would never need him in proper hand-to-hand combat. Gabby would be much more efficient.

"I left because I saw you with Lionel the night of the party. I went to search you out and I found you in his arms sitting on the bed."

(*So that's who the shadow belonged to…*)

"I did want to fight for you. I didn't want to leave, but if there was a chance that the baby was his, how could I fight? It would only be selfish. Lionel can offer the child the world, give it the best education, simply the best of the best. I can't. I can only offer to love it and care for it for the rest of my

324

life." He broke off here, his serious, penetrating gaze leaving me weak and rather breathless.

"It's enough for me." The words slipped out without me even thinking. "The only gift I would ever want you to give your child would be just that. Unconditional love. Material wealth, fame and fortune pales in comparison." For a moment we just stood there. His arm still around me. My hands had found their way up his arms and rested on his strong, powerful shoulders. I could feel his body heat through the layers of his clothes, and the urge to hit him had disintegrated. I now found myself fighting the urge to sink my hands under his jumper and pull it off. I would say rip it off, but that only happens in films, and anyway, there wasn't a hope in hell I could tear this thick yarn with just my fingers. But before things got any more intimate, I had to clear something with him first.

"Robbie, Lionel isn't the father. He can't have children. I only found this out recently, but I'd already made up my mind that my future lies far away from Lionel and his world. I'm not the woman for him. I don't belong in his world, I don't understand it, and I could never take it away from him. But it's not just that. It's because I love someone else, and it wouldn't be fair to anyone if I betrayed my heart."

Robbie pulled me closer, one hand around my waist, the other went up to my face and gently caressed my cheek.

"And do I by any chance know this someone you're talking about?" he asked, words deep and throaty with pent-up emotion.

"I'm looking at him right now."

And with that his face lowered to mine. As our lips touched, I knew that Robbie was, and always would be, the best mistake of my life.

EPILOGUE

As the early sun's rays filtered through the soft curtains and fell on her face, he fought the urge to wake her and join their bodies once again in a union so primitive that it left him breathless. He smiled to himself as his tenderly placed his hand across her still flat stomach. His brother Lionel may have the world at his feet, but Robbie had his whole world in his arms.

She stirred under his touch and slowly opened her eyes to look at him. Eyes as golden as the sun, a beam of light that warmed him to his very core. She smiled and snuggled close to him, fitting perfectly into his arms.

"There's beautiful," he whispered as he leaned over to softly kiss her on her lips, "and then there's you, Chantelle Rose."

***

Life is short, break the RULES.
FORGIVE quickly
KISS slowly, LOVE truly,
LAUGH uncontrollably,
and NEVER REGRET
anything that made you SMILE.

Your friend,

Valentina Mendoza.

THE END

ISABELLA
(Book III of the <u>Chantelle Rose Series</u>)

Who is Isabella Gravachi, and what's the mystery behind the trail of heartbreak left in her wake?

Having lost her mother as a child, Chantelle is desperate to trace this side of her family and confront the ghosts of her mother's past. So when a surprise invitation arrives, promising to take her to the place that holds the secrets to both Isabella's past and Chantelle's future, she doesn't hesitate.

But unravelling this Sicilian mystery that's been locked away for centuries, under the guard of looming Mount Etna, will test Chantelle in ways she never imagined.

As new love challenges old, and bonds are formed and broken, will Chantelle's quest for the truth destroy everyone she loves or will it bring her peace at last?

OUT NOW!

Buy link: <u>Isabella (Book III of the Chantelle Rose Series)</u>
On Amazon!

Sign-up to Cristina's Newsletter **for all the details and exclusive content.**

www.cristinahodgson.com

THANK YOU FOR READING!

Dear Reader,

I hope you enjoyed *Valentina*. As an author, I love feedback. You are the reason that I will continue to explore Chantelle's story, now through her mother Isabella Gravachi. So tell me what you liked, what you loved, even what you hated. I'd love to hear from you. You can write to me at: hello@cristinahodgson.com or visit me on my web page: www.cristinahodgson.com

Or my Amazon Author page for all my books including my free short story *"Simply Anna."* And whilst you're there, I'd really appreciate a review. Reviews can be tough to come by these days and you, the reader, have the power to make or break a book. If you have the time, I'd love to read your feedback. http://author.to/CristinaHodgson

Thank you so much for reading *Valentina* and for spending time with me.

In gratitude,

Cristina Hodgson

FREE EXCLUSIVE CONTENT

Sign up for the author's New Releases mailing list and get a free copy of her short story *Three Against One* a true story about love, hope and survival.

Click here to get started:
Cristina's Newsletter
www.cristinahodgson.com

19947567R00199

Printed in Great Britain
by Amazon